CM Harris is the author of novels *Mother Lamp*, *The Children of Mother Glory*, and the psychological thriller *She Never Left*. Her writing has appeared in *O Magazine*, Pseudopod podcast, as well as various journals and anthologies.

CM Harris lives in Minneapolis with her wife and their twins. She is also the singer/guitarist for indie band *Hothouse Weeds*.

authorcmharris.com

twitter.com/flammablewords
facebook.com/cmharrisauthor
instagram.com/flammablewords

# SHE NEVER LEFT

## CM HARRIS

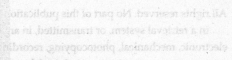

This book is produced from independently certified FSC™ paper to ensure responsible forest management.

For more information visit: www.harpercollins.co.uk/green

One More Chapter
a division of HarperCollins*Publishers*
1 London Bridge Street
London SE1 9GF
www.harpercollins.co.uk

HarperCollins*Publishers*
1st Floor, Watermarque Building, Ringsend Road
Dublin 4, Ireland

This paperback edition 2021
First published in Great Britain in ebook format
by HarperCollins*Publishers* 2021
1

A catalogue record of this book is available from the British Library

ISBN: 978-0-00-847284-9

This novel is entirely a work of fiction. The names, characters and incidents portrayed in it are the work of the author's imagination. Any resemblance to actual persons, living or dead, events or localities is entirely coincidental.

Printed and bound in the UK using 100% Renewable Electricity
by CPI Group (UK) Ltd

certified FSC™ paper
management.
rcollins.co.uk/green

*For the Elim Girls*
*(whether you want it or not)*

I am out with lanterns, looking for myself.

– Emily Dickinson

# Chapter One

## KETCHUM, ILLINOIS

## Two Decades Ago

The girl waved goodbye to her friends and pointed the ten-speed toward the center of The Thicket. Girdled by fog, the forest appeared to levitate before her. Warm air closed in, bringing with it the sweet scent of pine sap. The girl grinned wide with the strangest notion, a complete satisfaction for once, and sensed there would never be another night like this one.

She was right.

The Thicket opened to her like the gullet of a whale, the hard-packed dirt its depressed tongue. As the bike's narrow tires stuttered in and out of rain ruts and across exposed tree roots, she remotely questioned the logic of this short cut. She'd been showing off for the other kids. *Oh, I'm not afraid of the dark.* But now the moon had disappeared and the only light in the woods gleamed from an amber pinpoint halfway in.

Branches clawed at her as she sped past them. The faster she rode, the more the distant limbs vibrated and smudged as if motioning for her to come further. She plowed through a spider web and its strands clung to the hairs of her arms and eyelashes. She let out a screech and flicked something meaty from her shoulder. But she was doing it, really doing it! In fact, she could even close her eyes and stay on the trail without veering off. She cackled at her newfound ability.

The Thicket laughed back. A coyote, she reckoned.

When she opened her eyes again, the amber light was gone. Out. Disappeared. Relocated. Definitely not where it had been before.

The bike's momentum halted in an instant as her front tire struck something hard and simply refused to roll over it. The girl's butt lifted from the saddle. She sailed through branches—the black of the woods, the deep velvet blue of the sky, the black of the woods again—all of it a sickening spin until she landed with a thud on her face and chest.

Eat dirt.

Um, yeah, she got the meaning of it now. Gritty clay stuck to her teeth, thick as peanut butter. The girl spat it out and kept spitting until saliva ran down her chin. She rolled woozily back onto a bed of pine needles, blood dripping from her stinging knees and palms, shorts torn at the inseam from one hell of a cartwheel. Nearby, her bike lay tangled in tree limbs, the front wheel spinning off-kilter. The ground tilted. She pulled herself up on stinging palms, leaned back on a rotten stump to get her bearings, then wiped her chin with the back of her hand.

She looked around for the amber light to orient herself.

It was still out, still gone.

Around her, the crooked forest faintly glowed with that gooey fungus she and the other kids had smeared on their skin so they could see each other in the near dark. Foxfire, one of the boys called it. Its pale-green slime still striped her forearms.

A high-pitched buzz rang in her ear. The whir of the county road faded. The scent of licorice grew stronger than when the kids first discovered the cache of fungus. It sickened her now. *Do you get nauseous with a concussion?* She needed to rest a moment, come to her senses; then she could push her busted bike home. *Crap*, she was going to be in so much trouble for being out this late—her driver's permit revoked, maybe even her allowance cut.

She shivered in the gathering fog. At least it cleared her mind a bit.

The dewy grass by her legs fluttered; something small and slight wound through the blades. She squinted. A colony of ants on the move? Difficult to tell by the faint glowing light. She craned her neck back and the tops of the conifer trees spun. Stars had come out, but they blurred into stripes.

All around, the splotches of fungus pulsed.

She shuddered and considered calling out for her friends, running back to them before they rode too far away. Just forget the shortcut, leave the bike, suffer the consequences with Mom and Dad. She tried to push up from the ground, but her brain sloshed in her skull with the effort and she slumped back. Hopefully, the ants wouldn't bite her; hopefully, they would march around this giant blocking their path.

She rubbed her eyes and blinked.

*That's no ant colony.*

Her lips parted as a small black tendril tapped at the skin of her thigh. She thought of a tiny fairy in an old fable with arms like burnt matchsticks, knocking at a neighbor's toadstool. Her skin tingled with a slight electric current. The buzz in one ear rolled into the other, rumbling and pinging as if she were underwater.

The forest clarified, growing brighter. The effect was like switching on her brother's night-vision goggles. But instead of a green cast, everything glowed amber. Rabbits huddled where shadows used to be. A deer stood rapt between trees, its antlers crosshatching the limbs for camouflage. Down the path she'd just ridden, a fox loped off toward the bean fields. As a leering white opossum waddled past, three babies on its back, the soft crunch of leaves and pine needles tickled her eardrums.

The tendril advanced. It climbed her bare leg, winding around it three times, and found the deep scrape on her knee. She drew in a great gasp of air, but as pale webbing bubbled up across the wound, the scream died in her throat. She'd forgotten how. Not an hour before, she had played an epic game of Ghost in the Graveyard and savored the terror of the chase, her squeals ripping through the air. But now her jaw hung mute, eyes watering from the refusal to blink. Her torn skin stopped stinging. The once oozing blood rapidly dried from bright to dark, then cracked and crumbled away. Her kneecap faded to a chalky hue. Her eyes grew wider, dry mouth gulping in fascination. She sat up straight. The webbing had repaired her.

More tendrils came scouting, more than she could watch all at once. In their wake, foamy pale webs knit across her limbs. She lifted her hands for a moment, but they dropped back to the dirt as if ten times their weight. The tendrils fastened them to exposed tree roots for safekeeping.

Far off in the woods, something moved through the trees, something glowing higher and brighter than the fungus. It floated toward her with the bobbing weightlessness and transparency of a sea creature. True fear finally hit with an electric shock through her spine, brief and all-confirming. The tendrils wrapped tighter. She fell limp—a rabbit resigned.

And then she saw the boy. He stood stiffly, watching her and the growing webwork, the whites of his eyes wide and bright with fascination. It was the kid from her class, the weird one no one hung out with. If she could think of his name, she would call out to him, but she couldn't place it. She'd known him since kindergarten! She tried to call up the rest of her friends' names but could not. She wasn't even sure of her own name anymore.

It didn't matter.

She shook her head and it lolled on her shoulders. The webs dried her tears and knit her eyes shut. The tendrils found her ears, her nostrils. She let out a wry little huff, bundled there like a mummy.

*There is no point in mourning, child. This is what you wished for, after all.*

The girl burst into laughter and didn't stop laughing until the tendrils entered her throat.

Soon after, the foxfire burned out and the amber pinpoint deep in the woods lit up once more. And the boy who had watched backed slowly out of The Thicket until he felt safe enough to take his eyes off the woods and sprint for home.

As for the deer, the bugs, and coyotes, they all returned to the task of staying alive another night.

## Chapter Two

### CHICAGO

### Last Spring

I stood in a trance on the Blue Line platform, waiting for the train that would drag me away from my horror show of a presentation. Hot wind from the tunnel bellowed a sour breeze of urine and ketchup across my sweating skin, like the breath of an oncoming dragon, its belly full of passengers. Down the east end of the tunnel: darkness. And from the west: light from the street above flickering on the rails. There gleamed freedom in that light, freedom beyond this trapdoor I'd fashioned for myself. I am a child of the woods and I don't belong here, though I keep trying to deny it.

I yearned to close my eyes but didn't trust the crowd. Just a week before, a man had pushed another onto the tracks, and a passing train brutally ground him into a bloody twist and decapitated him at the archway. I yearned to close my eyes, but I didn't trust my memories.

Standing next to an iron beam, one of many that must carry the weight of this city, a street musician strummed her acoustic and crooned Carly Simon's "Nobody Does It Better". Passersby threw coins and dollars into her open guitar case, which was all red velour inside. If my train hadn't just hissed up, I would have gladly paid her ten dollars to stop echoing it throughout this subterranean passageway.

My phone buzzed. I nudged my way onto the train, grabbed a handle, and checked the texts from my boss:

DAVID: Sorry I had to come down so hard, kiddo.

(No, he wasn't.)

JANE: I understand.

DAVID: I have faith in you.

(No, he didn't.)

JANE: I know.

Someday, when I rewind this shattering year for the entertainment of my fellow patients, I will leave out the alternate routes I could have taken on this exact day. Whether for expediency or self-preservation, I won't be sure, but only the FBI and the DNR will know of my many blunders and where I might have put a stop to it all.

My first mistake was not walking out of that meeting at

Stuben Fisher Literary before promising the world. I wasn't fit to present a damn thing that afternoon. The morning had already started with a nightmare about my stalker. And true to form, his latest email had arrived with an annoying buzz during the sketchiest pitch of my career. Harrying me in my dreams was bad enough; my inbox unconscionable. I didn't think I could hate Lincoln Metzger any more at that moment. Stupid me.

While my boss, David Stuben, and the rest of the staff had sat around the conference table reading my client's sample pages, I'd shot a glance at my phone notifications.

That was my second mistake.

———

Good morning, my love. Sleep well?
— Lincoln

A pinch between my eyes; something rotten ascending my throat. More than my breakfast bowl not sitting right. Fear gone bad; fear congealed to resentment.

*If you make me angry enough, I'll fight back. Make me angry enough and I'll have my cousin murder you in her next novel.*

My phone buzzed again.

*Ignore it.*

David interrupted the reverberating silence. "That's all we get?"

I jerked, sweat gathering on my upper lip. "What? Oh, yes, for now." At this rate, I'd soak my favorite silk blouse by the end of the meeting. I sat there woodenly, fighting the urge to raise my arms.

"Three pages, Jane? Really?" He spun the papers across the conference room table. The other agents and interns shrank from them as if I'd laced the pages with anthrax. "*That* got TJ Render an advance?"

"Actually, no. We got an advance for the synopsis."

David closed his eyes and pinched the bridge of his nose between his fingers. His voice grew low and measured. "Where is the stalker you promised?"

I sneered at my phone. "Oh, he's coming, believe me—"

"And what's with the fungus?" He walked across the broad lofted room, old floorboards creaking, to the whiteboard hanging from exposed brick.

"Um, well, magic mushrooms feature prominently"—I wiped my lip—"in the story." I knew how it sounded and tried not to cringe. More heat rose in my cheeks.

David uncapped a marker and scrawled *The Thicket* in orange, next to the other client projects. The abrupt squeak of the wet felt, the chemical smell, that color—God, that color—twisted a new knot in my gut. A few of my cohorts flickered smiles of support. The intern responded to tweets on his phone.

Rarely did we all gather like this, in the rehabbed wing of a 1920s warehouse just off Lumber Street. Most of the agents worked from home now, save for David, me, and the occasional intern. But I hadn't left my shabby small town for the big city only to work out of a stuffy apartment when I could overlook the rippling jade of the Chicago River. Still, the eyes of the other agents asked: *I changed out of my pajamas for this?*

I'd soon understand that David had meant this get-together to be a celebration of sorts, and we had thrown him off his narrative. TJ and I excel at that.

David capped the marker. He ran a hand through his cropped gray hair and crossed his arms. "And she's going on vacation with an advance hanging out there."

"No! It's … for research. And reconnaissance."

He blinked with a condescending pity that sunk me. Kind of like the look my ex-boyfriend used to flick in my direction when he realized I sucked at finance, just like he thought a girl should.

The others sipped their coffees and teas, and jotted fake notes.

"Jane, you need more from this client. TJ's got to go deeper or, well, I don't think we can keep her on. She's too niche."

"Trust me," I said, nodding at the pages, "this *is* deep for her. She knew that girl."

We *both* knew that girl. And I hadn't thought about her in years. Until this morning.

David raised an eyebrow at the desperate gleam in my eye. The others traded cloudy glances. They'd never seen me this shaken.

I raised my hands, risking armpit exposure. "We are going deep. I promise." I hoped.

TJ would kill me. Her bloody heart lay in those pages, torn from her chest. And here I had stolen it, tossed it on the poker table like a stack of chips. But dammit, TJ owed me.

She owed both of us. She'd been M.I.A. for two damn weeks. What did she expect me to do?

Allergic to stress, I wrung my itching fingers. "David, it's her thriller about where we grew up. This is the one." I could picture TJ's face: a soft hurt blooming into fury. She didn't know I'd scoured her laptop that morning for something—anything—to bring here today. Heck, I would write the whole manuscript for her if I had to. All she would need to do was slap her name on it, once she got over her outrage.

Of course, first she had to come back.

"So, here's the set-up," I said, nodding with insistence. "Divorced woman returns home for her twenty-year class reunion."

"Too old." David turned to the windows and gazed down at the river. "Should be ten."

That stung, but I wrote it on my notepad. "Okay, ten. Divorced woman goes back home to her reunion. She's the belle of the ball. But she's forgotten all about the disappearances and the weird boy who fell in love with her in school. The one who can't let it go. Well, there he is, and he still can't let it go. Super creepy vibe. And now he's a city councilman."

David tilted his head and peered back at me. Another agent nodded, chin in hand.

My phone buzzed again.

For God so loved the world,
That he gave his only begotten Son,
That whosoever believeth in him should not perish

"And an evangelical!" Then, as if grabbing the waiter to add last minute appetizers to my order, I said, "With an extensive gun collection. Plus, he's a Civil War re-enactor. Oh! And a tornado chaser."

The intern snickered through his nose.

*Ooh, that little worm in his NASA T-shirt!*

David clasped his head in his hands. "Okay, we got it! But she needs a first draft soon, Jane. Elaine called and she's *not* happy. No more of this six-months crap or you'll have to pay back the advance."

My cheek twitched. TJ had already blazed through most of the money.

"You've got two months to present something workable." He came back and poked the table until his knuckle bent white. "And the research is on your dime."

"Got it!"

David clapped hands. "Okay, folks, since I have you all here, I have a little announcement. Well, actually"—he fidgeted, rattling keys in his pocket; he'd already forgotten his annoyance with me and had gone red-faced and, dare I say, frightened of our blank stares—"it's a big one. Now," he chuckled, "stay with me here."

He grabbed another marker, a red one this time, and blocked off a new quadrant on the whiteboard. There he scrawled:

### A NEW ERA: DOWNER'S GROVE!

Audible gasps puffed throughout the room. The intern's phone dropped to the hardwood floor with a clatter.

The light in the train car flickered, then gave in to darkness. The crowd murmured as we rumbled down the tracks. I swayed with the train's momentum and braced for a mugging.

Instead I got the damn dream.

*Six feet above me, Lincoln looming in his baggy white tux, dirty at the knees. His mouth forms a simper that twitches with hesitation. He wags his finger, and because I won't stop screaming, lets loose the trapdoor. With a slam, he leaves me suspended in a pit of black. I hang by the wrists, not in silence, but marinating in the continual loop of his mother's easy listening records meant to tenderize me for his sham of a dungeon wedding.*

Nobody does it better. Yeah, my dreams are epic. They always have been.

The lights flashed back on and everyone looked around at each other with sudden kinship, grateful to all be in one piece.

*Should I tell them we're not?*

We never were. We're all so many pieces.

*We're relocating to Downer's Grove,* David had admitted to the staff.

No. No. No. This couldn't be happening.

David moving the agency to the suburbs meant Stuben Lit was headed to the minor leagues. In two years, we'd be down to a couple agents, three if we were lucky. To our Manhattan-based peers, a Midwestern literary agent was already akin to a horse-drawn carriage salesman in Detroit circa 1915. But we had a (mostly) dependable crop of writers appealing to readers from Ohio to Utah. We knew our market. All the more reason for TJ and me to swing for the fences on her next book, and earn David's downtown rent.

But there was just so much to do, piles of words and dozens of chapters and drafts upon drafts and none of it starting without TJ's skills.

The train stopped at the next station. New strangers pushed together, our bodies jostling on the edge of intimacy. The car rattled beneath me while I gazed absentmindedly into the lush brown forest of a beard on the hipster a foot away. As we emerged from the underground and passed through downtown, sunlight flickered between the skyscrapers and strobed across my face. It reminded me of an ancient threat I had once known, but I was too distracted by every other thing in my life to place it.

I nibbled the inside of my cheek. Maybe I wouldn't need to tell TJ that I'd stolen her chapter. I could interject ideas for this manuscript, and she would believe she'd thought of them. It was a common tactic. How hard could it be on this one? I'd helped her research her last novel so extensively I could pass as a hard-boiled lesbian detective if pressed into service.

Around the car, stares alighted on me: some greedy, some apathetic; mostly men, a few perturbed older women. With wild red hair, I'm hard to miss. Some days I swear Lincoln is lurking behind the window of the next car, and I will cower in a corner seat until my stop, and then dash to my apartment, glancing over my shoulder all the while. I hadn't sensed him today but I still felt a strong presence behind me. Or rather, smelled one. The burning juniper stench of gin. Fanfuckingtastic. At least my stop was next. The engine disengaged as momentum carried us to the station.

I held my shoulder bag close and pretended great interest in my phone, only to be greeted by Lincoln's latest:

What dress did we choose today?
Something pink to match your freckles, I hope.

I yearned to respond, just once, *We chose my black suit, asshole. And pitted out my favorite blouse. Sexy, huh?*

The man behind me moved closer, his fermented whisper in my curls. "Does the carpet match the—"

I dug my heel into the stranger's toe.

"Yeowch!" The man bent over to grab his foot. The brakes screeched and the train lurched to a stop, sending him tumbling. TJ would be proud. In fact, I could swear her brand of giggles erupted from one of the other women in the car.

I stepped over the man and his wet paper bag of Seagram's, pushing my way out before the doors shut. Emboldened, I willed Lincoln to be here too so I could unload my can of mace in his eyes and demand to know why he was still emailing me, why he was invading my dreams, why he wouldn't give up after two fucking decades. If he were here, I would push him off the platform, onto the third rail, into the path of an oncoming train.

Okay, maybe just into the eternal puddle of piss that's always pooling by the turnstile.

I slogged down the metal stairs onto the sidewalk by Belmont Avenue, tears welling in my eyes. I tried to be brave, but with TJ absent without leave, the nightmares were getting worse. They felt so real; half of them were recollections, if we're being truthful.

"TJ," I said to the sky. I didn't care how it looked. "I can't do this without you."

## Chapter Three

In the foyer, my keys hit the sideboard next to the class reunion invite. I'd left it there to entice TJ when she sauntered in. It hadn't moved, and was only collecting dust. So were my credit card bills and a manila envelope addressed to TJ Render marked, *Foreclosure: Final Notice*.

The room rang with silence, but maybe that was just me feeling sorry for myself. I bolted the door, slipped out of my pumps, and padded to the bathroom. I splashed water on my face but the mascara refused to budge, and I opened the medicine cabinet to look for the make-up wipes. There, a honey-colored bottle stared at me, as it had every day for a month:

NICK STONE

TAKE 1-2 TABLETS EVERY 4-6 HOURS

OXYCODONE

Just one would feel so good, would smooth over the day's humiliation, soften my newly single status, blur my financial woes, and transform it all into a warm chuckle on the couch. Two would ease me down to the edge of sweet oblivion. And three? Oh, three…

My hand hovered by the bottle. I would dump them in the toilet. *No, that contaminates the water. Makes the fish high.* I could turn them in at a hospital. *No, why let them go to waste?* I should call him, give them back. *No! I'm so done with him.*

I slammed the medicine cabinet shut and closed my eyes. The pressure dropped. I took a deep breath and opened my eyes, slowly exhaling between my lips.

In the mirror's reflection, TJ sat hunched behind her computer in the darkness of my den, her sometimes place of residence. She wore a tank top and cut-offs, an act of defiance this early in spring, as if she could summon summer just by dressing for it. Her gaming headphones smushed the middle of her spiky blonde hair as she peered at the screen, clicking away at the online game *World of Warcraft*.

I leaned against the bathroom doorframe and barked across the hall, "When did you get back?" All around the den lay bags of clothes, licorice wrappers, and empty Pringles cans.

TJ pushed one headphone aside. "Huh?"

"Where the heck have you been?" I demanded. "It's been two weeks!"

She wiggled her eyebrows. "Here and there."

A bed here, a bed there, no doubt.

TJ tapped the keyboard with rapid-fire blows. If only I

could stand before her with a big yellow question mark above my head, a dangerous quest to accept, a shiny new set of armor for her to earn.

"Goddammit," I whispered and stomped to the foyer, bare heels pounding the floor. I snatched the invite and thumped back to the den.

I slid the card next to her keyboard.

TJ kept on clicking, her face made lavender by the monitor light, her lip piercings like gleaming pinpoints. My best friend of three decades—once the hammer to my nail, the drama to my peace, the gravity to my orbit—TJ sat there, a slave to the endless quest for e-gold and e-glory, as entranced as an assembly line worker wishing on the lottery.

After a while of my glaring, she looked down at the invite then back to the screen.

"Mmm," she said. "Pass."

I forced myself to merrily state, "Oh, we're going."

TJ grumbled. "Eh, I blacked out at the ten-year reunion. Really not keen on discovering what brand of asshole I made of myself."

"Come on. I'm sure everyone has forgotten by now." They hadn't. "How's the book coming?"

She returned a nudge of the shoulder. "I toldya, April. April … fifteenth."

"When taxes are due."

"Yeah, so?" TJ mashed the keyboard buttons. "I can last-minute more than one thing at a time."

"Actually, you suck at that. Seriously, Teej, I got my ass handed to me today because of you."

I wished I hadn't said that. This whole agent/author arrangement had wedged a burr into our relationship. Before I took her writing on, we had never questioned each other's life choices. If I chose a twit for a boyfriend, TJ made every effort to like him, and never said, "I told you so" when it fell apart. If she picked up goat yoga or poetry slams or—dear, God—absinthe, I tried it too. Now it was all me harrying her like a mom. Come to think of it, that's also how it went with her lovers too until they nagged her out the door and on to the next.

"Really?" she said. "*Really?* You're going to do this?"

"Listen—"

"Not you, Janey." *Click-click-click.* "The healer. Oh my God, what a nozzle! Ha, I'm droppin' group. Try to find another tank now, ya newbs."

Thirty-seven and still playing axe-wielding Brunhildes. I turned to the hall. Plenty of laundry needed doing. "Okay, you seem busy with very important stuff."

"You know this is how I relax, Jane," she said.

Yes, I knew she had her reasons. We both knew what she was running from. Over the years, we'd talked so much and yet broached so few topics concerning her father. But a trip back home could equalize us, remind her why we sought the yellow brick road instead of the small-town life in Ketchum, Illinois.

I poked my head back in. "Did you know the Norway gunman played Warcraft to relax? He killed seventy-seven people."

"Uh, I'm sure he ate Nutella too. Am I supposed to stop using spreadable chocolate?"

"It *is* high in processed sugar."

The clicking stopped. "Hold up." TJ sat back, crossing her arms so that the thorny tattoos encircling her biceps bulged. "Okay, now let's think about this, Jane. Why exactly do we need to go back downstate? That's like the definition of loser in Dictionary-dot-com."

"Since when is visiting friends and family being a loser? You haven't seen your mom in years!" How deft I am at switching arguments, I thought, then realized we were no longer talking about her writing. "It might be good to make peace with it all."

"I'd rather visit your parents in Boca."

"Okay, we could drive to Florida after the reunion," I nodded, "drop off the rental, pull up some beach chairs, get down a solid fifty pages, then fly back?"

She puffed air at her bangs. "Heard from Lincoln lately?"

"All effing day. Going on and on about the evil in the woods and the end times. I'm sure he'll email me again this weekend for his birthday."

TJ snickered. "To tell you what presents he got from himself?"

"And what steakhouse he went to. Party of one."

"*Bake potata.*" Her head shook, mockingly.

I snorted. "*Side a corn.*"

"*Slice a pie.*" TJ straightened up. "Why don't you just fucking block him?"

"He keeps changing his email address!" I shook my phone at her. "This is the second one this month. Remember the woman in Lake Forest who blocked her husband on

Facebook and he shot her? Maybe if Lincoln feels like his messages are being read then that's all he needs. He just wants to be thought of."

"You still feel guilty about high school." TJ nodded, so assured of knowing my every thought. "You don't owe him any—"

I closed my eyes and moaned. "Can we talk about something else?"

"Well, we'd be going right down there to him. You sure you wanna tickle that bear?"

"No! But why should we let him ruin it? Besides, if the others see that he's still doing this to me, maybe they'll help. I can't run forever."

"What about Nick?"

"That's over. And you know I can't go alone. Lincoln might … abduct me."

TJ's eyes slid left to right. "Could be source material for a homecoming romance, I guess. Or a story about stalkers."

"Exactly!" I looked away, out into the hall again, trying to tamp down my enthusiasm. I have a terrible poker face and TJ's moods were as skittish as those of a stray cat. "Plus, it could be fun?"

"Or it could be a massacre," she said, eyes now half-lidded.

"Both, most likely."

TJ pulled her best geek voice, lisping and nasal, "I do have the highest damage-per-second."

*Go deeper.*

We stared at each other like that, sarcasm teetering on something more honest. The last thing I needed to do was mention her dad right now. Her stare drifted back toward the monitor, the game flickering in the blue-gray of her eyes. *Play me!*

And then I thought of the one word that could yank this once-promising novelist out of her video game and make her cough up a magnificent hairball of sentences that might save both our careers.

"Also," I said, waiting. I wanted her full attention for this.

She raised an eyebrow.

"Mushrooms."

Her gaze drilled through me. "*Dude,*" she whispered, "I haven't tripped since we left Ketchum."

"Me neither." A half-truth. I watched her ponder it as she pushed back her cuticles with a thumbnail.

"You could stand to loosen up a bit, Jane," she said. "Widen your horizons."

I nodded with a shrug and a good-natured smile. "So?"

She chuckled. "Oh, don't get your tits in a knot."

I raised a fist into the air. "Quest accepted!"

## Chapter Four

### KETCHUM

Lincoln Metzger sat in the fortified basement of the Metzger family's abandoned farmhouse and logged into *World of Warcraft*. TJ Render was on. Unlike his dear Lady Jane, TJ had been easy to watch. Egotists always were. Her blathering in an interview about videogames had opened the door and then it had taken only a few weeks of combing servers until he found her character. He didn't chat with her at first, just followed at a distance and joined her guild: *Eats Shoots And Leaves*. Over the months, he moved up the ranks and didn't engage her, even after becoming an officer under her reign. Then she asked him for a favor— ever the user—and now they were friends of a sort. And that put him one step closer to his beloved.

Not that Jane would ever play. Sometimes a low-level sorceress did show up in the guild, and Lincoln would introduce his paladin only to find out she was some guy in Topeka or Orlando. And then he would scoff at himself for thinking Lady Jane would ever waste her time killing pretend dragons and battling through imaginary dungeons.

It wasn't that Jane couldn't be found online, with the right techniques. Her bio and literary agency popped up in search engines, but while Jane had been easy to find, the depth of information stopped at her work. She did not need to exist online. Unlike TJ, Jane had a professional reputation to protect, not an ego to burnish. Jane existed in the real world. In Chicago, two hundred miles away of course, but right now she felt as close as the next room. The idea that she could be just upstairs, in the kitchen frying up liver and onions, or in the laundry room folding their towels, filled him with pure love.

Lincoln reached for the cylindrical device he kept nearby, the one with the soft pink opening on one end. He gazed at photos of Jane that he'd mounted all along the basement wall over the years: enlarged shots from the high school yearbook; candids taken without her awareness on the streets of Chicago. Some of the photos hung loose, fluttering above the space heater, their tape coming unstuck.

He unzipped his khakis, flicked on the device, and it came to life with whirring, annoying insistence.

Beneath Lady Jane's gallery grew a black, veiny fungus that had made inroads on the old stone walls over the years. There was much work to be done in this old house—good work—before he could bring Jane home. He turned off the device and zipped back up. *Not tonight, sweetheart.* He really needed to consider saving himself for her. Jane would fit him, just so. He knew she would. Better than the toys, better than the hitchhiker he'd made the mistake with. The one who'd stared up at him blank and disappointed at what he'd done to her. That one who'd had to be dealt with in an unclean way. God had forgiven him. That was all that mattered.

The game dinged at Lincoln. He peered at the screen, like a spider gazing down the long strands of its web as the fly buzzed in for a landing.

Mindrender: Hey there, Night.

Lincoln cracked his knuckles, and his fingers glided across the keyboard.

NightTemplar: Good Evening!
Mindrender: You raiding tonight?
NightTemplar: Most certainly. You?
Mindrender: Nah, I gotta work. My boss's belchin' fire.

His breath caught, pulse quickening, and his thighs flapped together.

NightTemplar: He's a real jerk, aye?
Mindrender: She. Yunno, they're not all guys.
NightTemplar: Most are.
Mindrender: Whatevs. She's a good egg. Friend since high school.

Times like this when the planets aligned for Lincoln, he

knew he wasn't imagining it. The Lord was bringing his Lady Jane back to him. They would fight their problems together. He would show her what a real hero was in this ugly world.

> NightTemplar: That's interesting. That you work with an old friend.
> Mindrender: Yeah, cousin actually.
> NightTemplar: Does she play WoW?
> Mindrender: lol. no, she all biznuz.

Lincoln swooned.

> NightTemplar: You should bring her in. Help her relax.
> Mindrender: I should go. Just popped on to check my auctions.
> Mindrender: Made twenty Gs off that crappy sword.
> NightTemplar: Grats.

Lincoln's shoulders slumped. He didn't bother saying goodbye.

Warcraft, he scoffed. All the adventure and none of the death, dismemberment, or PTSD. TJ didn't know the meaning of war. Typical liberal. When a real person died, there were no easy resurrections. This he'd seen first-hand.

His Lady Jane though, she valued life. Ever since her recovery stint at the Hazelden Clinic, Jane was all business. Well, Jane needed a break. Jane needed to get out of Chicagoland. She would be thirty-eight in July. Despite the danger sprouting up around Ketchum, it was time for her to let go of the big city dreams and make a family with him before it was too late. The rot that had been growing in and around Ketchum had reached his doorstep, and it was make-or-break time.

Lincoln clicked the email program icon. In that infinite moment, as he waited for it to open, he prayed Lady Jane had responded to his latest email. She hadn't in years, but he always prayed anyway.

His breath caught.

**From:** Render, Jane [jRender@stubenliterary.com]
**To:** Metzger, Lincoln [hansolo99@frontieronline.net]
**Subject:** RE: Trouble in The Thicket

Please stop.
There is nothing wrong with those woods.
I do not love you.
Nor have I ever loved you.
I have a boyfriend already.
It's time to move on.

The power of prayer was a mixed bag. He read it again. And again. Then, licking his lips, fired off a response:

**From:** Metzger, Lincoln [hansolo99@frontieronline.net]
**To:** Render, Jane [jRender@stubenliterary.com]
**Subject:** RE: RE: Trouble in The Thicket

My Dear Lady Jane,

My aim was simply to discuss something important.
You can't mean the things you have said. It is Chicago
and TJ talking, not the Jane I fell in love with. I just
want you home and safe.

Come home, Lady Jane. Come back to me.

Love forever,
Lincoln

He combed his fingernails down his mustache and
started another email.

**From:** Metzger, Lincoln [hansolo99@frontieronline.net]
**To:** Render, Jane [jRender@stubenliterary.com]
**Subject:** RE: RE: Trouble in The Thicket

Jane,

Do not shut me out. You must never shut me out.
And do not lie to me again. I know Nick is gone.

Lincoln

Okay, Jane was playing demure right now; she needed
to miss him. A new dream had been brewing, and he knew
from experience that nostalgia was a heady elixir. Even his
levelheaded Lady Jane would be downright inhuman to
ignore a taste of it.

Maybe today was the day. He'd overheard at the diner that the reunion invitations had gone out weeks ago. Why hadn't he gotten his? Didn't matter. He would show up anyway. It was his right as valedictorian.

Lincoln shuffled upstairs, across the worn blue carpet to the front door. On the porch, he peered eastward toward The Thicket on the far side of his farm. The rain on the fir trees had blackened their trunks so they looked burnt. Mist obscured the depths of the woods so that no faces stared back today, but the voices hissed all the same. The girl, the woman, his brother.

*She's coming home, boy. She's coming home.*

Lincoln shuddered and drove his sockless feet into high tops. All this moisture meant he'd have to go out and spray the perimeter of the house twice today just to keep those rooting webs at bay.

He peered up at the sky, searching for the first delicate hints of a funnel.

Electricity gathered in the air, raising the hairs on his neck. The earthy scent of nitrogen hit the back of his nose.

He would need to be quick.

Lincoln sprinted down the gravel drive to the mailbox, raindrops pelting him, and jammed his hand into its metal mouth, scraping around for every last bit.

"Danged postcards."

He sprinted back toward the house and the air went white. He leapt for the door just as the boom rattled the windowpanes.

After drying off in the kitchen with a hand towel, he

flipped through the envelopes, the latest *Manosphere* newsletter on men's rights, the Fleet Farm circular, and found the formal invite. He tore open the lip and ripped out the card.

## CLASS OF 1999:
### I'LL STAND BY YOU

## Chapter Five

"That's all you're bringing?" I pressed the key fob and the SUV tailgate rose skyward.

TJ flung her messenger bag into the cavernous trunk. "Jeans, shorts, coupla shirts. What else do I need? I'm going off-grid. You should too. You didn't bring your phone, did you?"

"What do you think!" I clutched at my full suitcase, packed with two weeks of clothes and shoes for every occasion and weather pattern. The nail of my forefinger bent backward. "Feck."

"We should really just go dark," TJ said. "Live dangerously." She grabbed my suitcase by the side handle and swung it into the back like a bale of hay. She nodded at me. "Move." I hopped back and she slammed the tailgate shut. "If we're connected to the city, how are we supposed to get a feel for things? How we gonna do this authentically, organically?"

Like most things TJ spouted, it sounded good in theory. I

loathed the tether of my iPhone, weary of the constant flow of query letters and the nag of social media, but I still had manuscripts to read, contracts to negotiate, authors to promote.

"Um, hello? I do have a 24/7 job, you know. I can't just faff off down to The Thicket and frolic around like some *artiste*."

"This was your idea, not mine."

We piled into the SUV and pulled away from the curb. The interior smelled like a leather bar—cologne, animal hides, and a sweaty hint of past indiscretions.

I waved in the rear-view mirror, "Goodbye, Lakeview." It would all feel surreal when we returned. It always did after a vacation, as if walking in on a stranger's apartment, the angles and smells foreign. "Well, at least you brought your laptop," I said.

"Did you know new-car smell is carcinogenic?"

"You brought your laptop, *right*?"

She hesitated and then grinned. "Of course! You even know how to drive this thing?"

"Of course!" I mimicked her braggadocio.

So there we went on the first Friday in June, negotiating a hulking SUV down the crowded streets of Chicago toward the Kennedy Expressway on-ramp. Though it had cost more than I could justify, nearly maxing out my remaining credit card, I was wary of my driving skills after a decade of hailing Ubers and taking the train. I could feel TJ's judgment upon me. But surely I'd earned enough carbon credits by now to warrant this wasteful choice?

TJ turned on the radio and classic rock blared from it.

Normally, this should have resulted in elaborate gag reflexes for each other's amusement, but neither of us reached for another station. Supertramp's harmonica riff cried as we hit the Dan Ryan, the sun setting on the glass towers and lighting up the tar repairs in the roads like tributaries of molten gold. My teeth throbbed from two weeks of hardcore whitening, but something else brimmed inside me too.

We didn't speak as the road whirred beneath us, knowing we were about to create a memory that would last into old age. And one day, on a beach somewhere, we would lie baked and spotty and wrinkled and sloshed on rumrunners, croaking our amazement at how funny and outrageous it had all been and how we'd written a best seller in the process. All I had to do was look at TJ to seal the import of this moment. She nodded back at me from a passenger seat much too far away, and I took a deep breath.

Long way home. Long way home. Long way home…

Soon, the buckled asphalt of the south side slid to a stop and we sat partially deflated in traffic.

"Not exactly Fast and Furious up in here," TJ said.

"Why are you in such a hurry?"

"I'm not. But when I'm in a car I feel it should actually go somewhere."

"When's the last time you were on the interstate?"

She shrugged. "So, um, how's it going at work? David still mad?"

"He's on low boil. If we don't come up with something this month—"

"Hey, it's not my fault, y'know." TJ gazed out the

window, tracing distant graffiti onto it with her finger. "You were supposed to be the writer in the family."

True. I was the one who'd completed the prestigious Iowa writing program after my bachelor's. She had shuffled through odd jobs and DJ gigs. All the while, I clawed my way out of the quicksand of the slush pile to finally take on my first client. I read soul-crushingly bad manuscripts in the day, and mind-broadening books at night—the old greats like O'Connor, Faulkner, James; the new greats like Murakami, Whitehead, Jemisin—and wondered how the hell I could ever say anything as remotely important.

TJ, on the other hand, was so blissfully unaware of the giants that had come before that every cliché popping up in her first pulpy manuscript felt somehow fresh. It didn't take long for me to grasp that no one had handed her *talent*. Boundless ideas had flowed from her ever since we were teens, while we were smoking pot or eating psychedelic mushrooms with our friends in The Thicket. And since then, every damn thing that happened to her or someone in her orbit became "material."

I just needed to scratch that itch in her again.

Eventually the interstate cleared out, the sight of big box stores heralding the suburbs. We passed the giant navy-blue warehouse with its iconic yellow sign.

*Go deeper.*

"I suppose a trip to Ikea on the way back is out of the question?"

I held my breath.

TJ took a moment from watching the highway scroll at us at seventy miles an hour to shoot me an aggravated look.

I had received my answer, but that wasn't the point of course. The point was to tickle.

TJ had once discovered a dead woman in an Ikea living room showcase. She had gotten lost in the maze, refusing to follow the arrows—TJ, that is (though perhaps the woman too, come to think of it)—and she kept seeing the same lady in denim slumped thoughtfully at the center of a Söderhamn sectional. It scared the shit out of TJ, so much that she didn't leave my apartment for a week. And then she had gone on to spout, "*It changed my life*" at many a party and bar. I could have told anyone listening that every month a random encounter on a living room sectional somewhere in Boystown changed her life.

TJ shuddered. "I wrote that down, you know. I thought she was following me at first and just sitting whenever I walked by. Like a fan of my books or something. Then I thought she was one of those promotional mimes you see in Grant Park. Then some other lady started screaming. Her sister, I think."

"Would make an interesting route into a story. The Lady in the Denim Suit."

"Mmm." TJ's merciless eyes thankfully returned to watching the suburbs fly by. "So would Lincoln."

*Aha!* "You think? Hmm. Maybe so." I smiled out the window.

"Why can't I have a stalker?" TJ asked. "Like, a female stalker. A cute one. One that doesn't die on a couch at Ikea. Why can't that happen?"

"I'm sure if you snapped your fingers any one of your readers would oblige."

"Yeah, but I want them to come to it on their own." She laughed. "Like Lincoln. I mean, you sort of like it on some level, right? That constant affirmation?"

I balked, the SUV swerving over the middle line for a moment. "Um, no! You don't want that because it sucks, TJ. Besides, women don't feel entitled to our bodies the way men do. Why would you want that? Sometimes I swear I see him on the street following me."

"Ooh, what if you do?"

Making her writer's mind itch hadn't turned out as I'd hoped.

TJ changed the radio to a Top 40 channel and soon we were air-drumming to Imagine Dragons. Eventually, neighborhoods grew sparse, the sky darkening until stars winked on. I set the cruise control and turned the fan down on the air. What had taken years to escape would come into view in two hours or less.

"How much of the last one do you remember?" I asked.

"The reunion? Not much." TJ shuddered. "How about you?"

I tried not to smile.

TJ raised her hands. "Please don't tell me."

Even a distant drunken summer night in the last decade was immediately retrievable. In a mere ten years, the small-town kids we'd known were already starting to bloat, time exacting its inexorable price. I hadn't even considered I might be paying the same cost.

We Render girls were basic European farm stock, but we glammed-up well enough. TJ was a lanky, short-haired blonde—a real Valkyrie—accustomed to captivating book club ladies and fangirls. My curves, curls, and feminine charms were of more use at the high school reunion banquet. We just knew, even before walking into the Ketchum VFW, we had to be the top story.

However, the actual top story was of another disappearance, an all too common occurrence around Ketchum. The next generation of Thicket Kids had lost one of their own. A gay seventeen-year-old boy had walked into the dense forest bordering our hometown, and never came out. The local paper used the term "hate-crime"—a step forward for our neck of the woods—but we all knew better.

That night ten years ago at the VFW, TJ and I arrived unaware of the pall that had already fallen over our classmates. I had overdressed in a white wrap-around full-on Marilyn Monroe dress, still far from an age when poorly conceived lighting was a concern. TJ had gone back to dorky sidekick, just like in high school. I had been sure my graduate studies in southern gothic literature would finally be the inscrutably sexy topic I had always dreamed it would be. By 11 p.m. we'd managed to stomp the top story below the fold. At least for one night.

Awkward Lincoln Metzger had hung about in the shadows with the same bowl haircut, same baggy jeans, unable to gather the nerve to approach, while his small eyes followed me everywhere. I'd known he would email something epic the next day when I couldn't tell him to get lost. But the other guys, like my ex-boyfriend Paul, had fawned all night, their wives withdrawn and gossiping. I had wanted to assure those women I had no designs on their husbands, but where would the fun be in that?

Meanwhile, TJ had challenged our class to blindfolded karaoke, the Cha Cha slide, bucketloads of warm sake, and day-old sushi. She'd managed to entertain the guys, piss off the girls, middle-finger salute all those she swore had called her an art-fart, and then she'd vomited an orange and green mélange onto the one teacher who had bothered to show up. In fairness, he should have known it was way too late in TJ's intoxication process to test the stomach-calming benefits of pickled ginger.

Oh, they hadn't forgotten us. I cringed out the window. *This better be worth it.*

---

It was full-on night as we sailed through Illinois farmland. Outside the SUV windows, giant monolithic silos stood like silent sentinels of a land from which we'd been exiled.

"You know what's odd," I said, "I can't remember what Paul McKenna looks like."

TJ tilted her seat back, stretched her legs out onto the dash, and into her pile of empty candy wrappers. "Paunchy probably."

"Naturally, Lincoln is clear as day."

"It pays to stay in touch, I guess." The backs of TJ's fingernails drummed on the window. "Not sure I can do this without getting high. Wine or edibles? Your call."

My brow furrowed. I still hadn't admitted my pill problem and the trip to Hazelden last year, when TJ had been off gallivanting. I was afraid she would put it in a novel. She would love it; she'd give it a chapter and name it something precious like "Her Velvet Troubles." No squalid detail is ever safe around a novelist. Besides, I had it under control now. Control is my strong suit. Soon the pills would be an embarrassing memory I could wipe.

"Maybe we should roll into town eyes wide open," I said.

"Then let's lie low tonight. Get something to eat and fuel up before Ketchum, all right?"

"Affirmative," I said with a single nod.

We passed a giant metal crucifix, six stories high, lit by massive spotlights and standing next to a trucking plaza. "Mmm, maybe the next stop."

"Gas, donuts, and Jesus," TJ said with a wry chuckle. "Mankind's final irony? Self-inflicted extinction by belief in an afterlife."

Until this trip, I had never once suggested TJ go back to visit Ketchum, not even to see her mother or come down with me to visit my parents before they moved to Florida.

It had been twenty-five years since her father's service revolver discharged in his own face, killing him instantly in front of his wife and daughter. So, it was a given that TJ undertook this trip knowing dark memories lay ahead. But there were good memories too, weren't there? From when we were preteens and some even after his death. She'd made the most of high school after all, not letting anyone see her pain, turning it into art and music, class clowning.

The stars came out and the lights of Birkenham glowed to the west of the interstate. The closer we got, the closer the heart of the matter grew.

TJ sat up. "Did you know that from 1975 to 2005, Rand

county had a higher incidence of death per capita than Cook county?"

"No. I didn't know. That's, um, quite specific," I murmured, chancing a peek to gauge her stress levels. The cool blue light from the dash revealed nothing.

"And the majority of all those murders, accidents, suicides, and kidnappings, they happened around Ketchum," TJ said. "Isn't that weird? Jacob Metzger, Dad, the woman in the trash bag, Roy's crash, the girl who disappeared near the train trestle?"

"Evie Weiss." We both knew she remembered the girl's name.

"Yeah, Evie." TJ nodded out at the bean fields.

"So … you've been researching this." *Finally*, I thought, we can get this out in the open and I can tell her that I know about the chapter, that I've already presented it, and that that's what's bought us some time.

TJ hadn't even been there the night Evie disappeared. But the chapter was as good an explanation as any we kids had coughed up for our parents about that night. Setting aside for a moment that the whole story might save our skins with the publisher, I was dying to know what else TJ would excavate. I wanted answers on so many levels.

"Well, you wanted me to come here to write something deep, yeah?"

"Yes, but not if it's too painful." I cringed at my selfishness. "You haven't ever thought about hurting yourself, have—"

"God no, Jane!" She looked at me and laughed. "C'mon! I want to see how life turns out. Come on, Janey. Seriously."

I nodded, licking my lips. Should I wait and let her tell me about the chapter?

"I mean…" she added.

"Because if this is triggering you in any way we can turn right back around." *Dammit, why did I say trigger?* "It's definitely not worth it to me."

A massive lie. It was worth everything to me. I gritted my teeth, hoping she didn't ask to turn back. Because I knew, deep down I knew. Even if we had to tug this story out by the roots, even if its thorns bloodied our hands, even if it left us with disfiguring scars, we needed to remember.

"Jane. I'm fine." TJ cracked her knuckles and her face went soft, lacking guile for once. "Not saying it isn't going to be hard, but it's not hard in that way."

If anyone could make something beautiful out of something hideous, it was TJ. I released a calming breath.

But it didn't take.

## Chapter Six

The engine of Lincoln Metzger's truck pinged as it cooled off at the end of his long gravel drive. His heavy eyelids fluttered, having stayed open a full twenty-eight hours after saying goodbye to the Missouri storm chasers. He would have to go inside eventually. He'd left the porchlight on and it beckoned warmly to him. But there was movement in The Thicket to the east. The voices huddled close and whispered, as if they knew where he'd been.

*You'll find no answers in the wind, son.*

*Come to us, you'll find them here.*

*How about a ride, big boy?*

"No," he muttered. "Go back to hell."

He opened his phone and thumbed through the album of storms he'd captured. The image of daylight, even daylight blanketed with wall clouds, soothed him a measure.

The night before Lincoln Metzger turned five years old, a fleetfooted EF3 tornado touched down on Birkenham's outskirts, danced across the countryside into Ketchum township and through the Metzger cornfields. On its heels followed a brilliant light show of a thunderstorm that pelted the roof with marbles of hail, then gave way to a nightlong shower.

The next morning, Edith and Byron Metzger sat weeping as Lincoln ran through the house in his Winnie the Pooh pajamas, looking for birthday presents and for his older brother, who he knew was hiding a new drum set for Lincoln in his closet.

"Where's Jacob?"

His mother could do no more than sputter, her face all pink and wet and stretched into a horrible mask.

"The Lord took your brother up in that funnel with a flash of lightning," his father said.

Two days later, Lincoln sat between his parents in the front row at church, smiling chin-up at such an honor for they normally sat in the back. But then he stared confused at the gleaming black box in front of him.

"If God took Jacob up there," he whispered, "how come he's also down here in that box? Can we open it? And say hi?"

His father glared at him. "You want a whippin'? I will take you outside right now."

"No, sir."

His mother wept and never stopped.

Off and on over the years, Lincoln thought back to the fading thunder strikes he had counted as he dozed off that stormy night. Had he heard the holy bolt? Was it the one that had rattled the leaded panes of the farmhouse? Did the funnel whisk Jacob up high into the clouds when it shot back up? Why did God want a teenager? Could Jacob persuade God to let him come back to visit? If Jacob had also been in the box that went underground, he must be able to be in more than one place at a time. God surely was a mystery.

As Lincoln grew older, he suspected he'd been lied to. A twister hadn't vacuumed up his brother into Never-never Land. Something far uglier had occurred involving lightning. But Lincoln still held out for the possibility of a tornado as an express elevator to paradise.

He also suspected his brother wanted no part of returning, that heaven had better scenery, better people, better everything. This made sense at least. But no one else seemed ready to accept it, not least his mother. Edith locked Jacob's room so no one could enter.

When Byron saw that the ghost of his son was seeping out from under the door, in little corrosive ways—sunlight catching the crystals Jacob had mounted on his window, an AM radio alarm set to a Chicago rock station that went on every morning because Edith refused to turn it off, even the change of carpet at the door frame because Jacob had insisted on purple shag—he threatened to tear the house down and build anew. And for a spell, Edith went along with it. They drew up plans for a newfangled ranch home that would level all that had gone crooked.

Lincoln grew excited for the move to his new room. But on the day of the farmhouse wrecking, Edith ran out in her housecoat. She leapt in front of the backhoe, coming within an inch of its diving scoop, so close that Lincoln nearly became motherless too.

Edith would allow her husband his new house. But the old farmhouse would stand empty, just fifty yards away, a haunted monument to their favorite and firstborn. Every tornado that crossed the prairie would remind the Metzgers of what they'd lost, for the old home's bulkhead housed the storm shelter.

———————

Tonight, the old farmhouse stood dark before Lincoln's truck, inking out the stars, its pitched roof a black arrow to heaven. The Thicket whispered again.

*She is here... She is here...*

Lincoln's weary eyes popped open, a fresh jolt of adrenaline coursing through him. He peered into The Thicket. Within its depths, pale lights surged west, like a runway.

*She is here.*

*She is here.*

*She is here.*

*She is here.*

*She is—*

## Chapter Seven

"The trash bag with body parts they found out in The Thicket, back in the 90s?" TJ murmured at the dense black of the forest passing by on either side of us. "Was that real? Or a campfire story?"

"I think it was real. She was a sex worker, from Champaign or Birkenham. But we also made it a campfire story because we were callous little brats."

The SUV had just rolled out of the last large town, on the twenty-mile stretch of blacktop to Ketchum, when we entered our old haunt, what some old-timer had dubbed "The Thicket," a compact but dense woodland that butted up to the ditches on either side of that diving and climbing county road known as Seven Hills. The twisted oaks and towering conifers threatened to blacken out an already dark sky.

"I used to picture Pan out there," TJ murmured. I knew she didn't mean Peter.

"Meanwhile, the rest of us were picturing Freddie Krueger."

TJ scoffed. "Yeah, bush league. No, I always imagined the Greek god Pan, all cloven-hooved, with huge antlers and furry legs. The trickster lord, with eyes gleaming like amber."

"Amber as the Donzerly Light?"

"Oh my God, you read my mind!"

I smirked. "It's not hard."

Tucked back in those woods was the Donzerly Light. An enchanted place. At least to us kids. A magical, cursed light anointed by tales of drunken teens.

"I wonder if it's still there," TJ muttered.

"I wonder if it still works."

"We can't leave town without checking, you know."

I nodded and squinted out into the trees flicking by, searching for the amber of the light. Or Pan's eyes.

"'Member Ms. Van Laar showing us those old filmstrips in grade school when she ran out of VHS tapes?" TJ gazed over at me. "The creepy ones from the 1960s, with fables in them. One had Pan in it. Remember that?"

"Sorta?" I lied. Of course I remembered. It had petrified me.

We could not have been more than seven years old, sitting in a darkened windowless A/V room. We watched agape as faded images, some partially obscured by lightbulb burns, flashed up on the screen of a hairy-legged cartoon man with hooves chasing a screaming cartoon nymph into a river. Each slide put them closer and closer until Pan was almost on top of her. I'd shielded my eyes with every *kerchang* of the slide carousel but peeked out around the edges. The nymph escaped, only to be "saved" by the gods who turned her into a reed. A reed that cried when the wind blew through it. Such a raw deal. Meanwhile, Ms. Van Laar watched us all with an intensity that didn't feel proper.

"He was going to rape her, wasn't he?" TJ asked, still staring at me.

"Probably. But at the time, I thought he was going to eat her."

TJ sang, hushed at first: "Pa-an, Pa-an, Greek god Pan, One half goat—"

"—the other half man," I finished for her. "And do you remember when Lincoln was the first boy to grow hair on his chin and we called him Pan and we made him chase us around the schoolyard?" Faster and faster we had scrambled, chanting, laughing, until a line of screeching girls ran from this thrilled little boy.

*Pan! Pan! Greek god Pan!*

*One half goat! The other half man!*

"Hmm, I recall kicking him in the knee when he tried that with me," TJ said with a sniff.

"God, it was *Lord of the Flies* back then, wasn't it?"

TJ balked. "No way could a teacher get away with showing that now."

"I think it was about how the flute was created."

"Right, he cut down her reed and made a panpipe out of her. *Jesus*. What sick fuck would write such a thing?"

"Ovid, I believe," I said with a chuckle. "Just think how

far back it all goes. Maybe Ms. Van Laar was trying to prepare us."

"Or recruit us into paganism," TJ burst out. "She was sort of a hippy after all."

True. Sabrina Van Laar, the only remotely interesting teacher, suffered ridicule for having camped out in The Thicket in the 1960s with her gal pals, playing acoustic guitars and bongos instead of going to church. Rumor had it she'd gone off to train at Julliard to become an opera singer and had traveled the world, but at age thirty-five settled right back in southern Illinois, content to teach grade school upstarts "Hot Cross Buns" on a recorder and feckless juniors and seniors European literature.

"I had such a crush on her," TJ said, and I knew she was picturing the necklace.

That necklace.

Ms. Van Laar had worn a silver necklace that either settled on one of her breasts or wedged in her cleavage. TJ and the boys fixated on its location on any given day. From its chain dangled a silver rod curved into the shape of an S and along the curves were seven circles, like planets. The largest circle sat in the center of the S, each becoming smaller in size so that the two smallest circles hung from the ends of the S. None of us knew what it signified, though many boys asked. She said it was a gift from a genius, intriguing us further, but that was that.

"She's dead now," I said. "A cancer of some kind."

Ms. Van Laar had chosen a green burial in The Thicket. Nobody knew where. She'd been illegally planted under the cover of night by her own generation of Thicket Kids. For all I knew we'd just passed her.

The highway before us narrowed, entangled brush overgrown in the ditches. Our headlights pried it open and in the red glow of the rear-view it knit shut behind us. As adults we hadn't put words to the power of The Thicket, though as teens its magic had been a given. Surrounded by it again we grew pensive in its shadowy hug.

Memories reached out for us, some pleasant, others a bit greasy. Hours spent foraging in the woods for magic mushrooms, waiting for a basic amber light to turn off or on and the ensuing screams when it did? How bored were we country kids that this was our entertainment?

The road grew more treacherous, asphalt rising in the center, slanting downward on both sides, so that when a car passed and I veered close to the gravel, I was higher up in my seat than TJ.

"Jesus, was it always this small?" she asked.

"Yeah, you're used to the Dan Ryan, remember?"

"It's so dark. I don't remember it being this dark either." With no oncoming cars on the horizon, TJ leaned forward and peered out the windshield. "Turn off the lights for a sec."

I switched off the headlights to the fog lamps, backed off on the gas, and leaned forward too. "Wow, I haven't seen the Milky Way in years."

We marveled at the pale swash of light that arced softly across the velvety blackness. We knew if we let our eyes adjust, the stars would grow and grow and overtake our thoughts. That's what entering the Thicket did to you; it showed you your size in the universe. But it also gave you hope that one day you'd be up there exploring other worlds.

TJ pressed her forehead to the glass of the passenger window. "Whoa, foxfire's on too."

I gasped. The base of the forest glowed in faint smudges, just as it used to. Perhaps even more. Flashbacks tapped at my subconscious, awaiting their turn in my dreams tonight.

*Welcome home, girls.*

"So cool." I leaned back, flicked the lights on, and gunned it.

"Yeah."

"Hey," I said. "I never told you about the night we lost Evie and you moved back to Ketchum." I shot her a glance. "I made a wish in The Thicket. That you would come back."

TJ gazed at me with such innocent wonder she looked seventeen again.

"Seriously?"

"Yeah, I was kinda embarrassed because—"

There was a flash on the road before us of fur, a black nose, glowing eyes, and antlers—massive antlers. Then came a thud and rumble as we hit the creature and it clattered up the hood, cracking the windshield, and slid over the passenger side, the antlers scraping the sheet metal in a deafening screech, all of it occurring in that eternally brief moment under the stars.

## Chapter Eight

As we skidded, we dragged the deer along with us, its antlers tangled in the passenger mirror, its hooves rumbling in the wheel well. When we came to a stop, it tore free and tumbled into the ditch.

TJ and I got out and stood beside the SUV, hands over our mouths.

The deer lay twisted in the ditch, mewling a hollow cry, like a lost calf. I couldn't shut it from my mind.

"I'm so sorry, buddy," TJ murmured. "Please forgive us. I'm so sorry."

The headlights of an oncoming vehicle lit the buck as it wallowed, broken, in the weeds. We squinted into the glare as the truck pulled up on our side of the road, facing our SUV.

A door slammed and a man stalked toward us.

We stood dumbfounded in his high beams. Through the flaring light and the tears in my eyes, I couldn't make out his face so much as his jeans and western shirt, a farmer's mesh hat, and the knife on his belt.

"This happens all the time," he said with a gruff voice and nodded at the steam coming out of our grill. "You're lucky he didn't do more damage."

The deer still mewed. The man walked away then, back to his truck, and came back with a rifle. I reached for TJ and she grabbed my hand. The man pointed the gun at the deer and the ripping crack made me yelp then moan. I covered my mouth, embarrassed, tears flowing down my face.

The mewling in the ditch stopped. Mine did not.

"Calm down, Jane," TJ whispered. "You gotta calm down."

The man scrambled down into the ditch, pulled the knife from his waist, and drew a line down the center of the animal. Its insides slid out in a slippery pool. I thought the convenience store sandwich might come up then, but it didn't. Nothing was working right in me.

"Get in," TJ murmured, grabbing behind herself for the door handle. "Quick."

I backed up, slunk around the SUV, and slid into the driver's seat. I eased the door shut and tapped the lock button. I bit my lip and gently pulled the T-shift down, clicking into reverse, and rolled us backward, cringing with every rubbery pop of gravel. Then I rammed it into drive and veered around the man's truck.

He looked up from the ditch, the truck headlights brightening half his face. Something dropped inside me, that small organ of dread tucked between my heart and lungs that fires up at the worst possible times.

"It's him, isn't?" I said.

"Yeah."

I wheeled around in my seat, staring through the rear window at the man scrambling back up the hill, trying to imprint the awkward boy I'd once known onto the figure of this burly man.

"Go!" TJ said with a bark. I nailed the throttle.

In the rear-view mirror, Lincoln Metzger stood shrinking in the red flame of our taillights, hands on hips, something black covering both his arms. I forgot how to breathe.

When I remembered, I began moaning again, because I am physically incapable of screaming like any self-respecting woman. It always comes out sounding like a hyperventilating cow.

TJ yelled back at me, "Shut it, Jane. Jane, *please*!"

The SUV lagged, jerked forward, shimmied up to forty-five miles per hour, then lurched back down to thirty.

Eyes still locked on Lincoln, TJ bellowed, "Go, go, go!"

He would surely run to his truck and whip it around, then come after us with that rifle and knife. Or worse, start galloping at us in an inhuman way, breaking through the back window and dragging us out into The Thicket.

Once he faded into darkness, TJ turned back around. The Ketchum water tower stood there, bulbous and foreboding, a toadstool from a lost land of giants emblazoned in an eroded font from decades gone by. She glared up at it as our hobbled SUV coasted past. "This does not bring me joy."

The lights of a Casey's General Store beckoned like a holy place – discount civilization. The upper façade of the building was a silkscreened red roof made of folksy cartoon shingles that on any other occasion I would deride for their absurdity. Tonight, it seemed fitting that reality had been reduced to comic architecture.

We didn't need gas or food and so hightailed it inside to huddle by the freezer section.

My teeth chattered. "Should we call the police?"

"Why, exactly? The wreck or the woodsman?"

"Call your mom?"

"Come on, Jane. Get real."

"Whoa. We can't come here and not see her—"

The savage light of the convenience store cast dark shadows under TJ's eyes; it made her stylish haircut look blunt and severe, warning me not to proceed. In the freezer glass I looked ten years older myself. And I laughed with a huff at the power of my vanity to cut through this moment and exert itself.

"Do you think the rental will start again if we give it a minute? Make it to the motel?"

"Do I look like a mechanic? Don't answer that."

"I don't want to walk"—I peered over the aisle of donuts —"with Lincoln out there."

"Yeah, that's an odd fucking coincidence, Jane. How was he the first one to find us?"

"There are no coincidences. He's probably been sitting there waiting for us to arrive! Like a tarantula!"

"No, you're thinking trap-door spider."

"Who cares! They all jump on you superfast."

"Don't know why you're so worried. He loves you. I'm

just the sidekick," TJ was hissing now, "the expendable one. He'll kill me first to show you what's at stake."

A short bleached-blonde woman in a red smock that said CASEY'S on it approached us.

"You okay?"

"We hit a deer. Busted our rental."

"Oh, kid, that happens all the time."

"So we've heard."

"They're really running rampant. We're all eating venison these days."

TJ grimaced. "Don't suppose there's an Uber around here?"

"Closest taxi's Birkenham. Where you headed?"

"Here actually, for a reunion."

"Oh! The class of '99! Render, right?"

"Yeah, how—"

"Well, I'm Sadie Pullham, Jaylene's sister. Three years ahead of you, remember?"

I didn't, but TJ claimed to, her charm cranking back up. "Oh my God, how are you, Sadie?"

"Good, good, Jaylene's so excited to see everyone. Where you staying?"

"Le Grand Motel."

"Oh, that flea pit? You can't stay there. Got Indians running it. It's filthy."

I was unclear which stereotype to picture, the Indigenous peoples of America or South Asia. The easy brashness of her bigotry would have provided no end of mockery for us had we not just seen my stalker gut a large mammal.

"It'll be just fine, I'm sure," TJ said, trying to stay polite while mitigating the insult.

"I'll call Jaylene; she'll find you a place."

"Seriously, we're good. Maybe if we called there, they could get us a ride."

And they did.

A quiet middle-aged man named Ranveer escorted us in his four-door to the motel on the other side of Ketchum—population now dwindled from four to three thousand, TJ handily noted on the sign as we passed.

From her place in the backseat she sat forward, sticking her head between the driver and passenger seats.

"Hey, what did you mean you made a wish in The Thicket?"

I gazed out the window. "I'll tell you later."

"Excuse me?" Ranveer said with a clipped London accent.

"Oh, it's nothing."

# Chapter Nine

## OUTSIDE TIME AS WE KNOW IT

S ince acquiring the Illinois basin, its spores had circled the planet a thousand times over.

A hundred cycles of children passed through its domain, nameless and just as inconsequential as the other animals. Throughout those centuries, young humans rarely differed in their play-practice of adulthood: chasing and laughing; fighting and crying.

A few who now gathered—three boys, two girls—held potential. A fourth boy hovered, a foul pest, broken, unusable, dangerous even. The others would join the legion along the way. Some quite soon, some in years to come; all drawn to its knowledge, all a blip in its existence.

One girl held the undercreature's focus over the others.

She contained legions, multicamerate, latently eternal. Like the foul boy, cruelty had altered her mind, but unlike the boy, pain galvanized her.

This girl tranced—raw with sadness, more than the usual

*juvenile. Surging with estrogen, testosterone, progesterone, cortisol. A soul scoured by great loss.*

*The undercreature intended to reach her before she doused her neural network with alcohol, THC, opiates. She sparked with enough creativity on her own, just beginning to form abstract concepts, desires to grasp at in the years to come. The undercreature could fulfill many of them. It would reveal itself to her, and provide all she needed to prepare for a new era.*

*Whether or not she made proper use of the knowledge was another matter.*

*The undercreature had subsumed many before who had failed the task. They had joined its library of souls, fruiting its domain, and served no greater purpose than as a welcoming committee.*

*But first she would need to make contact.*

*It wouldn't take long.*

## Chapter Ten

### Two Decades Ago

**B**rian stood in front of the fire pit, juggling their empty Mountain Dew bottles with deft hands. "I heard the hooker in the bag had mold all over her. White mold."

"Blort," Evie said, phoning in her distaste, more interested in the delicate katydid crawling up her sleeve. Her forefinger was poised to flick it off if it ventured too close to her face.

Paul balked. "Where the hell did you hear that?" He shot Brian a glint. A warning.

But Brian's gaze remained occupied, arcing round and round as the green bottles spun through the air, ducking and weaving when the bottles got too low. "Gary's dad knows the coroner in Birkenham."

Next to Paul sat Roy, the new kid in town, who had brought his beat-up acoustic guitar and stopped playing

Oasis's "Wonderwall" for the twentieth time to glance Jane's way.

In the fresh silence, she blushed.

After the sheriff died, the kids had been hesitant to mention anything grisly around the Render family. Though Brian's concern now waned (it had been a year now, after all), Paul and Roy kept themselves in check.

Jane wrinkled her nose and offered an obligatory "Sick." But it hadn't disturbed her that much. She wasn't looking forward to growing mold someday either, but that day was so far off, wasn't it? Too far off to be imagined. And she had no plans for getting herself dismembered and glad-bagged.

Paul turned to her, cringing for Brian's sake. She smiled back and threw him a shrug. It was all good.

Brian caught one bottle at a time, tucking them under his arm. The last one he held up to the kids and wiggled his eyebrows. "Wanna play?"

"Nuh-uh, Ghost in the Graveyard," Evie stated, still fascinated with the little katydid. It rubbed its fairy-like legs together, unconcerned by her enormity.

"Jesus," Brian said, "what are you, five?"

Evie glared at him. "If we can't play Ghost—"

"Okay, okay, but then Spin the Bottle."

Evie rolled her light-blue eyes at Jane but snickered just the same. Three boys to two girls. They were getting kissed tonight for sure. Then she looked back down. "Aak!" Evie leapt from her log, screeching and jumping about. "Is it still on me? Where is it? Oh my God."

The guys laughed, delighted by the katydid's surprise

attack. Brian murmured to Roy something about her being "a real screamer."

Jane checked Evie's striped crop-top and cut-offs, then brushed down her curvy body, stuck between envy and admiration.

"You're fine. It's gone," Jane said. Her cheeks tickled. Something had happened with her face. And it dawned on her that she hadn't smiled like this in months. The ride on their ten-speeds to the clearing between the Metzger farm and The Thicket had been magical—warm wind in their hair, sweat cooling under their arms, and a candy-red sunset over the cornfields that rivaled any she had seen from an ocean beach. Sweet hickory smoke hung in the air and Jane drew it in, savoring her first taste of nostalgia.

On the weekends, the older kids sat around this rusty tractor wheel while a fire blazed inside it. They drank beer and apple schnapps, shooting the shit, encircled by their beater cars and trucks. But on a Tuesday night like this, most of those older kids were already in bed, resting up after a day's work and preparing for the next.

This new crop had not gotten steady jobs yet and they were on that cusp between rounds of Bop It! at sleepovers and studying for college entrance exams. They hadn't started drinking or smoking pot yet. They hadn't divided up into factions yet either—boys vs. girls, geeks vs. jocks, rich vs. poor. No, that would come in the fall.

Hormones well past the brink, Jane was a morose young thing that wavered between missing TJ and bouncing around different friendship groups. Her legs had gone from being scratched and scraped with childish play, to burnt from boat rides on the river with the juniors and seniors she'd just met. Her freckles were in full bloom.

Paul sat poking the fire with a stick and gazed into the coals, shooting Jane the occasional side-eye from underneath his bushy bangs. He wore torn jeans and a red plaid flannel shirt with the sleeves ripped off, which revealed that sculpted V-shape at the triceps that some of the luckier boys in her class had sprouted. This was the night, Jane was sure. The night they would kiss for the first time. A dewy chill settled in the air and inside her too. It wasn't love; she wouldn't fall in love with a man until her twenties. And yet, it wasn't quite lust either. More like curiosity on jet fuel. And she sensed the same burning interest in him.

Evie skipped around them, patting their heads. "I get to be ghost first."

Brian jumped up and chased her down, grabbing her and swinging her around as she screamed. "Nope, we spin for it." He set her down and grabbed a bottle.

Roy set down his guitar and got to his feet. "Okay, I've never played this before."

The five of them gathered in a circle and pointed one shoe in. Brian set the bottle in the middle and spun it. It made a crooked twirl and stopped with the open end pointing at the toe of Paul's dusty Air Jordans.

"Damn," Evie said.

As they walked toward The Thicket, Brian laid it out, "Okay, fire pit's home base. Paul's the ghost. We give him"—he formed air quotes with his fingers—"*twenty-four hours* to find a hiding place. At *midnight* we look for him.

The first person who finds him yells, 'Ghost in the graveyard run, run, run' and we hightail it back to base. The last one he catches is *it*. Unless he can't catch any of us, in which case, last to base is it."

Paul blew a gust. "Easy-peasy. You guys are mine."

"One o'clock!" Brian yelled with a boom.

Paul sprinted into The Thicket, leaping branches as he went. The scuffing noise of his shoes died off. The kids turned around to face the fire pit.

"Two o'clock!" they all yelled out. Evie grabbed Brian and Jane's hands; Jane took Roy's. As they counted off, they all looked to the dying light in the sky as if making a pact. Jane's eyes started to tear up, though she didn't understand why.

———————————

Fifteen had been the hardest year yet for her – surrounded by well-wishers, but somehow still alone. People spoke in hushed tones as she wandered among them, dreamlike and mute. Many discussed the details of Sheriff Render's demise, after church, on the sidewalk, in the halls of KHS.

Jane overheard plenty.

With these stray words she pieced together a gory tableau that stuttered into her thoughts at the worst times: the sheriff cleaning his service revolver right in front of TJ and her mother. The man peering down the barrel. She could almost taste its metal in her own mouth—electric, like a penny. Then a faint ringing, because Aunt Ellen said she hadn't heard the shot yet lost her hearing and it hadn't come back until the next day. Pink spray on the living room drapes and the ruined deer head over the fireplace. The family dog, Cookie, licking the carpet and getting taken to the pound for it while TJ wept. The Birkenham remnant factory staff arriving at their door to donate new drapes and flooring.

At the time, it was lost upon Jane that the man could have accidentally shot his daughter instead. But to young Jane, TJ was gone either way—moved three towns over to ward off gossip. Gone to "help" their grannie, a strong-limbed woman who didn't need attending to. When Jane picked up the phone to call TJ, no one answered. And soon her mom thought it best if she gave TJ a rest.

Around the same time, Paul McKenna noticed her braces had come off and had clearly decided to take another gander. Plus, Jane's glasses had been upgraded to gas-permeable contact lenses, which made her feel like she always had lint in her eyes. But at least people could see how pretty they were now, like a doe's eyes. Near the end of their freshman year, Paul handed her a sheet of paper with two groups of dots on it, labeled, "The Jane Nebula Supercluster." She recognized them as her own freckles. These little pink-brown dots she'd hated so much before were now her trademark, her special thing – to one person at least.

So Jane's heart balanced this addition of Paul and its loss of TJ. One feeling could not be placed in or on top of the other. They just stood ready at opposite ends of her mind for her to explore when she tired of the adult voices tut-tutting around her.

She was ready to feel again—happiness, pain, whatever.

———————

"Midnight!" the kids yelled. Then Evie called out, "Ghost in the graveyard, here we come," and sprinted toward the trees.

The path inside The Thicket rose and fell, a ridged hardpack that tunneled off into darkness.

Before long, Evie's scream blasted out from deeper within. "Ghost in the graveyard, run, run, run!"

A thrill shot through Jane. She looked to Brian, his face muted in the near dark. The whites of his eyes flashed at her. The two took off.

A consistent first-place finisher on the KHS track team, Paul nabbed Evie before she could get up to speed. She howled in defeat. He picked off Roy next. In front of him, Brian and Jane wove through the conifer—off the path, onto the path, making it difficult to choose between them.

Brian yelped as Paul brought him down in the dirt and they wrestled.

Jane slowed her pace when she caught sight of The Thicket's edge and the smoke rising from the fire pit. As she caught her breath, Paul looked up with a grin.

He tried to tear after Jane like a sprinter out of the blocks, but Brian held onto him by the ankle and was dragged along, ripping off Paul's shoe.

"Run, Janey, run!"

"Cheating!" Paul laughed and ripped himself away, hopping back into his shoe.

His feral growl sent an electric zing through Jane, half-fear, half-delight. Instead of aiming for the clearing, where she knew he could close the gap, she leapt sideways into the brambles, where thorns raked across her like cat scratches. The brambles condensed and she could no longer find the path in the murky light. Broken limbs jutted outward like blades and sap left Jane's grasping hands sticky and dirty. She crouched behind a fallen tree—heart pumping as Paul's footsteps thumped closer—and tried to muffle her giggles.

Paul hurdled the dead tree and tumbled into the dirt beside her.

She screeched and scrambled backward.

He held his knee up to his chest and winced in agony.

Jane hesitated, then knelt next to him. "Oh, my God. Are you okay?"

He grabbed her by the arms. "Gotcha."

"Dammit, Paul!"

She laughed as he laid her down in the weeds, where pine needles drove exquisitely into her back and neck. His shirt smelled like a forest fire. The night had grown so dim she could only just see his smile. It was too dark to play inside The Thicket now.

All around them, the forest floor had come alight in yellow-green patches, like the tails of a thousand lightning bugs clustered together. The two lay staring at each other, trying to make out the other's expression. Paul puffed Jane's hair out of her face and then brushed a thumb across Jane's upper cheek where her freckle constellations lay.

"You're glowing," he said.

She sniffed. It was a bit too romantic, even for Paul. "Very funny."

"No, seriously. You've got that stuff on your chin." He reached across her and into the rotten tree, where a mound of glowing fungus grew on the soft bark. "My dad calls it foxfire." He pulled out a stalk and ground it between his fingers, then drew a line across his upper cheeks and across his nose like a warrior.

"Cool!" Jane bobbed up over the log. "Hey guys, check this out!"

"Damn," Paul said, just audible enough.

***

The five kids wandered deeper into The Thicket, the whir of traffic on the country road now muffled, to collect glowing fungus, as if it were treasure. Little greasy mushroom stalks that smelled like licorice. Meanwhile, creatures that they never fully saw fled from them. Branches cracked. Mating calls ceased. Soon, Brian, Roy, Evie, Paul, and Jane had marked their faces and arms with streaks of foxfire, no second thought about whether it might be toxic. With glowing skin, they could keep playing Ghost on a whole new level.

"Hey," Roy said, "check it out."

He'd discovered a small round clearing, hugged by the tall blackness of the forest and graced with a moonlit pond at one end. They made it their new home base.

For an hour, they choked on laughter, running faster than death, unafraid of the night that had swallowed all but their glowing faces and limbs. Feral children raving in a forest instead of on a dance floor; their music was the draw of their breath, the beat of their feet, the boil of insects, and distant rumble and howl of freight trains.

As Jane searched the woods, Evie's radiant face poked out from behind a tree and she couldn't help but giggle.

Jane pointed at her and sang out, "Pan, Pan, Greek god Pan, one half goat, the other half man!" then sprinted past Roy and Paul.

"What the heck does that mean?" Roy asked.

Paul laughed as they jogged backward from Evie, who trudged and held her side as she reached out for them.

"Long story," she huffed, and bent down to catch her breath. "Before you … moved here. Grade school. It was like tag, on the playground."

"Eh, I'm tired too." Brian halted and let Evie smack him on the arm. "Can we just spin the damn bottle already?"

"Yeah, but you gotta go get it," she said.

Brian found his second wind and was off in a glowing blur that stuttered through the trees.

Jane called to Evie, "Race you to the base!"

As the two girls sprinted for the small clearing, Jane glanced over her shoulder. Evie came at her like an angry witch, her bright cat-like eyes flaring and long black hair whipping, another of her trademark banshee wails brewing in her chest.

Jane heaved with laughter and her side cramped. As she turned back to face the clearing, a dark monolith blocked the path and she ran straight into it. The hulk was tall, warm, unyielding. The strike blew half her breath out and her fall backward into the hardpack knocked out the rest.

A leering creature towered over her, a man with long branching horns. Jane gulped for air to scream, like a fish out of water. She writhed in the dirt, scrambling backward, hands clawing in the dust.

"Jesus, Lincoln!" Evie ran up and knelt by Jane's side.

Jane raked in huge gasps of precious, wonderful air, and let out an abbreviated squeak.

Lincoln Metzger bent down, filling her vision.

Jane felt sure he would smother her. This time, the pine needles in her back didn't feel so enticing. At least his horns were gone. She closed her eyes and re-opened them. The horns must have just been the tree limbs above him. The dark must be playing tricks on her mind.

Paul yanked him backward. "Lincoln, what the fuck?"

"I didn't mean to scare her. I couldn't see. Her-her face is glowing. I wasn't sure if she was real. I'm sorry, Lady Jane. I-I—" He looked at all of them, wide-eyed.

The kids looked at each other. They did resemble ghosts. Roy honked a laugh.

Jane sat up. "I'm okay." Paul extended a hand and helped her up.

"I don't feel so good," Evie said. "I-I feel a little weird."

Jane felt odd too but chalked it up to lack of oxygen and discombobulating darkness.

"You shouldn't be here," Lincoln said in a monotone. "It's not safe."

Jane envisioned the moldy girl in the bag. A hand.

"I see things in here sometimes," he said. "People who've died. I thought you were... I thought—"

"Oh, come on, Linc. It's fine," Paul said. "Nothing's out here but some deer and rabbits."

Brian ran up then, bottle in hand, gawking at the new arrival. "What are *you* doing here?"

"Dad sent me to check on the fire pit. It's still burning. Nobody was tending it. Then I heard screaming."

"We were just playin'," Brian said with a scoff.

"Well, you have to put out the fire if you're not going to be there."

"We're gonna play Spin the Bottle. Wanna join?"

Evie turned to Jane and crossed her eyes.

It was one thing to kiss an average boy like Roy or Brian, but Lincoln "Logs" Metzger? If it got back to town, they'd never hear the end of it. They all knew Lincoln wasn't *one of them*. But neither were they the sort of kids who would tell him to buzz off either. The infamous tree where lightning had killed his brother Jacob was only a few yards away and they all knew it. It now stood half-gone, a tall limbless splintering reminder with a ferocious rip down its center.

So now there were four guys to two girls, and just one person Jane wanted to lay her lips on. *If only TJ were here to help balance things.*

Jane and Evie shuffled resolutely toward the center of the clearing.

———

From the nearby marshes came the wet rattle of boastful frogs preparing to mate.

Jane spun first. The bottle landed closer to Evie than to Paul. Off to a terrible start. Her shoulders sank. She grabbed the bottle to re-spin it, but Evie put her hand on the bottle and raised an eyebrow.

"You have to kiss whoever it lands on."

"Um…" Brian raised a finger. "Not that I don't like this particular scenario, but I just want to make it clear that I won't be kissing a dude."

Evie huffed. "Then I'm not playing."

The guys looked around at each other, weighed their options, then shrugged.

Evie grinned at Jane.

Jane had to admit that Evie was strikingly beautiful, in that goth way that dark-haired girls with pale skin can be. TJ had crushed on her all throughout junior high, really possessed by her. And if girls had been her jam, Jane would have been thrilled. So, she kissed Evie to be a good sport and, for a moment, understood what TJ had liked. The tenderness. The smell of her, like orange blossoms. But then it just felt like kissing herself.

Evie spun next, eyeing Lincoln as if trying to work out the physics of avoiding him. She landed on Brian and they went all-in with tongues so that Jane had to turn away. Brian spun and landed on Paul and they made a show of who got to be the man but in the end just touched lips. Then Paul landed on Evie and Jane felt anger rising in her gut. Evie kissed him quickly for her friend's sake, then she landed on Roy, then Roy landed on Jane and she obliged, thrilled at his lips and whiskers and the possibility that Paul was getting jealous and might work up the nerve to ask her out now, or else they would never get to kiss.

Jane laid her glowing grubby hand on the bottle again and this time swore under her breath to The Thicket that it *had better freaking clearly land on Paul this time*.

And it did. She took it for granted that it would, just as you do when you're young and think the universe must align to suit your wishes.

They both nodded and went slowly toward each other, pretending this was a chore.

Paul's kiss was sweet, his breath like corn on the cob. His hands clasped her neck and he drew her to him. She rolled into his arms.

The others cheered, their voices far off.

Jane truly felt odd now, untethered, but not just from the kiss, the fall, or the dark. Now, each time someone touched the bottle, *the kids* spun, instead of the bottle. She grew dizzy, blinking, giggling. She felt amazing. No, she felt amazed. The others sat laughing too, gaping at each other as if they were in on a joke they'd forgotten until now.

All save for Lincoln, who sat hunched over with bulging eyes, watching the others with confusion. They were laughing too loud.

Paul landed on Evie again, Evie on Lincoln.

When it was his turn to spin, Lincoln closed his eyes, murmuring, and placed his hand on the green glass bottle.

It spun and spun, quickly and evenly, like it was floating above the grass, a blur of kinetic energy. When it finally decelerated, it rotated slower and slower as if toying with them. They all sat, mouths agape, unable to speak or believe what they were seeing.

It finally came to rest, the open end pointed at Jane's sneakers.

She nodded, unconcerned about anything such as lips or reputations and crawled toward Lincoln. She'd lost her sense of self. *Jane* was now a part of something greater and this boy needed her to kiss him for all of life to line up. She brought his chin to hers and pressed her lips to his while he sat staring at her.

After that, no one said anything for a while. And Lincoln didn't touch the bottle. He just kept staring at Jane.

Though she sensed that she'd helped start something deeply irreversible, it didn't seem to matter in the moment, not in the context of this grandest of nights.

Roy squinted at the sky. "You know, I think I got some of that glow-shit in my eyes or my mouth or something. I'm not seeing things right." He turned to Paul. "How about you?"

"I'm fine. I think." Paul stood up and pulled Jane up with him. "Or maybe not."

Jane's eyes throbbed. She gazed upward at the pulsing stars. And then down into the pond, where they burned cold on its glassy membrane, as if the water were a hole in the earth and one could see through to the outer reaches of space. It made the land around them appear meager and precious, reminding the kids that they stood on a rock floating in a universe that was vast beyond comprehension.

*Jane?*

She looked around. No one spoke. She spun toward the black woods.

*Jane. I'm here.*

It was TJ's voice.

Jane couldn't move, didn't dare ask anyone if they were hearing it too.

Lincoln peered at her.

"Yeah, I think there's something in that foxfire." Paul chuckled, peering at the backs of his hands, and flexing his fingers into fists.

"Cool!" Evie pointed up at the three-quarter moon.

It undulated in the sky like a pale jellyfish in the darkest depths of an ocean trench. Roy howled at it like a wolf, his voice cracking to more of a coyote call. And then they laughed again, too loudly, except for Lincoln. Soon, everyone but Lincoln howled until their voices broke too.

Jane gazed around at her friends. She wasn't too young to realize she should cherish them all and never let them go.

But she would forget. Jane would forget a lot about those times.

"Let's make a wish on The Thicket," she said hoarsely, and reached for Paul and Evie's hands. All of them, even Lincoln, joined hands in that clearing by the small pond as whippoorwills burbled their song throughout the woods. The glowing fungus had faded, but now the moon had risen enough that they could see each other's faces again.

"I wish for a good career," Paul said. "One I love, not like my dad's nine-to-five pencil-pushing. A scientist or something."

Brian shook his head, incredulous.

"What?" Paul said.

"New car," Roy volunteered. "A Supra would be nice!"

"Dude, really?" Brian laughed. "A million dollars please!"

Evie gaped at them. "What about world peace?"

"*You* ask for it!" Brian said.

A grin spread across her face. "I won't need to; I'll be able to make it happen." She raised her face to the sky. "I wish to know everything there is to know."

The kids oohed, all except Lincoln. They looked to him, but he just stood staring mute at the moon.

They turned to Jane.

The tears in her eyes smudged the stars and moon. "I wish … I wish for TJ to come back."

Her friends glanced at each other and bit back words.

Evie squeezed Jane's hand and offered a wistful smile. "I do too."

"Who's TJ?" Roy asked. Paul shook his head at him. Roy cringed and nodded, turning to the newest arrival. "What do you wish for, Linc?"

Lincoln looked at the ground. "I don't wish. I pray."

Evie rolled her eyes. "That's the same thing."

Lincoln dropped their hands. "I don't pray to a moon or a forest. Especially this one. This place is rotten. And we need to get out of here. You don't understand what you're messing with."

Paul sighed.

Though they all thought Lincoln was a special kind of troubled, they also knew there *was* a presence in The Thicket. They assumed everyone had their own enchanted forest, or magic lake, or haunted hill. But none of them ever thought it was evil like Lincoln did, at least not evil enough to snuff them out. They could run faster than the ghost in the graveyard after all.

"Yeah, well, I need to get home anyway," Brian said. "Dad'll tan my hide."

"Me too." Paul took Jane's hand and they walked out toward the fire pit.

They all gathered their bikes and watched Lincoln shuffle off through the soybean rows toward his family farm. For once, they did not throw shade behind his back. Even Brian kept quiet.

"Ride each other home?" Paul said.

Evie pulled her old Raleigh ten-speed up from the ground. "I'm taking the short cut."

"Whoa, over the trestle?"

"Yeah," she swung a bare leg over her bike. "I'm probably already in deep shit." She rode off and the shadows swallowed her.

Jane and the boys pushed their bikes out west, toward the county road.

"Fun night," Roy said.

"Yup."

"Uh-huh."

"Let's do it again next week."

"K."

From deep in The Thicket, Evie screamed.

The kids stopped pedaling, freewheels buzzing.

Her laugh echoed out to them. "Spider web!"

Jane, Paul, Brian, and Roy pedaled along the county

road. When they crossed the railroad track on the edge of town, Jane could swear she heard Evie laughing again and made the guys stop and wait for a moment. She squinted into the blackness of the trees but could not see the amber streetlight deep in The Thicket from this direction. Either that or it was off.

She shrugged. "Wind in my ears."

———————

At home, Jane crept through the front door, locking it behind herself without too much clatter, only to be grabbed by her mother.

*She wasn't supposed to be out this late!*

*Didn't she know how many disappearances there had been lately?*

Jane's mother dragged the girl to the bathroom mirror, where Jane's hair hung clumped with pine needles and her face grinned from beneath the smears of dirt. She didn't fight back, her limbs rubbery with exhaustion. She smacked her lips. Grit had found its way everywhere, from the crooks of her elbows to the corners of her stinging eyeballs. It *was* shocking, Jane had to admit with an uncontrolled giggle. How little time it had taken for her to transform from mild-mannered bookworm to wild animal, ravished by the lips of four boys and a girl. In one night! Her reflection had a life of its own, laughing and snickering while she stood amazed. She flicked off the vanity light to show her mom the streaks of foxfire, but this sent the woman further over the edge.

Grounded. No bike or boat adventures for two weeks. Well worth the cost.

---

The next day, Jane sat alone at the edge of her backyard, with a half-smile still stuck on her face, and watched eddies swirl in the creek. Her reflection gazed darkly back atop her gathered knees.

"Hey, loser," a voice called from behind her.

When Jane looked up, there stood her cousin with wild blonde hair, wearing her favorite Nirvana T-shirt, the one with the wobbly smiley face and X's for eyes. She grinned like the best of days was yet to come.

"Oh my God! Teej!" Between this and Paul, the rest of high school would be a breeze now.

But TJ's smile dropped.

"Evie. She's gone."

## Chapter Eleven

Present Day

"Day one," I said into my iPhone, "we survived the night, the sun has thankfully risen, and we must now hunt for sustenance and other signs of life."

"I'm sorry," said Siri. "I didn't get that."

I tossed it onto the blankets.

A column of golden sunlight glared between the dense curtains and fell across the room. The sheets on my queen-sized mattress were over-starched and scratchy but clean at least. The room smelled of bleach and last year's cigarettes. I hugged the second pillow, yearning for the calm essence of my ex and peered around. It had been decades since I'd seen a room fully paneled in knotty pine and a burnt-brown carpet designed to hide all.

The desk, its chair, and my suitcase still stood stacked in a precarious tower against the door where we had heaved them the night before, fearing Lincoln would bust in sporting a bloody grin with a deer head in hand.

TJ lay curled into a blanketed lump on her own bed, and I made a noisy ruckus on the bedside table with my water glass, smartwatch, and the TV remote to make sure my sidekick hadn't been expended. She rolled over, stretched out, and with one eye squinted at the barricaded door, then buried her face back into the pillow.

"So, I didn't dream that deer?"

"How are we going to get around?" I asked. "Bicycles? Skateboards?"

"Eh, nothing's all *that* far." TJ yawned and stretched. "What time is it?"

"Seven. I'll call the rental place at eight."

"Suppose a continental breakfast is out of the question."

I grabbed the TV remote. "It's certainly not as bad as Sadie Pullham made out."

"Nah. Y'know, I feel kinda shitty leaving Lincoln. He was probably going to help us."

"Help us what? Who does that? Who unzips a deer in front of city people!"

"A bit warped, I guess," TJ said. "But good material." She rolled out of bed in her tank top and striped jockey shorts and padded to the window, parting the curtains. "We need to re-acclimate." She walked past me into the fluorescent-lit bathroom—"I get the shower first"—and shut the door.

Outside the bathroom, the bulb above the vanity blinked and grew ever more annoying with its threats to turn off. It reminded me of the flickering bulb I once had above the built-in desk in my childhood home. I had never been the kid who wanted a light on at night. No, I was the little girl who much preferred the dark to a flashing beacon that telegraphed to hooved and horned monsters: *Hey, there's a twenty-four-hour all-you-can-eat buffet of little girl in here.*

*Nope, nothing to see here. Move along, goat-man!*

I scrambled out of bed to the vanity and snapped off the damn light.

"Maybe you could work on your first chapter while we wait for the car!"

TJ's muffled voice: "Remember what the dormouse said? Gotta feed my head, Jane." The toilet flushed. "I'm starved."

While TJ showered, I haggled with EconoCar, arranging for them to bring us down a second car from Birkenham that afternoon, in time for the reunion. A cheaper sedan this time. They would cart off the SUV on the back of a flatbed. Costs were adding up.

––––––––––––

As we walked the road toward the center of town and whatever breakfast could be scared up, TJ pulled her hoodie over her head and hid in the recesses, fists tucked into jean pockets. She sneered at my athleisurewear. *So basic are we.* But I loved the way my yoga pants shaped my hips and my long-sleeved thumbhole shirt cuffed over my hands. My Asics would be a heck of a lot faster in a sprint than her flat-soled Vans and I would have challenged her to a race if it weren't for the parting of nearby curtains and rustling of blinds.

Skirting the base of every home, dark gray stains grew upwards in uneven stripes like an ombré of soot. This consistent appearance on every house we passed would have left me uneasy had the morning sun not lit the dew of wonderfully imperfect lawns and begun warming freshly cut grass, so that I could smell my childhood reaching out to me. The lawn ornaments! Oh, how I had forgotten the metallic gazing balls on stone pedestals, the black iron cutouts of a woman's butt bent over gardening, the Dutch windmills.

"Jeez," I said, "feels like going back in time, doesn't it?"

"I forgot there were no sidewalks."

I had too. The only sidewalks were on Main Street. On the side streets you walked in gravel along the side, or down the middle if you cared to, since there was barely any traffic.

The breeze picked up down the street. We were accustomed to the wind off Lake Michigan, but I'd forgotten the prairie could be this blustery. One minute we were enjoying the sweet scent of lilacs, the next minute we were making faces at the rotten mulch smell of cow manure from a local farm.

"Global warming wouldn't have made it windier, would it?" I asked.

"Probably."

There were kids out, running between the houses screaming and laughing maniacally. When they saw us, they stopped for a moment and giggled.

One with hair straight and scraggly like hay pointed at me. "Hey, crazy lady!" Then they all ran behind the house.

TJ shuddered. "Children of the corn."

"*We're* children of the corn."

"So, speaking of kids … you said you wished me back. I remember you guys talking about the wishes by that pond. You wasted a wish on me?"

We passed a double-wide trailer on which the dark grunge swept in a dipping arc along its length, resembling a broad black-toothed grin.

"Yeah, I did. It felt weird to tell you at the time. You know how proud teens are. But, I really missed you. I felt kinda lost."

TJ nodded. "I'll be here as long as you need me. You know that."

"You do tend to run off on occasion."

"That's 'cause you don't always need me!" She grinned inside her hoodie. "And, well, booty calls."

I shook my head. "Have you noticed that moldy stuff on everything?"

"Yeah. I don't remember that crap when we were kids."

"Me neither. Maybe the river flooded the town this spring."

The residential streets opened to the heart of town and its towering grain elevator alongside the train tracks.

Other than the mold, nothing else seemed changed about downtown Ketchum. It was the same sleepy town it had been when we were kids; we just hadn't realized back then what sleepy meant. The main drag held the same meager brick buildings built a hundred years ago. Same tiny library, save for new books in the front window. The train depot stood quaintly with its old switching sign but now it was an antiques store. Our old video arcade had turned into a nail salon. And thankfully the diner remained, with a row of pick-up trucks angle-parked out front.

We entered mostly unnoticed until we stepped on the mat, which connected to a bell that at one time surely rang out, but now only made a buzzing warble. At the front counter a row of men turned to us, one of them a deputy dressed in brown polyester. TJ betrayed no apprehension and sauntered off to a booth by the window.

The haze of smoke, stale grease, and the scent of burnt coffee beans instantly transported us to a time when one could still enjoy a cigarette after one's artery-clogging meal.

"Wow," TJ said, widening her eyes and sliding across the squeaky vinyl cushion. As I sat down to join her, her smile grew. With her fingertips she pushed the paper placemat with its ornamental edges around on the orange Formica tabletop. Then she flicked the lid of the little metal creamer container with delight.

"Whatever we order, let's get one of those little cups with a scoop of whipped butter."

An older waitress with thinning hair came over with a scuffed copper pot and I shook my head too, nostalgia overflowing. How many nights had the Thicket kids hung out here playing the Pac-Man in the corner? Along the far wall, all that remained of the video game was a shadow of newer paneling and indented linoleum.

"Coffee," the waitress stated.

"Yes, please!" I said with a bright smile.

She briefly returned it and flipped my mug. Then came the double take. When she recognized TJ, her smile dropped and tentatively rose again.

"Hello, kiddo," she said softly. "How you been?" And she stared with such compassion it was as if TJ had just been diagnosed with cancer.

"Good." TJ nervously glanced up. "Paulene, right?" But of course, it was there on her name patch.

"Uh huh. It's so good to see you. Have you been to your mom's house yet?"

"Nope." TJ looked down.

"Well, I completely understand. Give you some time with the menu."

"Thanks." TJ settled into the menu without further emotion and shrugged at my incredulous look. Was her ego so great and wide that she could take decades-old sympathy for granted?

The coffee woke me up in three sips.

Soon TJ and I were feasting on an omelet spanning the entire plate, loaded with greasy cheese, sweet peppers, salty ham, and an overabundance of fresh mushrooms so heady in flavor that I swear the cook had sautéed them in white wine. In between bites of this and slurps of tart orange juice, we stuffed our grinning faces with thick Texas toast until oil ran down our chins. For garnish, two flapjacks with TJ's cup of round butter that slid sideways as soon as it touched the pancakes.

All the while, over-the-shoulder glances were shot our way from the men sitting along the front counter. Our waitress spoke to them in a low voice and clucked from the side of her mouth. The deputy sadly shook his head. How could everyone still be that broken up about TJ's father?

"Oh, boy," TJ said, frowning out the window.

Another truck had pulled in, gleaming white, the man in the bill cap from the night before behind the wheel.

I tried to catch our waitress's eye, but she'd locked herself in conversation with two of her counter customers.

Lincoln Metzger climbed down from the truck cab, wearing a new western shirt, and moseyed in with a stilted bravado. He stood on the warbling mat and quickly stepped off. Though he stared straight ahead, the hairs pricking up on the back of my neck told me he knew we were here.

TJ used her odd sway with the waitress to get the woman's attention.

"Could we get the check?"

"No pie? It's coconut cream."

TJ looked at me. "Oh man, Jane, piiie."

My eyes bulged as I imagined all that thick custard and whipped cream and flaky crust made with real lard. Oh yes, oh yes. But was there even room? The meal so far was likely planning a hasty exit up my esophagus. I no longer had the iron gut of my youth. And my stomach had shrunk from my recent dabble with intermittent fasting.

"Nah, just the check."

Lincoln strolled up to the men at the counter. None of them turned, but the deputy kept the corner of his eye on him.

"My God, he's still uncool," TJ whispered.

He nodded to the backs of the farmers and deputy, as if

a conversation had transpired and then strode over to a booth diagonal to ours.

He leveled at me that strange, flat smile he always used to throw my way. Like a robot, like someone who never received smiles as a baby and therefore never learned how to mimic it properly. I resisted the urge to politely smile back, as I had been taught as a young girl. I had been in far too many close calls with men who demanded smiles.

"You should say something to him, Jane."

"What?"

She raised an eyebrow at me. "It's why we're down here, isn't it?" she whispered. "Go tell him to knock the stalkery shit off. Tell him to grow the fuck up."

"I-I…" Sweat beaded in the curls at my temple. The coffee, the hot, strong coffee, was surely the culprit.

*It's why we're down here, isn't it?*

*Isn't it?*

The entire diner—not just Lincoln—gazed at us, as if asking the same question. The deputy in brown, with close-cropped gray hair and a matching goatee that had turned a dull yellow around his lips from smoking, twirled around in his bar stool—the kind with the ridged chrome sides. He took a sip of coffee from his white mug, set it down, and would not release me from his stare.

I stood up, fingertips quivering on the table. My stomach cramped, as if the omelet were trying to escape. I took a few steps towards Lincoln's table and his flat leer spread.

The police radio on the deputy's belt crackled.

*"He's at it again,"* came a terse female voice.

In one fluid movement, the deputy slid from the stool, swiped the radio receiver off his belt, and stalked to the door. Everyone in the diner turned to watch him out the window as he stood in a wide stance, one hand on his hip, barking into the radio. He stepped into the street and strode north, picking up speed.

The farmers spun from their bar stools and piled out the door. The waitress hustled to the picture window, clutching the coffee container to her chest. "Oh, Jesus, Marvin."

TJ and I craned our necks.

Half a block away, a middle-aged man sat cross-legged in the road, yelling at a young girl passing by. It wasn't that we were unfamiliar with such a circumstance. But unlike the unfortunates we sometimes encountered in Chicago, this man was clean-shaven and dressed in khakis and a white golf shirt, which somehow made it even more disconcerting.

I glanced back at Lincoln. His leer dropped.

That was enough for me. I slapped down plenty of cash onto our check in its little plastic tray, bolted from the booth, and made for the door, giving TJ no say in the matter.

Out on the street the man yelled at the sky, "I have seen what is coming. It is coming for all of us. Some will be tested. Some will be taken." The man pointed at the deputy. "You! You will be tossed—like so much trash."

"Do we know him?" TJ asked. "He sure seems familiar."

The man looked at me then and his eyes grew wider, with a smile, as if I were a celebrity. "There she is. I'll be, there she is. She is the one!" His hands spread in supplication. "You have been chosen to spread the word!"

"Oh, good," I muttered. TJ chuckled a little hum in her throat.

"Your hubris will set the blaze, my child." Were those tears in his eyes?

"Come on, Marvin," The deputy said with an outstretched arm. "You're blocking traffic."

The only cars in sight were the trucks parked in front of the diner.

"No! The only safe place is the middle of the road. It can't get us here! Stay in the middle!"

The quick whoop of a siren behind us made me jump.

Another deputy, a woman, hopped out of her squad car and joined the first. As more Ketchumites gathered, the officers stood, hands on hips, and contemplated how to extract the man without causing more of an incident.

"Don't touch me!" the man yelped, batting at the first officer. "It's on me. I know it is. I saw it in my basement. In the dark."

"What's on you, Marvin?"

"The threads, the threads are on me!" He smacked the asphalt with both hands. "Just stay in the road. Stay in the middle."

The deputy turned away from the man, trying not to laugh. He caught my eye and his smile dropped.

The man in the street drew a revolver from between his legs and it dangled limply in his hands as he gestured. The crowd fell to the ground in a wave, as if their bones had collapsed.

"I can't take it anymore," he screamed. "This has already happened! Don't you see? I know how it ends!"

"Now Marvin, put that down, put that down."

Screams erupted along the sidewalk.

"Let's go," I said, backing up.

As TJ and I hustled back down Main, we took turns glancing over our shoulders. On the street, the female deputy had circled behind Marvin. When he turned on her, the other officer leapt at him and they fought for the gun.

It clattered onto the asphalt.

Marvin screeched and wriggled as the officers dragged him away. "Please don't take me into the grass. Not by the trees. In your car! Yes, just the car! Close the door! Close the—"

The door of the squad door slammed shut.

TJ shuddered. "Same shit, different city, eh?"

"You okay?" I peered at her, gauging the effect of seeing another man raise a gun to his head.

"Of course." She shrugged it off. "Hmm. The only safe place is the middle of the road," she said thoughtfully. "How profound."

"I don't think he was being rhetorical. Although, who says hubris down here?"

"Don't be such a snob. We're just city hicksters, remember?"

Again, the kids swarmed out from their houses to gawk and laugh at everything we said. Did we honestly look that different from everyone else? The hairs on the back of my neck prickled. Now that we were actually home, I was losing my grasp on the point of this trip.

"You know," I said, "maybe we should consider just

heading out when the new car comes. I mean, do you really want to see these people? They never really liked us."

TJ laughed loudly, ignoring the brats pointing and running alongside us.

"What?" I picked up my pace to keep up.

TJ skipped backwards in front of me. "I knew you were gonna choke. I knew it!"

"I'm not choking!" I wanted to kick her. "It's just that it's even weirder here than I expected."

"Hell, yeah, it is. Isn't that the point? If you want the material, you gotta be brave enough to face it."

I sighed. Deep down, not only did I know she was right, the mischievous girl in me hungered for more. "Maybe it's just that Lincoln always being just around the corner—"

"I feel bad for him in a way," TJ said, settling in beside me. "They still don't like him."

"I wish you'd stop feeling bad for my stalker!"

The kids finally gave up and went back to their mold-stained houses.

"Sorry. It's just that—"

"I suppose it is kind of odd though, that he has that effect on people. I mean, his brother died and your father died, but nobody feels sorry for Lincoln like they do you."

TJ retreated inside her hoodie and said nothing for a while until the motel was in our sights. "What do we do now?"

"Um hello? Material has presented itself, remember?"

TJ let out a dramatic sigh.

"And your head *has* been fed. Time to fire up the laptop."

"All right! God."

As we crossed the motel parking lot, Ranveer stood power-washing the brick veneer with a long wand connected to a whirring motor.

His wife Harini, her purple sari blowing in the breeze, shot a desperate smile at us. "My apologies. There is a grime of some sort that covers the whole of everything. Ranveer says it's that illegal corn still they run on the west end of town." She set her palms on her face and shook her head. "Have you heard of the angel's share? That's what they call the vapor that leaks out." She drew her hand down the air in distaste. "Feeds whatever *this* is. More like the devil's share if you ask me. Wasn't in the photos the real estate agent sent us, I can tell you that."

"Devil's share," TJ murmured. "I like it."

**From:** Metzger, Lincoln [hansolo99@frontieronline.net]
**To:** Render, Jane [jRender@stubenliterary.com]
**Subject:** Finger of God

Jane,

I am so glad you're back. It was a blessing to see you this morning, even under such disturbing circumstances. You see, I've been trying to convey this to you. Ketchum has changed.

You, however, are beautiful as always.

I was just coming home from a particularly successful storm chase when I came across your wreck last night.

See attached. An actual stovepipe tornado shot from a quarter mile away! That rectangular speck is not confetti. It's the roof of a grain silo that was tossed hither and yon like a tumbleweed. Storm roared like a monster and I do believe there is still dust in my every crevice.

Lady Jane, I brim with so much energy that I can barely contain it. Could it be power from the finger of God? I was surrounded by scientists who would laugh me right out of the chase team if I asked them that.

I am convinced that a tornado is the only thing that will fix what is wrong in The Thicket. An EF5 should just scour the place, right down to the bedrock.

More pictures to come. Looking forward to seeing you at the reunion!

All my love,
Lincoln

## Chapter Twelve

Bullets flew in rapid succession.

—*tat, tat, tat*—

The Savage MSR's tight bucking at Lincoln's shoulder felt good, like the nudge of an old friend, the bark of a good hunting dog.

—*tat, tat, tat, tat*—

Fifty yards away, the target he'd nailed to the fence post fluttered and the black silhouette of a person shone with points of light.

His body taut, Lincoln felt strong, invincible. The steam and the sulfur, the gun oil—this was the best cologne a man could wear. Unfortunately, the wind blew from the south today, pushing insulting wafts of pig shit up the prairie from Chesterson's hog farm.

They used to oink at him. The kids.

—*tat, tat*—

Until they came up with a better taunt.

—*tat, tat, tat, tat*—

In first grade, the P.E. teacher made Lincoln run extra laps to work off his belly. He'd asked for a bathroom break three times, but the coach said he was soft and needed to feel a little discomfort. The man knew nothing about discomfort. Lincoln tried to tell him this was about more than bladder control. He could hold it no longer. It was coming with or without approval. With the Metzger farm on life support, money was tight at home, and therefore his underwear was not; the elastic all but gone. Three short turds hit the basketball court for all to see, like the notch connectors on a Lincoln Logs set.

The class—no, the whole town—never let him forget it. And the nickname stuck.

Sure as pig shit on your boots.

—*tat, tat, tat, tat*—

But Lincoln Logs was the least of it.

It wasn't until the last day of school in third grade that Lincoln knew for sure that what some of the meaner kids had teased was true. Though he'd been having his doubts about God taking Jacob up into a funnel cloud, he continued to retell the story on the playground. It was the only thing they wanted to hear from him. And, like a bible parable, if you told it enough, to enough people, it became true.

"So, your brother's casket was really empty?" asked the freckled girl with cherry-colored hair. Her name was Jane Render and she reminded him of a dessert parfait. His favorite *Peanuts* comics were the ones in which Charlie Brown pined after the little red-haired girl. Though those chapters always left him with a knot in his gut, he was certain Charles Schultz would someday unite them. Someday, Charlie Brown would win.

"Probably," said another boy, who sat hunched with them under the jungle gym. "They do that all the time."

"They do?" Jane asked, pulling at the strands of her hair.

"Oh, sure," the boy said with a nod. "My cousin drownt' and they never found him. We went to his funeral and there was a casket at that one."

Gary Brown and Jaylene Pullham, who'd been swinging across the top of the bars to see who could reach the other side faster, hopped down onto the asphalt.

"You're such a liar, Lincoln Logs," Gary said. "You know your brother didn't disappear in a tornado."

"Lying is a sin," Jaylene confirmed.

"Did too!"

"He was out in The Thicket with the other kids, doing drugs," Gary said, his arms crossed. "Standing under the highest tree. Lightning hit 'im."

Jaylene nodded. "Yep, everyone knows that."

"I didn't know that," Jane said. "Are you sure? I believe Lincoln. He's the one who should know."

Lincoln tried to offer Jane a smile, but it had been so long he wasn't sure how anymore. He simply stretched his lips across his teeth at her.

"Wanna bet?" Jaylene said. "I'll bet you ten dollars! I overheard my parents whispering and they said it blasted the shoes right off him. His nose and toes turned into pink broccoli. Just boiled him right up." She made a disgusted face, by curling her lip down.

"Ooh," Gary laughed. "Nose and toes, Lincoln Logs. Nose and toes."

Lincoln sputtered. "You shut up!"

As Gary and Jaylene expounded upon all that had happened to Jacob's body, the pink welts forking all over his body, his melted eyeballs, Lincoln went into a state of gray. It was impossible to contemplate the ruined state of his brother amidst all those jeering faces. He clutched harder and harder on the steaming hot monkey bars until his knuckles went white.

Once they'd had their fun and taken most of the kids with them, Jane stood up and stared at the clouds inching across the blue sky.

"It's still a grand way to go though, Lincoln." She crawled out of the frame of bars. "If you've got to go." And she started toward the others.

"Lady Jane!"

The girl stopped. "Yeah?"

"Wanna be pen-pals this summer?"

Jane chewed on the inside of her mouth.

He squinted up at her. "You'll write me, won't you?"

She nudged a shoulder at him. "Sure." And she ran off.

He sat there long after the afternoon bell rang. He sat there until the shadow of the principal covered the ground before him.

---

Long after his parents called their truce of two houses and tried to move on with life, Lincoln's mother turned back to

Lincoln after years of either looking through him or walking away when he opened his arms up to her. Now she asked about his studies. She assigned him chores in the house alongside her. She drove him to basketball practice and stayed to watch. She met with the school guidance counselor when the bullying got worse. And she drilled him for answers all the way home, vowing to take revenge on the bad kids. Not because she cared that much about his feelings, he suspected, but rather the Metzger name.

He begged her not to.

But why, she asked.

Who knew why kids taunted the weird kids? He sure didn't. Nor did he care to ask.

She'd laid a hand on him then, on his shoulder, and he'd shrunk from it, unsure what it meant or how to act.

—*tat, tat, tat*—

It was too late for a mother's support. He was getting his driver's permit soon and then he would ask his new love, Jane Render, out on a date. For Lady Jane, he would figure out how to act.

But Edith wouldn't give up. Ever since she had commandeered his weekends, he almost missed the free afternoons after farm chores, when he could play by the stream that ran between the cornfields to The Thicket without anyone caring what he was up to.

But he no longer missed The Thicket itself. It was haunted for him now. And now a new generation of his classmates had started going there, not to fish or play games anymore but to make out and get high on the fungus, just like his brother.

He didn't know why it attracted the other kids like moths to a flame, because it repelled him. In fact, he could swear it felt the same about him. He'd once tried going back in it to fish at Ketchum River. But even standing on the woods' edge with his rod and reel, he could see things inside it for the briefest moments. It teemed with noise and movement some nights. Odd things hovered and glowed. Especially after a harvest, when dust from the topsoil and cornhusks hung low in the mist. Moldy white mounds pulsated along the forest floor. Agonized faces twisted in the knots of the trees. His brother with a pink broccoli nose and running eyes. The sheriff in uniform with a partially blasted and peeled-back face. A dead woman's limbs crawling in the underbrush. Inhuman voices whispering incomplete words. Conversations in foreign tongues.

—*tat, tat, tat, tat*—

It made him sick. His revulsion was God protecting him. God had given him a gag reflex for that place. Besides, there were bigger streams to fish now. Edith's doting and the fact that the farm was doing well had won him all sorts of prizes. A computer. A DVD player. A big-screen TV. A Nintendo.

And the more she gave, the more he turned away from her.

"Wish she'd leave me alone," Lincoln had said as he leaned over his dad while the man worked the farm's computer.

"Careful, boy," Byron said as he peered at the spreadsheet.

Lincoln showed his father where his numbers were off.

"She's just too much," Lincoln said.

Byron grumbled. "You were too much."

"What's that supposed to mean?" Lincoln stood as tall as his dad now, and wasn't afraid to talk back, no longer fearing the man's swipes. Though Lincoln still had the dent in his sternum from a punch at age seven—would have it forever—the older man had found new ways to injure.

"You weren't expected, if you know what I mean."

Lincoln did. He'd always figured the difference in his and his brother's ages—and his mother having been forty-five when she had him—was suspect. Having it confirmed left him cold. He'd feel it later, but not in front of this man.

"If it hadn't been for Jacob leaving us," Byron said, "you'd still be too much. So, count your lucky stars that she's taken an interest."

*—tat, tat—*

"Why did you lie to me about the night Jacob died? How he went."

"That was your mother's doing. She couldn't handle knowing he caught fire. His own negligence being out there high as a kite. And here she's gone and raised another sissy by not showing you how things really are."

Lincoln's jaw hardened and his eyes narrowed on Byron.

"Don't you give me that tough front, son. Boy, you're so lucky to have a mother. And to have this farm. You ain't gonna be good for nothing else."

*—tat, tat, tat, tat—*

By the time Lincoln was sixteen, Edith had literally clung to Lincoln in church, as if realizing a bigger force was coming for her baby.

Well, she was right. Lincoln could feel something coming for him, something big, like a raging inferno that would cleanse all around him and forge him into a man of steel.

He pitied his parents, at the same time as watching out for them, despite their inability to love him back properly. There was nothing meted out right in this world. That was for God to do. And now their time was ending, shrinking, and shriveling further.

He would take care of them as best he could, but then he started padlocking his room from the prying eyes and hands that were always concerned with the state of his sheets and the contents of his trashcan. The hardcore VHS tapes Gary had loaned him would send his mother straight to the asylum. But once he'd discovered what his pecker was for, truly discovered, nothing would stand in its way until he'd put it to the test. His guilt was inconvenient at worst, and a challenge at best. Sometimes he stood there admiring his length and girth in the mirror, and waited to see if his mom would barge in. He could bear the awkwardness of the intrusion if it finally got her off his case. Eventually, it just made him laugh, absurdity his constant companion. If he could bear such a shameful moment, he could bear anything.

He now left his door slightly open, closing his eyes and thinking only of Jane. Jane and the chase. The furious chase across the schoolyard and all the girls screaming. That kiss in the clearing of The Thicket; its unforgettable thrill set him on fire. And sometimes the blaze even burnt away the gray.

—*tat, tat, tat*—

Lincoln strode to the fence post. He tore the target from the nail and let out a whistle. He'd shredded it at the head and heart.

Okay, yes, he'd frightened Jane with the deer, gone too far by gutting it on the spot. But it didn't hurt for her to see him for the man that he was. A real man unafraid to make a decision, unafraid to pull a trigger and provide.

To provide.

Lincoln thought of the tenderloins he'd cut from the deer hanging in his basement.

He raced back to his truck, threw the rifle on the rack, and drove the chattery doubletrack road back to the farmhouse.

"Please don't be frozen, please don't be frozen."

## Chapter Thirteen

That black grime was even on the Dairy Queen. Blasphemy.

TJ mumbled around her Mr. Misty straw, "Gary was the guy who gave the titty-twisters, remember?"

"Oh, yeah. Friends with Lincoln."

"Some friend. He was beating on him one day, buying him lunch the next."

TJ and I lurked in the Dairy Queen across the street from the VFW, peering out as people from our past sauntered into the old brick building for our class reunion. When you go to school in a small town you know every kid, so it didn't take long to put names to faces.

Lincoln Metzger's white truck had yet to pull into the VFW lot.

"We can't stay here forever," she said. "Gotta lean into it, Janey. Although, I could handle another one of these. Grape this time. With vodka."

"*Teej*." But I craved a pill right then—just one, even a

half—something to smooth the corners. I would make do with wine, but it would be tricky. I hadn't had a drink in months and only ate organic whole foods. Now I was reeling from the tart sugar in the slushies she'd talked me into and the morning's diner food. The air conditioning cooled the sweat in the curls around my temple. When I'd planned my outfit of three-inch heels, and a tight green dress with sleeves cut just off the shoulder, I hadn't taken into consideration that our replacement car would not have arrived yet and we'd have to traipse a mile across town.

TJ slid out of the booth and sauntered past the gaping wait staff to the door in tight black jeans and a shirt striped like a pack of multi-flavor gum. She'd donned all four lip rings tonight and her hair stood up in a spiky golden wedge, ready for battle—the mod Valkyrie. Her walk from the motel had been a lot more comfortable than mine, even with the trip-hazard of her high-top sneakers stylishly untied.

Pfft. Trapped in Ketchum of all places. I would be on my best behavior just in case our stay extended past the weekend. TJ made no such commitment.

My trepidation was assuaged a level when we entered the VFW hall. Colorful lights danced across the ballroom and the music brought me right back. The loping braggadocio of "Gangsta's Paradise" blared from the DJ station in the back corner. Though we'd always known the song could never be about our lives, TJ joined me in lockstep, and we swaggered up to the bar like a pair of world-weary gangsters.

The first set of classmates had gathered by the snack

table across the room, Gary Brown the center of it all. He was a great icebreaker, laughing and grabbing guys by their necks, fawning over the women, showing them his new Apple watch. Gary was going to be one of those middle-aged guys who collected hobbies, if for no other reason than to argue about them—a jackass of all trades, who blathered on about the weight of a bicycle frame, the war in Syria, how to make a proper deep-dish pizza.

Next to TJ stood a slender bald guy in a loose white oxford and tan chinos ordering from the scruffy male bartender. He turned to me and smiled broadly. I smiled back, looked away, and then realized.

"Paul!" I leapt backward and he stood laughing. His face clarified as I matched the brown eyes, the strong jaw, the gentle smile with memories of the boy I had once known.

My high-school boyfriend opened his arms. "Jane, you look fantastic."

TJ slunk off.

"Oh my God, how are you!" I hugged him tight. His once-athletic frame had gone slight.

"Just finished my last round of chemo actually. Cheers." He slid his beer from the bar and raised it to me. "Can I get you something? Or is this an open bar?"

"Open bar, folks," the bartender nodded. Paul slapped down a dollar and the man rapped his knuckles on the wood.

"Um, can I get a white wine?" I asked the bartender. He nodded. And I turned to Paul. "So, what kind of cancer?" I left a dollar on the counter as well, then laid a hand on Paul's arm for just long enough.

"Testicular. *And then there was one*," he said with fake portent then chuckled. "It's all good. Hey, have you met my wife, Amanda?" He glanced across the hall at the restrooms where two women were chatting.

"I think I did at the last—"

"Oh, you met my ex-wife. Amanda and I have been together for a couple years now." Paul waved at one of the women. She nodded, said goodbye to the other woman, and walked over to us. She was tall and thin, finely muscled, with only a slight hint of make-up, and long blonde hair. No knockout, but a contender. Okay, the winner.

I extended my hand, "I'm Jane Render."

"Aha! I've heard so much about you. What a unique girl you were."

I rolled my eyes at Paul and he laughed.

"I like her," I said to him. "Perfect choice of words. Could be taken a number of ways!" I had to yell now over the music because Nirvana had just begun rocking out of the speakers. "So, Amanda, what do you do for a living?"

"I'm a yoga witch." She nodded with a smirk. "Yeah, it's exactly what you're thinking."

"I dunno. I'm thinking something pretty wild."

A group of guys had arrived at the entrance, wives in tow.

"You ladies excuse me for a sec?" Paul departed to greet them.

"Well, we aren't brewing toads or riding brooms," Amanda said with a chuckle. "But, yeah, I approach the discipline from a pagan tradition. You'd be surprised how much overlap there is in the earth energies of Asian and Celtic societies."

"Is this something you started yourself? I can totally see this catching on in Chicago." And with TJ, I smiled to myself.

"We're small but growing. Paul and I live near the campus in Champaign-Urbana. We get a lot of students from all over the world. There's potential for it to catch on. So, you write books, correct?"

"That's my cousin. I'm her literary agent."

"Oh, that's right. TJ Render." She winked.

"Yeah, TJ's a card. You'll like her. Well, probably."

She nodded politely. "I'm sure I will. I'm going to go see what Paul's up to. Great to meet you. Let's chat later, okay?"

I nodded and as I watched her go, my gaze snagged on the tall man in a suit standing at the doorway, lit from behind by the sunset. My stomach dropped and I took a big, vinegary gulp of wine. Then another.

*TJ, look.*

TJ chose instead to chat up Beth, who was a stout, quiet woman who'd had a crush on TJ since we were kids. TJ had said they had danced together once and Beth's hands weren't soft enough. That was the end of all possibilities in her book. Tonight, Beth wore an Illini jersey and baggy jeans and listened intently as TJ tested dialogue on her. "There's no chivalry between lesbians either, Beth. This is what they don't tell you." Now a high-school guidance counselor, Beth gazed at TJ with no apparent distress.

As I stood entranced by the man in the doorway, the

wine hit me like a loving smack in the face. After ordering another glass, I scuttled over to chance it with Gary and his crowd of revelers. They were more than a few beers into the celebrations. All of them had dressed in jeans and button-ups with T-shirts underneath. I felt like an ass in my expensive dress.

"Jane Render!"

"Gary Brown!" I yelped back.

"Looking good, hot stuff."

"You too," I said, though I despised him. He still had pointy brows like a cartoon devil. And, though Lincoln Metzger's unrelenting erotomania exhausted me, I could never quite forgive Gary for what he had done to Lincoln in school.

The crowd of men and women opened their circle and they all re-introduced themselves to me. So odd to stand shoulder to shoulder with those I'd only remembered as slight, smooth-skinned children. Most of them I had shared a key memory with, either in a class or on the playground. Now they were large and fleshy, some of their faces pockmarked or lined with hard lessons. Naturally, I forgot to realize the same had happened to me.

Jaylene Pullham was there. The female equivalent to Gary, she'd held Beth down on the playground and tickled her until Beth cried out of her nostrils and got dubbed "Snotnose" for the rest of the year. Tonight, Jaylene wore jeans and a Make-America-Great-Again T-shirt. Clearly, still a fan of tanning booths, her skin was the color and luminescence of a grocery bag. She and I politely smiled then eyed each other warily.

"So, you write them lezzie novels, yeah?" Gary said.

Right then, I wished I could say yes, just to spit it in his face. "TJ does."

He smirked. "Oh, TJ does, right."

Thankfully, Paul and Amanda joined us at that moment —to save me, or at least share some of the teasing.

"Did you guys know Paul here studies corn smut?" Gary yelled. "Bet that's a genre you never heard of, aye, Janey?" And he said genre like *jenner*. "Bow-chicka-wow-wow! A-maizing. Yeah, Paul is a real fun-gi!"

Paul shook his head. "Gee, I've never heard those before."

I turned to him, "You're still in school?"

"Not exactly. I teach mostly. I'm a researcher. Mycology. I do actually study corn smut. And other fungi that grow on feed crops. Although, right now, my job is trying to solve the whiskey fungus issue."

"Oh!" I yelled too loud. "The devil's share!"

Paul nodded with a chuckle, impressed. "*Baudoinia compniacensis*. It's particularly bad south of here in Kentucky bourbon country. Everything's covered in it, down to the stop signs, mailboxes, and houses. It's a constant battle."

"We just saw it here too! Harini at the motel says it's going to cover everything if they don't shut that corn still down."

Gary eyed Jaylene, whose eyes fluttered upward with annoyance.

"That's rich," Jaylene said. "You're here for ten seconds and already telling everyone how to fix things."

Paul ignored her. "Oh, I have seen it. It's not bad yet, but you're right. It won't go away until they shut down the distillery. Or we figure out a fungicide powerful enough."

I smiled warmly at him, not meaning it as anything but friendly affection. "I remember you wanted to be a biologist."

"He was just saying that to get in your pants, Janey," Gary said, and the group chuckled along. "To study your organism."

"Gary, you are ageless," I offered, quite generously come to think of it. I looked to Paul. "Where's Brian? I was sure he would come. Lord it all over us." Brian had been Paul's best friend and was a millionaire now. When Paul and I hadn't been on a date, he'd been out with Brian. They were as close as TJ and me.

Jaylene shook her head as if I'd peed on the floor.

"Milhouse?" Paul asked.

"Yeah, he was such a party animal back in our Thicket days," I said. "He became a real estate mogul in Branson, didn't he?"

Everyone grew quiet.

"He did," Paul said. He nodded slowly, thoughtfully. "He left his wife and kids last year. Moved back into his parents' house here in town. Hanged himself on Christmas Day in their basement."

My mouth hung open. "I'm sorry. I had no idea."

"Clearly," Jaylene said, just loud enough.

"Yeah, it was … pretty rough."

I took another sip of wine. Paul's wife Amanda patted my shoulder. I smiled meekly at her. "I'm going to powder my nose." As I walked away from the group, its energy surged back to normal. They began talking, chuckling. Jesus, I was back in middle school all over again.

TJ found me in the bathroom and stood beside me at her own mirror.

"It's weird, isn't it?" I asked.

TJ nodded and hoisted herself up on the sink basin, kicking her sneakers in the air. "I can't seem to get drunk enough to deal. God knows I'm trying."

"Lincoln's here."

"You know, sometimes you seem as obsessed with him as he is with you."

I glared at her reflection.

She raised her hands. "Just an observation."

"Don't leave me alone near him, okay? Seriously."

"Of course not," TJ scoffed. "Dude. Let's get wasted. Schwasted even."

I nodded. "Affirmative."

We made our way across the hall and a dance floor now packed with classmates, their spouses, and friends from other grades who lived nearby. We danced through, twirling and strutting for those who recognized us, then landed at the bar.

TJ kept dancing. But through my sluggish haze of boxed chardonnay, I realized a few things that you don't notice when you're sober, and yet can't quite make sense of when you're drunk. For one thing, other than quiet, unassuming Beth, everyone had gone a little off in some way. And for another, everyone TJ and I had tripped with in The Thicket had left Ketchum. The kids who everyone had thought were going to be the burnouts, we were the kids who had gone out into the world to make our mark. The rest had stayed home, run farms, and made babies. But a more niggling connection remained: Of those who had died or disappeared, every one of them had hung out in The Thicket.

There was Evie, TJ's on-again off-again make-out partner who'd wished for knowledge; I dearly hoped she had found it before her ride across the train trestle. There was Roy who'd pointed his Supra at Seven Hills and floored it until he sailed over one hill and smacked into the other with no seatbelt on. And there was Brian. Bold, confident Brian who was the last person you would imagine giving up the game to hoist himself from a toilet stack pipe in his parents' basement.

It was certainly more than my sloshed brain could make sense of. But I suddenly loved everyone in this room for that one moment because I knew, statistically speaking, some of us would be gone in a few years.

"You are radiant tonight."

I didn't need to look to know who had sidled up next to me. I searched for TJ instead, but she had abandoned me for the siren's call of karaoke. And by siren's call I mean the wild keening of drunken white people.

Dammit, TJ, you're supposed to be researching this guy!

Just how far would I go for our careers? *This* was how far. I'd relit Lincoln Metzger's candle, making at least part of his dream come true. I forced myself to stare back defiantly while Lincoln stood there in his tan suit and bolo tie. Because this was my chance; I was safe here amongst our class. And emboldened by the drink of course.

"Okay, Lincoln, why are you doing this to me?"

He stood there for a second, puffed up and trying to smile. Then he reached up to his breast pocket and popped the little triangle flap with the pearlescent snap on it. I flinched as if a gun had gone off.

God, I hate snaps. I mean, I really, really loathe them.

He raised his chin to look down at me. "I want nothing but your happiness."

Lincoln laid his palm flat on the counter and when he removed it, three round white pills stared up at me. I knew what they were by the slit in the middle of one. And though I was losing my nearsightedness I could make out the *80* on the side of another.

Oxy.

His mistake was thinking this would entice me more than shock me into realizing he knew something incredibly private. He had either found records online or followed me to the Hazelden clinic in Minnesota. Neither were great options.

"I could have you arrested for stalking and for drug solicitation."

"Fine," he nodded. "But know this…" He said it strangely, stiffly, as someone in community theater might. Or someone on SNL just before they break the fourth wall and start laughing at themselves. Oh, he had rehearsed this. He had surely stood in front of his bathroom mirror and rehearsed it. "I would never hurt you, my love. You saved me once. And I want to do the same for you. But there is something in this town that needs taking care of. And I can't do it without my Lady Jane." Nervousness twitched at the corner of his mouth. Could he tell how ridiculous it all sounded?

He reached for my elbow. A chill ran down that arm and rippled around my ribcage. My dread organ looked for a new place in my gut to hide.

I tried not to make my lip curl, but it did, and I could see the injury far back in his eyes.

"Where's your boyfriend," he asked.

I stood there, unable to move, the deer in his headlights now. "H-he's got a broken foot." That was technically true, at one time.

His flat leer came closer. "If he were a real man, he'd be down here looking after you. Besides, we both know he left." Lincoln winced at his own words. "He didn't deserve you anyway."

TJ's face crowded in, bright and pink. She spat words at Lincoln and wedged her body between us.

"You fucking manbaby. Leave her the hell alone!"

He blinked. Like an animatronic, he blinked. Computing how to deal with the love of his life's best friend. Knowing that if he hurt her, I'd never forgive him. His nose twitched and his flat smile returned. "We are not done here."

"Actually, you are, dude. Have a beer. *Reeelax.*"

Across the room a cheer went up at the DJ station.

"Rend-er! Rend-er! Rend-er!"

An American flag waved on the TV screen by the karaoke mic stand.

"C'mon, Render!" Gary yelled. "Sing it!"

Lincoln had backed away, along the bar, but still glared at TJ as she strode away to Paul who offered the microphone up to her with a dramatic bow.

The DJ had set the karaoke machine to "The Star-Spangled Banner" and was shaking his head. As the first few strains wound up, my face flushed. I hadn't heard this surreal version since high school.

TJ puffed herself up, blew the bangs out of her face, and stared off above our heads.

> "Oh say can you bleed,
> By the Donzerly Light?
> Oh so loudly we wailed,
> As our jugular lay gleaming."

One could easily tell then who our classmates were and who the spouses were by the laughter and the stiffening looks of shock.

> "Whose broad beams and bright core
> Broke the blackening night
> O'er the whimpers of the girls
> And the boys who lay screaming."

Some of the guys joined in then to help her to the end. Paul, Jessie, Gary. Hell, Gary hadn't even been there in The Thicket when she'd written it, but it had caught on around school afterward and even the freshmen knew it. It was bizarre how many had remembered. And yet I hadn't recalled the words at all until now. They came back to me like a particularly dreadful bedtime story.

> *"And the quake broke our hearts*
> *Vessels bursting apart*
> *Gave proof to the rites that Cthulhu was still there.*
> *Oy vey, does that many-suckered tentacle yet wave*
> *O'er the land of old gods and the home of the*
>     *naïve!"*

And they all pronounced naïve *nave*, just like TJ did when we were kids because none of us had actually heard the word yet. This caused me to giggle along with everyone else, despite Lincoln storming out. It wouldn't have surprised me if he had stomped right back in with an AK-47 and mowed us all down. But I was so drunk by then, it felt somehow right, that we deserved it … and wasn't everybody getting shot these days?

I stared at the door, resigned to my fate, until TJ coaxed me over to a quiet table of friends. Across the room, Jaylene had commandeered the karaoke and was plowing through "Stand by Your Man" with her besties.

"Does it still work?" Paul asked.

"The Donzerly Light? I dunno," Gary said, legs spread and a Pabst teetering on his belt buckle. "Only the kids go out there nowadays to do 'shrooms."

"Same as it ever was."

"Well, we'll have to check before we go." TJ wiggled her eyebrows at me.

I wasn't so sure. That light had petrified me as a kid.

After Evie, it had made The Thicket less of a haven and more of a haunted place. After Evie. And Roy.

We all watched as Lincoln came back in and after a few stuttering turns about the room marched over to our table. I knew it took great courage to come back, but it still did not endear him to me; I just wanted him to give up already. Thankfully, instead of a high-powered rifle he held a paper grocery bag with the opening folded down. He dragged a chair, screeching, over to us, sat on it, and set the bag on the floor. Where his grip had been, there was a sweaty handprint.

"Let me get this straight," said Paul's wife, Amanda. "It's a light that turns on and off. And you're all scared of it."

Paul dragged a hand down his face.

"Okay, yeah, I know how it sounds," TJ chuckled, "but here's the thing. It rarely goes off. And when it does, there has always been a death or disappearance nearby."

"Well, people do tend to die on occasion."

"Yeah, but in high school we tracked it down to the time of death. Remember?"

"Only a few people," Gary said. "But yeah, that was weird."

Amanda nodded, still amused.

*Some witch she is*, I could hear TJ thinking.

"Did they ever find the kid who went missing ten years ago?" I asked.

Gary tilted his head. "Who?"

"The boy."

The looks of befuddlement and disinterest stirred

something in me. My voice rose a bit too much. "The gay teenager."

"Oh, him." Gary rocked back. "Nope. Family moved out of town not long after. The consensus was runaway. Those types often do."

"Maybe he didn't feel welcome," TJ grumbled.

Lincoln sat up. "The light still works. It turned off when my mom died. And my dad." Everyone turned to him as he stared at the floor. "I put a deer cam on it. Got the times and dates. It matches up. Goes off pretty regular in the winter months with the Masonic home being just down the road. An old lady breaks a hip, or a widower just gets tired of being cold and lonely at the holidays. Cam stopped working last month though. I think Fish and Game took it down. And I'm sure not going back in there to check."

These were the first normal, unstilted words I had heard out of Lincoln. Maybe ever. We all just stared dumbfounded at him. And then Gary had to open his mouth.

"Good old Lincoln Logs."

"Gary," Paul said, in a low voice.

Lincoln shrugged. Honestly, he was better looking than he had been as a teen. He had been a shlubby kid, speckled with zits, and he'd worn thick square glasses with his straight hair cut like a bowl. But since then, he hadn't abused his body with alcohol or cigarettes like others in our class. His skin was clear and unwrinkled. He was still a little overweight but no more than the average American. His mustache had filled out enough to make a gay bear proud. If I hadn't known that he thought about me night and day, if he'd just been reasonable...

*Nope, still not happening.*

There was something crucially wrong with him, beyond the stalking, that I couldn't quite put my finger on. And is it too much to ask to want a man who doesn't masturbate every single day to your senior class photo? Why is it that my choices have always been "creeper" or "man who needs to be convinced to think about me for more than a couple minutes a day?" Seconds even. Just attentive enough. Nothing gloopy.

"Well, I'm going back into The Thicket, I can tell you that," TJ said. "It's not something I get to see every day."

Lincoln sat up at that. "No, you're not!" He glowered at her, his breath puffing through his nostrils like a bull.

Her eyes widened at him with challenge. "Excuse me?"

Jaylene ambled over, a glass of red in hand. "What are you losers talking about?"

TJ and Lincoln eased up on their staring contest.

"The Donzerly Light," Amanda said eagerly. Her pagan curiosity was finally intrigued.

"Oh, for fuck's sake. You idiots and that light. It's just a water treatment facility. Probably goes off when someone flushes a toilet. We could have won state if half the squad wasn't obsessed with that damn thing."

TJ leaned slowly back in her chair and looked at me with a barely perceptible smile, then turned back to Jaylene.

"Hey, y'know, you should go sing that Dolly Parton song that's named after you."

"What? Oh. That's 'Jolene', ya nitwit."

Paul chuckled and Amanda burst out with a laugh and a

tiny fart, which sent us all into giggles and had Amanda covering her face.

"Eh," TJ leaned over to her, "even the Queen of England toots like a busted party horn."

Jaylene smirked at our group, her teeth lavender with wine stains, as if marking us all with a curse. She settled back on TJ. "You always loved being the center of things."

"Well, wouldn't you," TJ pursed her lips in a more feminine way than usual, "if you were me?"

We all went hysterical with laughter. Except for Lincoln, who held me in the corner of his eye.

"You think you're so funny and *special*," Jaylene spat. "You weren't innocent in school. Remember calling poor Carl 'Crusty Carl' because he had that skin condition? He never got over that. But I'll tell you one thing, everyone's really over the Jane and TJ shitshow. Always trying to get attention. Nobody thinks about you or talks about you anymore!"

"Jaylene." Gary stood up and snagged her by the arm. She stood there, solid and sneering.

TJ, unfazed, smacked her lips and turned to Beth who had been silent through it all.

"So, Bethhhh, I never see you on Facebooook. Why aren't you on sosal media?" Slurred speech meant we were done here.

I rose from my seat. "We should go."

"Wait." Lincoln lurched forward and grabbed the paper bag, presenting it to me. "I have something else for you."

"Something else?" Paul asked.

"I—"

Jaylene grinned, and with a hiss said, "O-pen it."

TJ shrugged. I sat back down, stares upon me while Lincoln carried on leering.

It didn't seem heavy enough to be someone's skull, and at least I was surrounded by friends. Mostly.

I unfolded the bag and lifted out a transparent old Tupperware container, stained orange with grease, the lid cracking at the corners. Something caught in my throat, my damned dread organ again. I swallowed it back down and cracked the plastic box open.

Two ten-inch phallic sausages the color of liver lay between ice packs. Sage, oregano, and fennel wafted up with just the slightest reek of gamey blood.

*Don't puke. Whatever you do, don't puke.*

Everyone leaned in to take a gander. Gary snickered.

TJ nodded. "Interesting metaphor."

"They go great with pasta or you can fry them at breakfast time."

Jaylene giggled with syrupy evil. "Oh, how sweet."

My voice quaked, "These are the—?"

"Yup, deer. From last night. Made from the tenderloins. Fresh as it comes."

Paul perked up at that. Amanda's face twisted in disgust.

I looked up at them. "We ran over a—a buck... on our way into town."

Lincoln shook his head. "Oh, that was no buck."

"But the antlers."

"I've only seen it once before. A doe in velvet with a

sizable rack. She had teats too. Probably a fawn wandering around out there somewhere."

"Shit," TJ muttered.

Gary nodded. "Chesterson's grandpa shot one of those by accident once. But it was the opposite. Presented as a doe and he got trigger happy. When he opened her up and she had testicles inside. Tasted same as any other."

Amanda clattered out of her chair, a hand clamped over her mouth, and ran to the bathroom.

Jaylene rolled her eyes. "Vegetarians."

Lincoln reached into his coat and pulled out a sixteen-inch bowie knife that flashed with all the colors of the disco lights a mere two feet from my face. The shining blade gleamed two inches wide with a curved sloping edge, its top side serrated.

I raked in a deep breath.

TJ boomed out, "Hey!"

Jaylene and Gary laughed. Paul took a breath, his shoulders widening, and slid forward on his chair.

Lincoln gazed at the knife with the pride of a father. "This is what I used to dress her. Super sharp. Went real fast. Just got it. New model. Laser cut."

"Sweet, lemme see." Gary said. Thank God, I thought. Annoying Gary was at least clever enough to disarm a man. He tested the weight in his hands, turned it this way and that, then stepped back and jabbed the air a few times. "Very nice."

Then he handed it back.

"But—"

"Calm down," Jaylene spat in my ear. "He does this shit all the time. Don't mean a thing."

"I can't accept this." I raised the plastic container in a reverse offering.

Lincoln went blank.

"Oh, let me guess," Jaylene said. "You only eat meat from a supermarket. You know, what he did was ten times more humane than what animals go through at a slaughterhouse. If you don't want it, I'll take it. Brad's too lazy to hunt these days."

Lincoln's hand was still on the knife, the blade drooping toward the floor.

"No," I said, "I'll take it. Thank you. Gotta ... honor the deer, right?"

"You're welcome. There's a lot more too."

"I'll take some," Beth said. "I can pay you."

Lincoln just kept staring at me, his flat smile returning.

"Welp," I said, slapping my knees, "it's late."

And thus began the requisite round of hugs, the business card presentations, the procession to the door, all the while skirting Lincoln as he wove through the scrum toward us.

---

Once out of range of the parking lot, under cover of a blackening night, I tossed the Tupperware into a mulberry bush.

"Hey, litterbug." TJ sprinted back and fished it out of the brambles.

Something flickered around the base of the Dairy Queen.

"Did you see that?"

"What?" TJ caught back up.

"The devil's share."

"The *what*?"

"That stuff growing on the buildings, it sparkles sometimes."

"No, it doesn't. You're seeing things. Lightning bugs."

"I could swear—"

"Ya drunk, Blanche!" She tossed me the Tupperware.

I sighed. "You know I'm just going to throw it out at the motel."

TJ raised a finger. "Okay, I hate to say this, but maybe Jaylene was right. It's our kill. We need to—"

"But I don't even eat meat anymore, TJ!"

"You ate ham for breakfast! And eggs!"

"That was a special occasion." I stalked down the road. "How are we supposed to keep it cold?"

"There's an ice pack in here. We'll grab some from the motel machine too."

"Oh! I know. We could give it to your mom when we stop by."

TJ shook her head. "No. No, Jane. Not gonna happen. She's dead to me."

"Oh, come on."

"Jane, she always hated me."

"No she doesn't!"

"You didn't know her like I did, Janey."

"But—"

"Race me!" And she took off into the shadows.

"Not fair!"

Then we were running, streetlights flickering past.

Ahead of me TJ twirled around, casting long, spiky shadows that bent unnaturally and frenetically in all directions. She sang out,

> "Pan, Pan, Greek God Pan!
> One half goat!
> The other half man!"

The last I remember was that sidewalk sprint, listing starboard, sausages pummeling around plastic, TJ at my side, my high heels threatening an ankle catastrophe, singing and laughing so hard our cheeks ached and we could barely breathe. Back, back across this deathly quiet town, into the darkness—running both from and into the past. Our laughter followed, bouncing off houses, splashing round corners, and chasing us down the street.

There was a low rumble and flash of white two streets over as a truck matched our speed.

## Chapter Fourteen

### Two Decades Ago

"You sure about this?" Paul asked Jane.

"We already ate them," Brian interjected. "What choice do we have? Throw them up?"

"I'm fine," Jane said, nestling closer to Paul on the blanket. "It'll be okay. Let's just all stay together."

It was the first time the kids had entered The Thicket since Evie's disappearance. Nearly a year gone now. It had taken that long to recover from the initial loss of their friend, the trouble they'd gotten into at home, the police interrogations, the shame.

It had been TJ's idea to trip on the fungus. And frankly, Jane's too. Brian had gotten on board next, then Roy, and finally Paul, who had to admit the foxfire fungus was the coolest thing he'd ever seen. He'd been reading up on mushrooms and had determined that these were safe. Brian said his older brother had eaten them years before with no long-term problems. As long as they didn't discuss negative stuff—Evie in particular—they should be fine. They didn't even rub it on their skin this time, for fear of thinking about her.

It only took fifteen minutes for the effects of the mushrooms to slide into the kids' minds, the taste of dirt and anise still strange in their mouths. Their vision seethed as the copper sun set behind a trembling latticework of branches.

Roy and Brian began laughing first. And they didn't stop until both were crying, snot running down their faces.

TJ sat on the edge of the big wool army blanket, cigarette behind her ear, like a ship's captain. "Everything's brighter when I close my eyes," she said.

This started Roy off again.

"Dude, you sound like a fucking goose," Brian said.

"Shut the fuck up," Roy grumbled.

"Well, you do."

Paul draped an arm around Jane. "Guys, let's not."

Roy didn't say much from then on. He seemed to detach from their shared thoughts.

Jane gazed up to the sky, which resembled a perfectly unwrinkled sheet of lavender satin, a satin so smooth you could touch it, wrap yourself up in it. She tried closing her eyes, but the loud swirls of color flooded her mind and it felt much safer to keep them open.

As darkness fell, The Thicket grew quiet, as if someone had switched off the world. No crickets, no snapping branches, no wind hissing through pine needles, no jet engines miles above, or traffic on the county road.

Jane released a calming breath, but it caught in her throat.

Something in the foxfire glowed brighter than the fungus itself, which seemed to tear open, to be birthing something into the air around it. Jane screwed her eyes shut then opened them again.

A tumbleweed of faint orange light rose from the foxfire, just above the forest floor. The color reminded her of their biology teacher's blood serum floating in a vial, that amber plasma that he'd spun out with a centrifuge during class.

Each of the kids drew in great gasps of air but could not speak.

The thing unfurled as it rose up a few feet, nothing connecting it to the ground. This revealed hundreds of glowing filaments, uncoiling from a central orb the size of a grapefruit. The root system pulsed light in sparkling hues Jane couldn't quite place.

*What color is that?*

*It isn't.*

Further within The Thicket, more glowing and floating root systems emerged to slowly gather around the first. Though all were of different shapes and sizes, all hung from their own central orb.

The kids sat motionless, unable to move. Time seemed irrelevant; for all they knew, the vision might have progressed over the course of minutes or hours.

At least two dozen of these filament groups congregated, pulsing in silence.

Jane's tongue dried in her gaping mouth and tears rolled

down her cheeks in a kind of awe she hadn't experienced since, well, since way too far back.

The filament systems moved in an oddly familiar up and down motion toward one another. Two of them entwined and sparks danced along their roots with an occasional flash.

Jane nodded slowly. *Yes, yes.* She knew what they were. It was on the tip of her cracking tongue. She'd seen this structure before, in a textbook, but her ability to label anything aloud to the others, to describe even the most basic thought, had fallen away.

She assumed the others had forgotten words too until Roy burst with his odd laughter and stuttered, "Ffthg, jllfthg, oook." Then actual words returned to him: "They look like jellyfish, fucking jellyfish!"

At the sound of his voice, Jane's muscles sprang back to life with a jolt of adrenaline and her fingers dug into the blanket.

Each of the filament systems halted. Their orbs lit up in the center and Jane could tell then that the orbs themselves were not one structure but merely a denser nest of smaller filaments. From this central core, light flooded downward into the main stem and branched off in waves. Angry waves.

Jane squinted. The beings—because this is what they had to be—moved toward them. Slowly at first, flashing on and off like the after image when you shut your eyes, closer with each flash. As each of the kids recovered their wits and scrambled to their feet, the glowing roots quickened their flickering approach and the foxfire pulsed a path for them like an airport runway.

Something tugged at Jane's legs, her arms, making it difficult to stand, like a tenacious spiderweb. She brushed down her arm and threads pulled out of her skin. It reminded her of the time she'd stepped on a dog whisker and had to pull it out of her toe.

She shrieked and twirled off the blanket, batting at her limbs.

Paul ripped at his own trap of webs then yelped, "Go!" He pushed at her, placing his body between her and the glowing filaments that were sailing right for them. "Go!"

Roy and Brian were already racing down the path.

With mere feet to spare, Jane scrambled away from the glowing creatures, her hand in Paul's. The forest around them brightened and blurred.

Something stronger than threads clasped her leg this time and she stumbled. She reached down to pry it off. A hand with no arm coiled tightly around her ankle, its fingers as cold as her arthritic grannie's.

The sudden vision of a dimly lit basement filled her mind, a tall man coming at her in a flash with a hard slap of his left hand, then a jaw-twisting punch from his right that sent her mind further reeling.

Jane loped alongside Paul, hands out, trying to grasp what truly lay before her and what was hallucination. The forest? A basement? Their glowing pursuers? The hand around her ankle loosened, yet still held. *I want to live*, it seemed to say. Jane shook her leg and the hand sagged further. *Please help me.*

Given the chance, Jane might have been able to pry the fingers off one by one, but there was no time. The glow of the filaments just behind them lit the trees in front of them.

The strange basement flickered back into her vision. Now the room was upside down as the man carried her over his shoulder toward a circular saw table. It reminded her of her childhood, when her father would carry her giggling to her bedroom and toss her on her mattress for story time. But instead of delighted squeals, a howl ripped out through her throat. The man in the vision flicked the switch and the motor screamed to life.

Jane sprinted despite her urge to vomit. By God, she would take this damn hand home with her if she had to. She wasn't waiting to find out if the glowing creatures were friendly.

With the edge of The Thicket in view, one of the beings overtook Roy. The boy shrieked and writhed, with great leaps forward, as its glowing filaments poured around him, its central orb attempting to cover his head.

"Oh, fuck, no. Mom! Mom, help me!"

Brian grabbed Roy's arm, yanking him faster. They stumbled out into the prairie and Roy rolled around in the dirt beating at his head and torso, kicking up a cloud of dust.

"Dude, it's gone," Brian said. "It's gone!"

A few yards over, Jane and Paul leapt out of The Thicket too. Paul kept running toward their bikes.

Jane stopped in her tracks. "No. Wait," she yelped. "TJ!"

Paul ran back and pulled at her. "Come on, Jane! Come on!"

Jane chanced a disgusted sneer down at her ankle. The hand was gone, having left a muddy black stripe of ichor along her calve.

Deep in The Thicket, the glowing creatures flashed and dimmed, dissipating into darkness as if they'd never been there at all.

"Jane, come on," Paul pleaded.

*Please, God, don't take TJ too.*

Together Jane, Paul, Brian, and Roy stood quivering ten feet from The Thicket, still high, still tripping. Above them, in a black sky, constellations blazed accusations at them.

Jane bellowed. "TJ! *TJ!*" She would holler all night if she had to.

A glowing red dot floated in the hollow center of the path and bounced toward them.

In the murky light, a figure emerged from The Thicket, a broad smile on her pale face.

TJ drew hard on her cigarette. She rolled her shoulders and blew a smoky cloud.

"Now, that … was *epic*."

## Chapter Fifteen

### Present Day

There came a delicate knock at the motel room door. TJ and I exchanged wary looks. I unwrapped the towel from my wet hair, tightened my robe, and tiptoed to the door. TJ leapt from her bed, grabbed the desk lamp, ripping the cord out of the wall, and held it like a baseball bat.

A quick glance through the peephole revealed Harini. I motioned to TJ to stand down and opened the door.

"Good morning," the woman sing-songed. Hers and Ranveer's were certainly the only English accents we'd heard in Ketchum. Her long pink *kurti*, golden slacks, and purple shawl stood in such a contrast against the drab gravel of the parking lot that it took me further aback. In her hands, she held an ornate silver tray with English tea and biscuits. My brain still a muddle from the night before, I gaped for far too long.

"Oh! Thank you."

Harini took one hand off the tray and tapped the lid of the silver teapot. "This is made with filtered water. You won't want to drink from the tap. Get yourself a gallon at the grocer if you plan to stay." Wind from the prairie whipped into the dark strands of her hair, threatening to pull it from its bun. "How long *will* you be staying?"

"Just a day or two more. Until the new car comes. Would you like to come in?"

She shook her head and handed me the tray. "That's good. I mean to say, you are welcome to stay as long as you wish. I simply meant that there's so little to do here."

"Right." I nodded, rolling my eyes. "How long have you—?"

"We hope to sell in the next few months. Before winter." She peered down at the brick foundation near our door. Ranveer had missed a spot with his power washer. "It's not … what we agreed to."

I walked back to the desk to retrieve my wallet. TJ had replaced the lamp and stood staring like a dolt.

"Oh, no." Harini fluttered her hands at me. "No need. Ranveer and I simply wanted to make sure you were well set." She stepped out of the doorway, backing toward the office.

"Oh, sure. We're fine," I said. "This is lovely! Thank you so much."

After shutting the door, I stood staring at the carpet while TJ grabbed the tray from me, sat at the table, and munched through half the biscuits.

What had possessed those two to move to this godforsaken town? Were they running from something?

Had they lived in London before this? Did they have a mafia in India? These are the types of ridiculous thoughts I get upon waking.

"These are more like graham crackers," TJ mumbled, crumbs flying.

I nodded and joined her. Though the round biscuits were dry, they went well dunked in the warm tea, which TJ had sweetened and thickened with an excess of sugar and milk. It smoothed the edge off an otherwise dreary start.

After our impromptu tea party, TJ jumped back on her bed, propped herself against the bed pillows, and typed on her laptop—a pluck here, a tap there. She sucked pathetically on an electronic cigarette from the convenience store.

The light above the vanity was on again and flickering. It pricked the hair on my arms.

I walked over and snapped it off. "I told you not to turn that light on!"

"I didn't!" TJ said with a bark. "You did to put your damn make-up on!"

"Oh."

We were a bit sick of ourselves and the sharded memories of the reunion. I had suckered myself into three too many drinks and needed to be careful now, or the desire to self-medicate would get its tender hooks back in me.

"What do you think Harini meant about the water?" I asked.

TJ muttered back, "Pesticides probably."

After dressing in a fresh pair of capris and a blousy T-shirt, I watched out the front window for our replacement car

145

to pull up. The prairie went on for miles, past fields fluttering with young corn, windmills slowly spinning, silos, and cell towers. I pulled out my phone and scrolled through the news: World leaders argued about $CO_2$ levels; an off-season hurricane made an appearance; a new virus was touring the globe; the south had flooded again, while drought ravaged the west; a Hollywood starlet teased a nipple on Instagram. Not that I had the luxury of watching the world burn. I opened my email. Each day my inbox grew heavier with book queries. New writers from across the country, each hoping for a shot at publication. I couldn't afford to ignore them. Anyone of them could be the next Zadie Smith.

"If I had a nickel for every white dude who sent me the epic tome I never asked for—"

"You'd have \$322.95."

"That's a lot of nickels though!"

"Gotta adjust for inflation."

My phone buzzed. A text. From my boss, David Stuben. On a Sunday.

DAVID: How was the reunion?

Shit.

JANE: So much fun!
DAVID: Any good material?
JANE: TONS!
DAVID: Great!
DAVID: Love to hear what you've got.

Double shit.

JANE: You're in the office?
DAVID: Nope. At the cabin.
DAVID: Jada and I are bored.
DAVID: Call me.
JANE: Okay!

I stared at my cousin, the laptop glowing on her face.

David's voice hounded me like a chant: Deeper—Go deeper—Or else we can't—keep her.

"I have to call David," I said with a sigh. "Tell him where we're at on the book— Oh my God, what are you doing?"

Behind TJ, in the reflection of the mirror over her bed, *Warcraft* glared from her laptop. Green orcs and blue trolls ran rampant all over the screen.

"Just checkin' to see if I made any gold."

"Seriously? It's not even real money!" I lowered my voice. "Listen, I get it. You get to be strong somewhere when you can't be strong in the real world, but it's eating up your creativity, TJ, and I can't—"

"Dammit, I'm not a sausage grinder, Jane!" This, TJ could not finish without an old-man voice and laughter, trying to brighten me up. She sucked on her e-cig and spoke from the side of her mouth. "God, I wish I still smoked. I need to start vaping for reals."

"Seriously, I have a lot riding on this. We both do, trust me."

TJ shrugged at my less than subtle threat. "Girl, you've only given me a few days to come up with anything."

"It's been *months*, TJ. This trip only bought us a few more weeks."

"Maybe it wouldn't be the worst thing in the world to stop depending on each other so much," she said. "Maybe you should settle down, make an honest woman out of Nick, have some babies. I'll figure something out. I always do."

I collapsed onto my bed and crossed my arms, staring at the reverse universe ceiling tiles with their little black pinpoints. I could just picture David and Jada right now, lounging in their cedar Adirondack chairs, growing bored with one another and wondering why I wasn't calling. She would be drinking a mimosa overlooking Lake Wisconsin ready for some grubby gossip from "Hicksville, USA." He would be smoking a Cohiba, its barnyard-on-fire scent annoying her into wishing she was back in the city.

"I can't believe you're saying this." I sat up and pulled at the strands of curls at the nape of my neck, untangling them as I often did when stressed out. How was I going to get out of this?

She glared at the computer, lips pinched. "I told you I didn't want to come here!" She rarely turned her ire on me. Something was wrong.

I sat up. "You mean because of your dad?"

TJ was silent for a while, peering at me, gauging something in me. She snapped her laptop shut. "Maybe I don't tell you every single thing."

"Well, maybe I don't either." I thought of my pill

problem, and whether the ones Lincoln showed me at the reunion were real. I was no longer concerned about how he knew I'd want them, so much as how I could possibly still get one—or two—without him making it into a bloody marriage proposal. *Hillbilly heroin, still a hick at heart.* The oxy would never be done with me, whether I avoided it or not. An empty brown bottle would be mine to tote for the rest of my life. That and a Tupperware of sausage.

TJ glowered at my expression, unsure. "Do you remember something? That he touched you?"

"Who?" Was she talking about Lincoln? Paul?

She looked away. "Never mind."

"*TJ?* What? Who?"

"Dad."

I balked, head cocked, squinting at the paneling, comprehending too much all at once, comprehending what exactly she was asking and why she was asking it.

"No, Teej? Why would he—?" I leaned forward, elbows on knees. "Are you saying your dad touched you? Molested you?"

She looked down at the bedspread. "There are no faces. Only feeling. I was … I was really young. I don't remember any pain, just something that didn't feel … right."

I went to her bed then, but the wall was up. TJ drew on the cheap e-cig and blew her cloying bubblegum vapor in my direction. She didn't want comforting. She was in that place.

"I didn't know," I murmured. "I swear I didn't know."

"Yeah, because the cops covered everything up for Mom."

"Everything?"

"The tapes, the photographs. But I called him out that night." TJ made a disgusted face, like she'd just eaten something rancid. "The last thing I remember saying to him is that I wished the gun would go off in his face. He'd mostly stopped hitting me, so he knew I wasn't scared of him anymore."

My lips parted.

"Yeah. He meant to shoot himself." TJ nodded. "He did it right there on the spot. Just to spite us. He'd been caught out. Detectives found his stash. He was done. Then I said that to make matters worse. It's like I killed him."

"No, it isn't! That's not— Then he was a terrible father, Teej. He—" I tried to picture her father. When we were small, he was just another mustached man in pleated slacks towering above me.

"Maybe I was the trigger though. And y'know, maybe I'm glad to be the widowmaker. Maybe it was up to me to suggest it."

I shook my head, confused. I didn't know what to say; it was all too much at once. It was beyond my capacity; I had no tools.

TJ spoke in a low voice, "After he shot himself, a detective saw me. Only once. She showed me one of the Polaroids I'd been in when I was really little. I didn't see the rest, the other kids. But Mom saw all of it. It was kids from around the county. Jaylene was one of them. Evie," she said quietly, "was another. Then Mom just shut down, wouldn't tell me anything more."

I could barely form words, just whispered, repeating, "I

didn't know." But deep down I'd always known something was off about the story. And I selfishly never asked, telling myself it would only hurt TJ to bring it up. Silence begets silence.

"Nobody did, for a while. It's easy to cover up the unfathomable. They did it for Mom and me. But mostly for the department, because they'd bungled the case so badly. Hell, they probably would have blamed his suicide on a cop-killing if they'd found some drug dealer to pin it on." She tapped her temple with her finger. "But then at the diner the other day, it felt odd, didn't it? Even before Lincoln came in. And before the guy in the street? And so, last night at the reunion I realized someone must have talked at some point. It's no longer a secret."

"That's why Jaylene went off on you."

"Yeah. She thinks I just make a joke of things, I guess. Well, that and the fact she's still a bitch from hell."

"Teej, what was in the picture the detective showed you?"

"It was just me. In the bathtub."

I huffed. "Every family has a photo of their kids in the bath!"

"That's what I told them too. I didn't remember anything that felt very solid, so I just kept quiet. But I asked Mom about it when I got older. I asked her all the time. And she never told me details. She wanted to put it in the past. Said I was only thinking of myself trying to delve into what Dad did. Don't know why she still protected him in the grave. He used to slap her around all the time too. So then, we just started to resent each other."

"I'm so sorry, TJ."

"It's okay, I just—" She looked to the ceiling. "I'm not sure I can write about this place. I love it, but I hate it, you know? If I could camp out in The Thicket, I'd be fine. But the people?" She shook her head. "And I don't want to go over to her house. Ever. Can you believe I just said that?"

I couldn't imagine such a thing. I loved my mom. She was always on my side. What would it have taken to stop loving her? There might never be enough fan adoration to fill the hole in TJ that her father had shot out. She must have figured that out long ago. No smooth-handed lover would ever soften that callus.

Or maybe I was wrong. Why was I sealing her fate? Plenty of people went through trauma and turned out all right. TJ was strong—strong enough for both of us most times. But one thing was certain: bringing her home had been a grave mistake.

I nodded. "So, maybe there's not a story here after all."

"Not one I can tell yet. Not about Ketchum. Even Lincoln. It's too damn close." TJ hung her head. My throat ached to cry. Then she asked what time it was.

"About three, I think."

"When do you have to call in?"

I didn't answer.

She turned to me. "*Now?*"

I said nothing.

TJ cracked open her laptop.

"Call him. I got this."

"Whoa... Are you sure?"

"Do you trust me?" She laughed. "Okay, pretend you do."

I pulled out my iPhone, called David, and stood behind TJ as her fingers spidered across the keyboard.

---

"You're on speaker now, Janey," David Stuben said. "Wow us."

TJ typed. I looked at her. She mouthed: *trust me*.

"Something different," I read and winced. TJ nodded calmly.

"Not the stalker?"

"We're still developing that. This is on top of that."

"Good. She's finally off her ass. Let's hear it."

TJ threw her middle finger at my iPhone and then got to it.

I read the first paragraph as she typed ahead of me.

"Okay, here's the set up. Black kid growing up in rural Minnesota in the 1990s. Name's Keith. Adopted from a young mom in South Minneapolis. Is one of only two kids of color in a small high school. Real smart, straight-As. Falls in love with a white girl. She looks like Baby from *Dirty Dancing*."

I gawked, incredulous, at TJ. Her shoulders shuddered with silent laughter. David's wife, Jada, was black. I hoped TJ wasn't walking me into a minefield.

"Her parents forbid it, tell him to leave her alone. He gets bullied, beat-up, but eventually graduates and leaves town."

The other end was silent. TJ looked up at me. I nodded and made that rolling sign with my hands that you do to keep someone going. She typed.

"He joins the Army, does a tour in Afghanistan, loses three buddies in a Humvee to a car bomb. Then he moves to Minneapolis, goes to college, gets married. But then he loses his pregnant wife in the I-35 bridge collapse."

I tossed up my hands. TJ drummed fingers on her lips, then started typing again.

"So, life's tried to break Keith in many ways. He's hard as granite. Well, now his dad is ill, so he decides to go back home to take care of him. On his way home, on this lonely old stretch of road, he sees a yellow biplane flying low over the cornfields, smoking out the back. He thinks, eh, maybe it's just crop dusting, but then it dives. Crashes. Ball of smoke. He's got all this pent-up survivor guilt from the bridge collapse and PTSD from the war. He wants to do something, to help. He's got nothing to lose anymore. He's a man of action. He pulls over, runs toward the fire, calling 911."

I stopped then, not because TJ wasn't typing like a madwoman but because David damn well owed this tour de force some sort of acknowledgment.

TJ had never mentioned this story or character to me before, and yet they felt so familiar. *My God, her ability to just conjure people from the ether, right here on the spot!* Was the trauma with her dad the source of such a skill?

"Jane? You still there, Janey?" There was panic in David's voice.

"Yeah." I smiled. TJ licked her lips.

"Well, keep going!"

"Okay, so he gets to the fiery plane, it's just roiling with black clouds. He struggles to pull out an elderly couple before it blows. Barely gets them out in time. Then police arrive while he's trying to give CPR to the old woman. They nearly shoot him cause he's black and they think he's attacking the couple."

"Of course," Jada yelled on the other line. I remembered then that she'd had a cousin from the South Side who got shot trying to help someone. The boy survived but he now used a wheelchair.

"So, our hero's down, on the ground, eating dirt with a white guy's knee in his back. But eventually the old man convinces the cops that he's only helping. Keith's shaken, but after the ambulance arrives, he goes on home to see his dad and they cry and all that good family stuff.

"The next day he goes to the hospital to check on the old couple. Someone else is there to see them too. Their daughter." I hesitated as I read it, my jaw dropping at TJ.

She grinned.

David yelled, "His girlfriend from high school!"

"Yeah. He just saved the lives of the people who ruined his childhood. And now he's looking. At. That. Girl."

"That girl!" On the other line, Jada sighed and laughed. "Baby!"

"Yeah, and she's looking right back. Just like she used to."

"Bam!" David said.

"BUT, hold on. Baby's in a corner. Next to her is one of

Keith's bullies from high school. The guy's her husband. And that's all you get for now."

Silence.

"Okay, but how's TJ gonna pull off a black guy voice?"

"He's not culturally black, David," Jada said, "he grew up in rural Minnesota! White straight ladies will read the shit out of this!"

David argues. "Hello, he's still had to endure bigotry!"

As they bickered on about who gets to write what story in our little world of make-believe, I grinned at TJ.

She took a celebratory puff of e-cig.

"Okay, yeah," David said with a snort and a cough, "this is Nicholas Sparks territory. Maybe a Lifetime movie, if we can get Tina to whip up a script. How far along is she?"

I didn't dare look at TJ and bit back laughter. "Oh, about halfway."

TJ balked and threw her hands in the air. She stretched her neck, rolled her shoulders, then got back to it, fingers dancing across the keyboard.

I headed for the door to finish the call.

Outside, my smile dropped. Parked in front of the motel office was an EconoCar van and beside that, our new set of wheels. Or should I say our next set of wheels. *New* did not factor into it. EconoCar was now hedging their bets with the notorious cousins Render. I frowned at the old Ford Taurus that had seen better decades. Something about that faded silver sedan spooked me. As if I'd seen it before. That very car.

And deep down I knew I had.

## Chapter Sixteen

A quarter mile down the road, Lincoln sat watching in his white truck as Lady Jane signed for the old, beat-up sedan.

"Look how you've fallen," he murmured. "Right back where you started."

Dusty wind across the gravel lot blew her hair wild and she struggled to keep it behind her ears, manage her iPhone, and scan the paperwork at the same time.

"A far cry from the hotshot literary agency, aye, m'lady?"

While his coworkers took vacations in Branson or Orlando, Lincoln's idea of time-off well spent had been driving up to Chicago to watch Jane Render go about her daily life.

Last September, he had sat patiently just like this, next to the old brick warehouse where Stuben Literary headquartered, wearing a Cubs baseball hat and aviator sunglasses. Only occasionally would he glance up at the towering buildings, his father's voice clear as day reminding him, you can always tell a hick in the city by how often they gape at the skyscrapers.

Sometimes Jane did not emerge from the warehouse until the end of the day, and he would follow on foot at a distance as she boarded the L-train. Most days she wore dresses or suits and high heels, her red curls bouncing and making him weak in the knees. He could count on her not looking up either. Save for the occasional glance at traffic, Jane kept her head down, eyes on her phone and out of those of passing men—men whom he was prepared to tussle with.

He would methodically work his way through the crowd and take photos of her with a small camera on a stick. Sometimes he would brush her arm, only to turn away swooning. Other times he would get too close, tripping her suspicions, and he would relent, disappear into the shadows as she picked up her pace on the street. He would trail her, letting her hear his footsteps. It felt so good, becoming significant to her, being important in that moment, no longer just another man in a crowd. It sent an electric thrill through him that only hunting could match.

On a few sunny days, Jane and one or more of her coworkers would emerge from the brick warehouse at noontime and walk the sidewalk down to an outdoor café to watch the tour boats on the Chicago River. Those days, Lincoln sat at a table in the neighboring restaurant. There he ordered light to keep the waiter away and placed his messenger bag on the table, angling it toward their conversation. In the bottom corner, Lincoln had cut a slit for a shotgun microphone and small parabolic dish for amplification. He wore white earbuds, as though he were listening to music or a podcast but was instead eavesdropping, eyes closed, on Lady Jane's banter.

Occasionally, the subject of TJ Render would come up, or other writers in their stable. But never did Jane talk about the manuscript Lincoln had sent, the western about the outlaw gunfighter and the prostitute with a heart of gold who marry and become the town preacher and schoolteacher. She probably hadn't finished reading it yet. It was 180,000 words after all. Every one of them important, of course, but still.

On his last vacation day, he drove to Lady Jane's apartment building as usual, to watch her walk to the train platform. He chose not to follow this time, but instead suited up in a ComEd utility worker uniform, complete with logoed hardhat, coveralls, reflective jacket, and toolkit. He then waited at her lobby doors for the next tenant to emerge and politely nodded himself in.

Lincoln took the elevator to the third floor, to the apartment number listed in the Ketchum High School class of '99 address book. There he unrolled his Peterson Ghost lock picking set and got straight to work as he had practiced many times on various doors throughout Ketchum and Birkenham. There were undoubtedly cameras stationed around the building, but he paid them no mind. He wasn't going to steal anything, and besides, he really didn't care anymore if security caught him. Now that his parents were gone, there was little left to lose and no one to embarrass.

Lincoln took photos of the entirety of Jane's apartment,

plucked strands from her hairbrush, then made love to her laundry pile.

In the den, her ownership of an iMac instead of a Windows desktop computer thwarted his efforts. He could forgive this one thing about her, the scamp. It was on him not to have found it out from TJ during their *Warcraft* chats. So, no, he didn't know how to launch a Trojan horse on a Mac and commandeer her webcam, but he would certainly settle for a copy of the hard drive, password keychain, email correspondence, her IP address, and yes, oh yes, her new cellphone number.

He toyed with waiting until the last possible moment to leave, or even staying. Just imagine the look on her face when she walked in. God knows he would like to deconstruct Jane, to peel her apart and slip his hands inside, to see and feel everything that made her tick, but then after that she'd be a mess, gone forever with nothing left to hold onto but a coil of red hair.

That day might come, but not here, not now.

———

Lincoln drove home from his Chicago vacation with hours upon hours of valuable material, enough to keep him satisfied until the reunion. Sitting pretty, his mother would say. He settled into the drive and turned on the radio. The conservative host was talking to folks; reassuring them they were winning.

Hours later, twenty miles north of Birkenham, a hitchhiker stood in the rippling heat on the road shoulder.

The low sun in the sky dappled her red hair. Lincoln's truck flew by her and he glanced in the rearview. She was all curves and curls.

Lincoln veered down the next off ramp, turned left and took the onramp north. He floored it down the highway, keeping the woman in his sights. She stood, arm outstretched, as semi-trucks blew past and swayed her body. Her shoulders slumped, losing hope.

Five minutes later he tooled south again, this time at forty-five miles per hour.

As the redhead came into view, Lincoln tapped the brakes.

She wore cutoffs, buttocks leaking out in pink moons, a neon yellow T-shirt off the shoulder with black bra straps showing. Not Jane's usual ensemble.

The closer he got, the older the woman got. She turned to the sound of his truck. Ten years on him probably but still attractive under those sunbaked lines. He eased onto the shoulder and slowed to a crawl. She grinned and tossed a white can into the ditch.

He rolled down the passenger window. "Headed to Birkenham?" His brow knit. Bottle-red hair with purple tips. A brunette. Just a brown head underneath.

"Yeah, thanks." She climbed up and slid in, revealing a half-inch of silver hair at her scalp, and unzipped her backpack. "Wanna drink? Gotta six-pack." She smelled like sweat and lilacs.

"I don't drink. Seatbelt please."

She buckled up. "It's not alcohol. It's B12 and all that

shit. No calories, all the energy. I can't get through the day without four of these fuckers."

"Sure, I guess."

She pulled out a can and cracked it for him, then threw her backpack on the floor. She growled at her hand, where only two of her fingers had red press-on nails. "Welp, there goes another."

The drink was sour, lukewarm, and tasted like soda gone off. He set it in the cup holder. "You shouldn't be out on the highway. People disappear round here."

"Oh, I'm tough." She kicked her backpack. "Got a knife in there. No one messes with me unless they want their balls cut off."

"That's no way for a woman to talk."

She spurted a clear spray at the dash and hooted a laugh.

His face went hot.

"You look like you could use a ride yourself," she said. "Loosen up much?" The woman pulled out a rolled cigarette. "Mind?"

"I don't smoke."

She chortled. "It's weed, Reverend." She laid a hand on his thigh and slid it back and forth until his pants warmed and his cock went hard.

"I said no," he said. "And I'm taken."

"Whatever."

Her mouth pursed and they rode in silence. She downed her drink and popped another. He tried to think of Lady Jane, but Jane judged him for his naked desire. Betrayal. Good. He'd make her jealous.

They barreled along in terse silence until the off-ramp to Birkenham when the woman let out a snort. She was laughing at him again. He slowed the truck, prepared to give her a piece of his mind and a shove out the door.

Bubbles formed at the woman's nostrils and her body heaved. A lathery foam poured from her nose and mouth. She grabbed the dash and her face went purple. Then she slumped forward in her seatbelt.

Lincoln swung the truck into the back lot of a shuttered auction house.

For five minutes he pounded on the woman's sternum, her face growing pale again, her eyes staring blank at the dome light. He dipped his ear to her mouth—felt nothing, heard … nothing. He'd seen enough death in the woods to know what this was.

And yet his cock was still hard.

And she still smelled of sweat and lilacs.

---

The truck idled at Lincoln's mailbox.

*You've left your spunk on her, you idiot.*

*I told you what you'd amount to.*

*And now you've gone and proved me right.*

Lincoln unbuckled his seatbelt, got out and walked to the graveled entrance to the driveway. No cars on the horizon as far as he could see down County 9. The sun had dipped below the trees.

*There's still time. Give her to us.*

What choice did he have but to carry the woman over

the threshold of The Thicket like a bride—the wrong bride —and let it deflate her like he'd watched it do to Evie two decades ago? He'd long wondered if he'd only dreamt his classmate's absorption. Years had passed since that summer night; it had been dark, and he'd been tired from a long day helping his father in the fields. But he'd been glad to be rid of Evie. She'd liked kissing Jane too much.

The corpse was slippery in his arms when he pulled her from the truck. Unwieldy. Her left hand had landed with a sloppy smack to his face and he struck her back instinctively. She didn't care one bit.

*You have that effect on them.*

"Shut up!" he cried.

With the hitchhiker in his arms, he crossed the wide-open purgatory between his home and the Thicket. The dry, sharp-cut grass crunched beneath his boots, grasshoppers popping off all around. Her head hung back over his arm, mouth open, so that each step produced a glopping sound from her throat. He stopped, slung her over his shoulder, and she shut up.

They entered The Thicket and the crickets ceased their calls.

Lincoln found the same tree, now twice the size as it had been in the 90s. It was as tall as the one that lightning had felled, along with his brother. He'd often seen Evie's face in its knots from his kitchen window, but up close it was just a random assemblage of bark and sap and broken limbs.

He laid the woman in a heap at its base and marched in place, careful of the tendrils that hid in the roots. It reminded him of the time he'd kicked in a massive red ant colony to expose their tunnels of pale eggs and observe a society in panic. A dozen or more had bit his ankles before he discovered that if he just kept stamping, they would never be rid of this giant.

Lincoln marched for five minutes. The woman lay slumped, staring at her shoes. He backed up to The Thicket's edge and waited another five. Nothing.

*We'll take it from here, thanks.*

While it took longer with the hitchhiker (he suspected because less of her brain worked) the fungus did the job nonetheless and left her tattered clothes behind like so much snakeskin. He took the rags to the same place he'd taken Evie's—a landfill on the northside of Birkenham.

———

The silver sedan pulled away from the motel and headed south instead of north. The Hindu woman gave one last wave and went back to the office.

He should have ended it all in Chicago.

Jane returning to Ketchum should have been a dream come true. But it wasn't going as Lincoln had hoped. Paul McKenna was back in Jane's orbit.

At least Paul was married. And if the guy was working on fungicide powerful enough to get rid of the whiskey fungus, he might still be useful with The Thicket.

No, it was TJ that was the problem. Jane wasn't dignified here like she was in the city. She was rougher, coarser, turning from him at every chance. If she didn't straighten up and fly right, she'd be no better than the hitchhiker. And today, under TJ's influence, she was headed for an even more dangerous place.

Perhaps Lincoln hadn't made himself clear enough at the reunion. The Thicket was not to be trifled with.

And neither was he.

# Chapter Seventeen

## Two Decades Ago

Jane held her searing hand and winced in agony. Her fingertips continued to throb as if they were still sizzling.

"Why the fuck did you touch it?" Roy demanded.

Along the walls, his black-light poster collection of neon unicorns, toadstools with eyes, and big-breasted women all looked down upon Jane with derision.

Words piped out of her in squeaks. "I didn't know it was hot!"

"Um, it's a lamp?" Roy reached up and pulled the little beaded chain, turning the glowing violet bulb off then on again. It did hang far too low from his basement ceiling.

"But it … it doesn't look hot."

"It's still a lightbulb, Jesus!" Roy bit the air as he spoke, teeth glowing a sickening green in the black light's rays.

Paul walked back into Roy's wood-paneled bedroom

with a damp washcloth that smelled like ass. "Dude, you need to clean your bathroom."

Roy shrugged. "That's Mom's job."

"You need to fire your mom then."

Jane touched the wet terrycloth tentatively, trying not to grimace at the sting or the smell.

Roy settled back into his gaming chair, a sort of curving J shape that sat low on the ground and rocked back and forth. He selected a new character in *Tekken*.

—*Round One. Fight*—

Soundgarden's "Black Hole Sun" droned on from his CD player.

They hadn't known Roy Irving that long, though they instantly got his wry depression. His mom had moved him to Ketchum only a couple summers before. But since that first night in The Thicket playing Ghost in the Graveyard, their faces glowing, and their subsequent loss of Evie, he'd become kind of family. He had frizzier and darker red hair than Jane's, a goofy grin, and a general vulnerability that made him easy to talk to. He could play the hell out of an electric guitar now and hoped to someday play arenas. But ever since their last encounter with the beings in The Thicket, he'd withdrawn from them.

"Dude," Paul said. "Where were you tonight?"

Roy shrugged a shoulder as his thumbs danced on the PlayStation controller.

"Thought you were coming out with us."

Roy stared blankly at the large TV in the middle of his bedroom, as the two onscreen fighters pummeled each other. The guy didn't want for anything. In fact, his parents had just given him the Supra he'd always dreamed of for his birthday. But lately he seemed more content to stay at home and race pixelated cars on a pixelated track or beat the shit out of these boxy-armed enemies.

"Is everything okay?" Jane asked.

His eyelids fluttered and he licked his lips. "Like you care."

"Whoa," Paul said.

"Of course we care," she said. "That's why we're here."

Roy sighed. His hands stopped moving. On screen, the computer character stomped his character as it lay there, jerking with every blow.

"I had a dream the other night," he said. "Might have done too many 'shrooms."

Paul laughed, "You're not supposed to do them without us!"

"I know. I know." Roy hunched over in his chair. He looked away. "Evie came to me." He gazed up at Jane with weariness beyond his years. "She took me by the hand and led me into The Thicket."

Jane drew a breath to calm herself, but her back straightened tight.

"She just said, *look*. But it wasn't the woods anymore. It was an office building, in a city. It… um—I was really high up. I could see a big river—maybe it was the ocean. I was eating some sort of pastry. I can still taste it." Roy squinted and licked his lips. "Like, all buttery, flakey, with chocolate. And there was hot coffee, with really thick cream."

Paul knelt next to him.

"There was this huge rocking explosion." Roy set down

the game controller, staring off across the room, his eyes glistening. "The building caught on fire. Got super hot. I could feel it pressing at me, like when you open an oven? Then everything just shook, really hard. I tried to find Evie. But she wasn't there anymore. I tried to find … Jessica, this woman I'd had an entire affair with. I can still picture what we did together. So real. Better than any porn. And how I always managed to fit it all in before going home to my family. Oh, my God, my family. How is that … possible?"

Paul laid a hand on Roy's shoulder.

"The walls." Roy raised his hands up and dragged them down in the air. "The walls started falling, sliding down, before the floor did. This woman who I-I was in love with, even though she wasn't my wife, I know I loved her. Jessica. She called for me. Then she jumped out the window." Roy reached out into the air before him, surprised, shocked as if he were seeing it for the first time. "And my wife, my wife was calling on this weird flat phone from our house with our—" Roy sobbed, "I had kids." His face pinched into a horrible mask, red and covered with tears. "A baby girl and a toddler. A boy. Bailey." He covered his face in his hands. "And then everything just broke in me. Inside and out."

Jane hunched down and hugged Roy. She looked up to Paul, who could only stare back.

"It was so real, Jane." Roy cried until he went hoarse, shuddering in her arms. "It *was* real. That was my life. That *is* my life."

---

Later that night, Paul drove Jane in his Plymouth Duster down the access road toward the cliffs by the Ketchum River. He pulled into their favorite make-out spot in a turnaround.

Jane fiddled with the radio. Reception crackled sparse this deep into The Thicket and Sheryl Crow struggled to sing "If It Makes You Happy" through all the noise. Jane rolled the knob and clicked it off.

Paul stared out into the darkness of the forest.

"You okay?" she asked.

"Yeah," he said, his voice falling away.

By day, the nearby beach brought tons of people from around the county, eager to cool off from a hard week of work on a farm or in a factory. By night, the park reserve was all black woods and starlight. There might be a stray fisherman or floatboater still out there, but most had motored back to the docks before sundown.

"I had a vision like that too," Jane said. "After we saw those glowing creatures. Kind of like Roy's in the sense that it was … the future, or some parallel life. I can barely remember it though. It's like, the further I get from it, the less I remember. But it was hopeful, you know? Not like his."

Paul said nothing.

Jane tried to make out his expression in the dim light of the dash. "How about you?"

He shook his head. But Jane wasn't sure if that meant *no* or *leave it alone*, so she joined him in staring out into the night.

Paul leaned over and kissed her with warm lips—at first

passionately, desperately, and then slowly, pleadingly. She welcomed him. Paul had always respected her boundaries, always gave as much as he took, and he always gave first. He kissed down, well into her open shirt, lower and lower and unzipped her jeans.

As light from an oncoming car splashed across her ecstatic face, Jane bolted upright and yanked on Paul's hair.

He yelped. "Ow. What the fuck? Oh, hi." He waved to the couple in the other car.

Jane recognized them as seniors from a neighboring town. She buried her face in her hands while Paul laughed. The other kids waved back, laughing too, then pulled away. Their tires crunched along the gravel and squealed on blacktop.

The stillness returned, with only the faintest slap of the river tide and the occasional Late Cretaceous squawk of a heron.

It wasn't completely dark. Down a dirt road in a nearby gulley stood a utility shed lit by a single lamppost. Jane kept her eye on that amber glare, half aware, as Paul's hands wandered back into her bra and jeans. She lost her thoughts in that light while tracers on her cornea swam like paramecium under a microscope. Laid bare and ready to climax, she *told* her thoughts to that light.

*I sorta want to get home in time to read the next chapter of Harry Potter.*

*I am so bored with this town.*

*No, not there, Paul. Yes, there.*

*What the fuck is wrong with Roy?*

*Did Paul see something too?*

*Brian?*

*TJ?*

*How am I going to tell my parents that I want to study literature, not nursing?*

*Oh, God.*

Jane always returned the favor. And this night, quite pleased with the results, she sat up from a particularly deft blowjob and opened her eyes to a darkness so unsettling it left her dizzy. At the base of the trees closest to the car, there glowed the faint patches of bioluminescence from the fungus they knew all too well. They were too old to paint their faces with grimy fungus and pretend they were glowing heathens, and they were no longer in the mood to trip without the rest of their gang.

Other than the foxfire, the night had grown black as tar.

Surely, without tripping, they would not see those filament beings, Jane thought.

Or rather, she hoped.

Fear gripped her hard and cruel, as if she might conjure a phantasm right on the spot with the strength of her growing unease.

"The light," she whispered hoarsely. "What happened to that light?"

"It's off," Paul said.

"Duh. Why?"

"How should I know?" Paul stroked her hair and offered a thankful kiss.

But they had seen one too many horror films together. Jane waited breathlessly for the claws that would soon scrape along the sheet metal, imagining an elongated face with equally elongated fangs rising at the passenger window. Her mind rang in anticipation. Was that the sound of far-off gurgling? Or a rumbling in her ears?

"Can we get out of here?" her voice warbled in her throat.

His eyes searched out the back window toward the shed. "Oh, come on."

"I mean it. Let's go back to town." Jane smacked the lock down on her door, reached across him, and did the same.

Paul shrugged. They'd got what they came for anyway. He turned the key and put the Duster in drive. "It's probably just timed."

"Well, it's never gone off before!" Jane abandoned the thought of a seatbelt and scooted up against him.

"We've never been here this late." The car rolled out of the turn-around. As it came around to face the shed, the light flashed back on, solar brightness in their dilated eyes.

"Yar!" Paul yelped. He hit the brakes, lurching them forward.

Jane let out a screech. A faint ringing settled into her ears like high-pitched laughter. While they'd made out, fog had gathered in the gullies and copper beams from the light streaked across the mist and through the twisted oak limbs and underbrush.

"Okay, see," his voice quavered, "it's motion sensitive." Beneath Jane's panicked grasp, gooseflesh prickled his forearm.

"It has *never* done that before, Paul!"

Paul looked around, out every window. "If someone is fucking with us, I will kick—"

"Please *just go*."

He nailed the throttle and the Duster spun sideways, shooting gravel out the back. The ringing in Jane's ears dissipated and the two laughed at themselves. As Paul straightened the car out on the access road, Jane looked back.

She loved to look back.

The blacktop unspooled behind them in the red glow of their taillights as if all the earth were falling away into nothing.

## Chapter Eighteen

### Present Day

"What a piece of crap," TJ said with a bark. The air conditioning in the mid-90s replacement sedan blew warm, musty air at us. We cracked the windows.

After the agent from EconoCar dropped it off, TJ and I had celebrated our latest literary Hail Mary by tooling over to a neighboring town for pizza. We agreed that it was too late to make it to Nashville, though we were both lying. We could have crawled into a Clarksville hotel bed before midnight.

But we had unfinished business in The Thicket.

Our bellies full of too much dough, red sauce, and bargain chianti, we headed down Seven Hills toward the Ketchum River access area. I drove slowly in the remaining daylight; the blacktop splattered pink with the remnants of fresh roadkill. TJ kept an eye out for Lincoln's white truck.

"It looks so hardscrabble nowadays, doesn't it?" I asked.

We passed weedy trailers and the occasional one and a half story farmhouse sunken past its foundations. Large hunting dogs ran down long driveways to cajole us, past parked pick-up trucks with gun racks reminding me *we're back in Kansas, Dorothy*.

"It always was," TJ said.

I slowed the car and peered around at every turn-off. But most of these roads were entrances to homes set far back in the woods.

"Beth seemed nice," I ventured.

"I will not date a rough-handed woman, Jane. I will not."

"You could buy her some hand cream."

"If you don't care to make your hands smooth without prompting, what other skeletons do you have? That's all I'm saying. Why you trying to pair me up all the time? You're a bit slut-shamey, I have to say."

"Well, you seem lonely."

"I like being lonely. I mean, I like being alone."

"Okay, Garbo." I tapped the brakes. "Is this it?"

A rusted yellow Fish and Game sign bolted onto the trunk of a dying oak confirmed it. That big old tree must have stood along this barbed wire fence for a century or more. Nearly leafless now, its arthritic branches and limbs seemed to shake their gnarled fists at heaven. On closer inspection, the sign itself wasn't so much bolted on but partially absorbed into the bark. And barbed wire too had become one with the tree so that the fencepost once staked here, now hung in midair.

"Yeah. Yeah!"

As soon as the rental sedan turned the corner into the access area, we rolled over smooth black asphalt, paid for by a separate set of tax dollars than the township streets. The Thicket grew deeper on both sides of the curving road, which unfurled like a child's rollercoaster.

TJ dared me to gun it for old time's sake. I did, but not without darting glances at the edge of The Thicket for suicidal deer.

She giggled as she rose up in her seat. "Oh my God, this brings it all back, doesn't it, Janey?"

"Sure does." My chest ached with nostalgia. We were teasing death back then. Letting it give chase. We were faster than it. Well, most of us.

"Roy thought he could outdrive it," TJ said. Not only had she started finishing my sentences, she was damn well beating me to them.

I checked the rear-view mirror again for a gleaming white truck. Nothing but a sports car passed us, a last straggler from the beach.

"I wouldn't worry about Lincoln," TJ said. "This has got to be the one place he won't follow you."

"With good reason."

"So, what was he saying to you when I came up to the bar?"

I thought of the three white pills. It was what he hadn't said that had me worried. Maybe it was time to tell TJ about my trip to the Hazelden clinic.

"Oh, the usual mumbling. He's much better at email."

I made sure to park the car at the end of the turnaround, so we had a clear escape, but I didn't mention that. I didn't want to bring anything to life by giving it power.

*I am life.*

A voice. Inside me or outside me? Faint. Not TJ. My mind simply imaginative with fear? My dread organ powering up? Best not to mention that to TJ either, lest she laugh, or worse, write it down and make it even more powerful.

A doe and a fawn wandered past the front of our car and down into the other side of The Thicket. TJ and I quietly got out and watched, transfixed, until they disappeared into the woods.

"So cool," I said.

"Yeah, let's not tell them about the sausage."

We stood by the car and took in a breath of country air, which had a note of brackish decay underneath, a scent I hadn't recalled smelling in the past. But the sound of the wind passing through the birch leaves, flickering like spangles high above, and the warble of the birds, brought me right back. I was home again. As much as I loved the city, this wooded portion of childhood would never leave me. And I didn't want it to.

The day was waning, its colors draining. The electric blue of the cornflowers along the roadside had muted to navy, the buttercups from neon to simple yellow. Around us, the short-circuit buzz of insects. Though the sun had now dropped below the horizon, there was still a creamy gloaming light in the sky, so we strolled down the narrow road to where the light pole stood.

"Huh," I said. "There it is."

A light pole. A freaking light pole. With the bulb unlit in the early evening, it held little portent.

The pole stood next to a small brick building, moderately more menacing. A six-foot chain link fence with rusted barbed wire on top bordered the immediate perimeter. I hadn't remembered that. We used to wander all over in there. At one corner, some vandal had cut the fence and peeled it back. Just as Gary had said, we clearly weren't the last kids to come here to get our adrenaline spikes.

Peering through the fence, TJ scrawled in her little Field Notes booklet—the kind that hipsters carry around with all their grand plans for the next iPhone app or curated pop-up store. Black vines threaded up around the crumbling corners of the brick building. Little clots of dirty-looking fungus grew out of the cracks in the foundation. Next to the building stood one of those big, pill-shaped propane tanks. And next to that, within a concrete slab, round wells were set into the ground and six pipes shaped like upside down Js jutted from the concrete. Jaylene had been right about something; it was a water treatment facility of some sort. I hadn't really cared much about it in the past and still failed to pinpoint its significance. It was the light that held our interest.

As I kept my distance on the road, TJ sauntered around the underbrush, unperturbed by the possibility of ticks, poison ivy, or axe murderers. Many of the trees surrounding the site stood ashen gray and leafless. She kicked over a cavernous stump and peered inside.

"Bingo."

TJ came back, eyebrow raised. "Say hello to my little

friend." She held up the stalk of a small mushroom. "Wouldn't mind having a massive batch of these around for fun and profit." She twirled it between her fingers, the cap spinning like a little doll and then stopped. "I never noticed this before." She peered at it, then extended it to me.

The cap had wet black droplets on it, like little spider eyes.

"A disease maybe?" she asked. She went and plucked another one. Eyes on it too.

I shrugged. "Or the wrong breed. Could be a poisonous variety, Teej." I took a photo with my phone.

"Yeah, Google that, mutha."

"Checking with Paul," I said.

Her grin developed into a snicker.

As I typed on my phone I muttered, "Shut up."

"Dude, that's like a dick pic for nerds."

Cellular reception was spotty this far into The Thicket. I only had one bar. While we waited on the hood of the car for dark to come and Paul's response, I made a modest proposal.

TJ's mom, Aunt Ellen, was like a second mother to me. It seemed petty not to stop by and say hi tomorrow morning before we left for Florida.

"No way." TJ stared straight ahead at the light. If her angst could have powered it, it would have come right on and shattered the bulb with a pop.

"I know a lot has happened between you, but it just takes one of you to reach out. You could do the right thing first."

"I tried a long time ago, Janey. You don't know how I

tried. It's too late." TJ sighed. "Listen, if you really want to go, that's fine. But I'm waitin' in the car."

I agreed to this, sure there would be a way I could get her to come inside. I'd figure it out tomorrow.

It was nearly dark. Storm clouds were piling up to the west, the scent of rain in the air. Maybe it truly was the mobile reception or maybe the number on Paul's business card was a landline. I thought of texting his yoga witch wife, Amanda. It would kill two birds with one stone: put her at ease about me, and get our mushroom identified. Not that Amanda appeared at all worried about me at the reunion, but I was growing a little concerned that TJ was going to ingest this mystery fungus at some point. Especially with a potential confrontation with her mom on the table.

I checked my email.

"Damn. Lincoln knows where we are."

TJ sat upright and glared out into the trees.

**From:** Metzger, Lincoln [hansolo99@frontieronline.net]
**To:** Render, Jane [jRender@stubenliterary.com]
**Subject:** Evil grows there

Jane,

I sit here praying that you have made it out of The Thicket.

I will not allow you to go back in there. It is not safe for you. If TJ is convincing you to go, you must not listen to her. I will find a way to stop her next time.

The gift I offered last night still stands. There is more where that came from. More sausage too.

Be safe, Lady Jane.

Love,
Lincoln

TJ leaned in, looking at my phone. "What the bloody? I will kick his ass." She scoffed. "And what's that about a gift?"

It was dark now, the only light my phone. "Maybe we should get in the car first."

My phone buzzed and I yelped, nearly dropping it. A current surged through my body. I put a hand to my chest and caught my breath. Paul had texted. We scrambled into the car and locked the doors.

PAUL: looks like the mushroom we used to trip on
PAUL: u got from thicket?
JANE: Yes.
PAUL: lol
JANE: Haha wanted some for the road
JANE: hard to get in chi-town
JANE: was wondering if these are safe
JANE: see the dots?
PAUL: yeah those are weird

JANE: disease?
PAUL: looks like more than just bruising
PAUL: don't eat them
PAUL: when r u leaving?
JANE: tomorrow morning
PAUL: i want to check them out too
PAUL: can u wait till afternoon to leave?

I licked my lips, thumbs hovering. We really had nothing calling us to Florida right this very second. Then again, we had Lincoln breathing down our necks. Paul might ward him off tomorrow. He had kept Lincoln at bay in the old days.

TJ nodded.

JANE: OK sure
PAUL: great. 2pm?
JANE: yeah. here at donzerly
PAUL: OMG u r rly at the light?
JANE: yeah
PAUL: is it on?
JANE: not yet
JANE: leaving soon
PAUL: see u tomorrow

As we drove away, the light powered up, weakly at first. TJ and I gaped at each other with stunned joy. In the cup holder, the little mushroom that TJ had picked burned a faint green and our eyes grew wider. All around us, out in The Thicket, foxfire on the forest floor matched its glow.

Something tugged at my chest—a bittersweet heartache I think, though I didn't understand why.

TJ turned around in her seat and set her chin on the leather to watch out the back window. "Do you think the Donzerly Light went off for Dad too? Does it go off when no one is looking, like a tree falling in the forest?"

"Quantum physics is not my strong suit."

In the rear-view mirror, The Thicket knit shut behind us.

## Chapter Nineteen

W its' end. That should be the name of a town, he thought. A place you were immediately sent to when you could take no more of this world. A place where they took care of you. That's probably what heaven was like. The end of your wits.

He strode around the farmhouse in the dark, fungicide sprayer in one hand, gallon canister in the other, to the side closest to The Thicket. He always saved this wall for last, though it scared him the most. The voices were louder here.

*Hey, Lincoln Logs, we've gotta surprise for you.*

"Die."

Lincoln furiously doused the foundation until liquid ran in stripes through the black mold. The sprayer sputtered empty just as fresh drops of rain pelted him and thunder rumbled in from the west. A cool breeze tousled his sweating head.

*Hey, you give me a ride to Birkenham? I could give you one too.*

"Die!" he cried and hurled the sprayer at the house. It clattered to the ground with a hollow sound, the canister rolling back and forth.

Would he ever get a good night's sleep again? He got by on a couple hours most times, but this was going to be a long one. He could rarely sleep during a thunderstorm anymore. There would be no sense waiting it out in his bedroom in the ranch house or the basement bunker of the old farmhouse.

Lincoln shuffled through the metal barn that housed the corn and bean fertilizers, pesticides, fungicides. While rain poured down in curtains outside, he kicked up dust as he walked, sneezing into his sleeve. The overhead lights flickered their lonely strobe effect like a long-forgotten dance hall.

The hitchhiker stood at the end of the rows, tapping the tall white energy drink can with her long press-on nails. She said it was diet. No calories, all the power.

*Can you give me a ride? I'll give you one.*

"You're not here."

He stopped at the shelves of fungicide. No doubt he was the right man for this job. The Metzgers had been doing battle with leaf blight for years. In fact, his fields were a haven compared to what lay in The Thicket. What his father used to call East vs. West Berlin: in The Thicket lay corruption and lawlessness; in their lovingly maintained fields, freedom.

Lincoln pushed back his green John Deere cap then tucked his fists on his hips. It would cost him a fortune. Failed applications had bankrupted his father twice, leaving the crops susceptible to the spores after a flood in the 90s and the drought of 2012. There was also the matter of logistics. He couldn't exactly fly a plane or helicopter over The Thicket. Dousing the tops of the trees would be a complete waste. No, each tree needed a dose at the roots. But between the farm and the city council, it would take months.

Lincoln rubbed his eyes and scratched his late-day whiskers.

He smelled his father. When he was a boy, the way dust and axle grease and sweat mixed meant important men were getting things done. He'd never really put a finger on it before. He supposed he smelled like that now. But there was no one to smell it on him. No one to appreciate it.

In the makeshift office by the door came the low sobs of his father. He tried not to look. But then his mother tut-tutted, comforting the man.

*We just need to pray on it, Byron.*

*That ain't gonna cut it!*

"You're not here." He muttered, walking to them, daring them to disappear.

They ignored him.

There sat Byron Metzger, drunk as a skunk, tears running down his dusty whiskers as Edith massaged his shoulders. Lincoln watched his father turn to a pathetic, sniveling heap.

*I might as well burn it all to the ground for all the good it'll do us, Edie! At least that way it takes the damned disease with it.*

Lincoln stood for an interminable amount of time, well after their ghosts had fizzled out. Then he stomped back to the shelving and hauled down four gallons of undiluted fungicide. There was no time to treat every tree. It took him an hour and a half each night just to spray the perimeter of his farm, let alone an entire forest. Instead, a cleansing blaze —the blaze he had seen so long ago when the kids made him stare into that amber eye—would do most of the work. But the water supply could use some insurance. This plan required a two-pronged attack. Because the evil seemed to originate by that cursed light his classmates had loved to call the Donzerly, he would pour the fungicide in the water treatment tanks and then set The Thicket ablaze.

Lincoln set the plastic canisters of fungicide by the door and marched to his tool bench. He grabbed the largest pipe wrench he owned—a real mace of a fellow. You could dent a man's skull right in with this red meanie. He could see it flying into Gary Brown's face, knocking out teeth in its wake.

Lincoln chuckled wryly and let the wrench slide down in his grip, to stand beside the fungicide canisters. He hustled out the door into the rain and strode to his truck, sorely tempted to send Gary and the others to hell in The Thicket; he knew just how he would do it. He also knew he should let it go after all these years. Gary sure had. At least the man liked to pretend it had all been harmless joshing. But their words still echoed in the night.

Once Lincoln graduated valedictorian, he thought he had finally attained the notoriety that would earn their respect, but halfway through his speech in the auditorium he heard it from the first row: Gary and Brian cough-yelling "Lincoln Logs" a half dozen times. Seventeen-year-old

Lincoln had smiled his flat smile throughout, pushing up his thick solid-state TV glasses without the rims and raising his voice over them. He heard it sometimes around 3.15 a.m. coming from The Thicket.

*Lincoln. Lincoln Logs! Look at the light, you pussy.*

The truck's pale high-beams danced across bony trees of The Thicket and he averted his eyes while he drove down the lane. At least he'd learned before the rest of them what life was about. Their sorrow was yet to come. And for some, it had and would also come courtesy of The Thicket. None of his concern.

That it had taken so many years for The Thicket to finally come for him indicated it must be toying with him. Though the new house remained clean, the evil encroached on the old Victorian, the one his mother had saved. Those cursed roots climbed the brick foundation and pried their stubborn fingers into the cracks as if hungry for the sorriness that still filled the place. Mushroom stalks grew in clumps all along the corners of the cellar, which Lincoln would stamp at with disgust even though he knew the fungicide did a better job. He wanted to see it suffer. The next day twice as many grew in their place. Out came the spray.

Lincoln considered selling it all, the houses and farm, to ship off to Arizona, where there were surely fewer mushrooms to contend with. There was something godly about the desert. Something about that barren landscape that cleansed your soul like fire. The more humid climes, this was the territory of the pagan. Plus, in Arizona he could wear a cowboy hat without a second glance. He might even learn how to ride a horse. Of course, Arizona would put him too far from Lady Jane. But once he was done here, they could go away together. She would love it there. She had to. At some point she had to.

Throughout the years, he had emailed Jane spectacular images of himself with tornados in the background, selfies with Dave Grohl of The Foo Fighters, skydiving shots of him conjoined with another man, views of Jupiter captured with his telescope and Nikon, umpteen photos of his woodworking projects. Gosh, he'd felled five trees in her name! Sold three homes' worth of exquisite furniture! All because he had read in *Christian Couples Today* that your spouse will remember why they love you when they see you outside the context of themselves, when they see that you can be exciting and special on your own.

Why wasn't it working?

The Thicket was clouding Jane's mind of course. He would never understand the pull of those woods. There was no mistaking The Thicket's malevolence. It had taken his brother and Evie and Sheriff Render; it had made his classmates do bad things to him.

TJ was surely the instigator. She held too much power over Jane. She would need to be taken care of, but to extricate her from Jane's orbit would be tricky. Unfortunately, his skills lay in surveillance, not mind control. He would have to wait for the right opportunity.

Lincoln drove to Heathrow Tire's back lot, which offered a sideways view of Le Grande Motel. There he sat with a pack of Slim Jims, a can of Arizona Iced Tea, his Nikon, and his laptop. He was glad to be away from the farm for a while, in the relative sterility of his truck. He might even sleep here tonight.

Lincoln logged onto the laptop he'd bought at a garage sale in Birkenham and joined Heathrow Tire's free WiFi.

It was ridiculous that he would need to access the dark Web for the exact recipe of components. The farm had some of what he needed lying around—ammonium nitrate, chiefly, which he'd used for fertilizer. Wiring the detonator would be simple enough. But where to find the blasting gel without drawing attention? That was the tricky part. He had a road engineering contact in the DOT who was currently at work on the new lanes through Carbondale. But getting Bill to just hand over a couple blasting caps or plastique sausages with a wink and a slap on the back would be impossible. Heck, just searching all of this might be enough to bring the EPA, OSHA, and the ATF down on him like a swarm of bees. He'd have to move fast just in case. And here he was, working to actually do some good.

But again, this was the logic of Wits' End, population one, the smartest kid in the class.

## Chapter Twenty

### Two Decades Ago

The morning after Jane and Paul's encounter with the amber light, the hallway telephone jangled. Jane yanked the covers over her head to grab another hour of sleep before church. A weight eased onto the edge of her mattress.

Jane rolled over, ready to smart-off, but the tired woman gazing back with an all too familiar dread sent energy through Jane like a strong cup of coffee.

Her mother set a soft hand on Jane's blanketed leg. "I'm afraid Roy was in a crash last night."

Jane sat up with a glower. "No way." Impossible. Roy had been way too tired for that, too settled-in for the night when she and Paul left. "Is he okay?"

Her mother smoothed the covers and stared out the window. "He was barreling down Seven Hills, Jane. Too fast. Didn't have a seatbelt on. Drunk, I'm guessing. You kids—"

"Oh my, God. Is he in the hospital?"

Her mother's eyes glistened. "Janey, sweetie. It was instant."

"No." Jane's voice shook. She leapt from the bed, stumbled out of the covers, and ran to her desk. She grabbed her Nokia cellphone and rapidly stamped out Paul's number.

It rang and rang.

---

Three days later, Jane and TJ joined a line of mourners that filed past a gleaming red casket, the closest color to Roy's car that his parents could find. It lay shut and silent before the pulpit of the First Baptist Church.

"Looks like a giant Tylenol," TJ whispered.

Ready to be swallowed, Jane thought.

She shook her head, sickened at such a dark flourish. Even if it went unsaid, that was TJ's realm.

*No more of this!* She decided right then that she would stop indulging in callow thoughts. Roy was gone from the world. They would never see him again. They would never again hear his guitar or honking laugh. Just as Evie had gone. And the sheriff. All of them: there one day, gone the next.

Jane joined the others in the pews and mouthed the words to old hymns. She stared up at the gothic arches of the ceiling that met like tree branches.

The dead weren't completely gone, of course. And nobody talked about that. Their thoughts and actions were gone, to be sure. But their inert bodies were still around, somewhere nearby, in various states of disintegration. Oh sure, Evie had been "gone" two years now. But she was surely buried somewhere, nearly bones, her stark beauty dissolved to an ugly jangle, perhaps still mottled with dry cracking gristle. Roy hadn't even started yet. They could pop open that Tylenol right now, peek in, and see his battered face. And TJ's dad?

*Enough! What did you just promise yourself?*

Jane rubbed her eyes. She had to be strong for the others. She would be strong for Paul. Even for Jaylene, who bellowed and cried in the back pews as if she and Roy had been the best of friends. Jane had to stop being so sarcastic and spiteful. She needed to grow up. That was the only way to deal with these things. That was adulthood, right? To just stop thinking about it, to forgive all, to learn from it, to move on.

After the platitudes, The Thicket kids gathered quietly outside the church, while old people wept and hugged one another. According to Brian, Roy had landed a hundred feet from the Supra, which was now a twisted heap of plastic and metal. Apparently, Roy had also left his own dent in the mud.

Brian shook his head in fascination. "You can see it when you drive by."

Paul glared with incredulity at his best friend for a moment. But his mouth didn't open. Nor did he meet the rest of their eyes. His wavy brown hair blew in the breeze and his hand hung limp in Jane's grasp.

Despite this, she held on and glanced softly up at him, trying to catch his eye. "Want to get together tonight?"

She would tell him her big news. She was going to be more mature about things. It was probably all dawning on him as well. They would be the mature couple.

Paul gazed back blankly and shrugged. He pulled away and shuffled to his car.

---

That afternoon, Jane and TJ stood playing Pac-Man at the diner and spoke to each other's reflection in the video screen.

"Roy had weird visions," Jane said. "He saw himself die. Saw his future."

Of course, if he'd seen his future, then maybe he saw an alternate one. That meant things could be changed. You could cut your future short. So, you could take control of it, but at the ultimate cost. Jane gulped. What was happening to her? Why was she even having to think about this? So much for getting to be a kid. She had to get out of this town.

TJ rammed the joystick right then left, up then down. "Hey, I did too! Except mine's really cool. I'm going to be a writer."

Jane shot a look over her shoulder to check if anyone was watching them yatter on like fools, which had become far too frequent. "Not exactly an epiphany; you've been saying that for years," she murmured. "Seriously though, Teej, I really feel we need to not live here forever."

"Of course not. Gross. I can't get famous here. *Please.* And what's this about a spooky light going on and off?"

"Oh, it was really odd. Down by the river. You know the overlook? We had just been over at Roy's..." Jane went hazy. "He must have gone out, right after we left..."

*Why did we leave him? We should have stayed.*

"Jane. It wasn't your fault. He's been depressed for a while. His toys never made him happy. Didn't you ever notice that?" TJ kicked the video game and their quarters fell out. She plugged them right back in and started another game. "Let's go out there after this round. I wanna see it go off."

---

But it didn't. Not that night. And Jane was glad for it. She wondered if Paul thought that the light had gone off around the time Roy left his home. She wondered if Paul would think she was a hysterical little girl for drawing such a correlation.

The two young women sat in the silence of dusk with Jane's car running, pointed toward the access road, just in case. The shed and light pole lay engulfed in shadows. It felt ridiculous. Nonetheless, Jane kept the car doors locked and forbade TJ to even think of getting out. So they sat there for a half hour, engine idling, while TJ played *Tetris* on her GameBoy.

"Of course, you realize," TJ said, "it's going to need a name. Branding is half the battle."

Jane sighed. The refusal of the light to perform had not impeded TJ's curiosity in any way. Ever since scoring an A in English Lit, she had decided she was more than capable of filing in the blanks. Jane knew few kids as self-assured as TJ, save Brian, who knew exactly where he was headed in life. Every step they took was one more step toward the goal.

For someone so organized, Jane couldn't muster any epiphanies. She suspected Paul had the dream. She hoped his hadn't been as dark as Roy's. But maybe that was why he'd gone cold. Could it be that she was in it?

Jane stared off into The Thicket. The foxfire was alight in its pale-green mystery.

"Do you think Brian had a dream about his future too?"

"Yep. For sure."

"How do you know? Did he tell you?"

"Nope." TJ turned off the game. "It was the mushrooms, Jane. Everyone who takes them … *knows*."

"God, *Teej*. That's just not even possible."

"Okay." TJ shrugged. "But what about those jellyfish things?"

"We ate magic mushrooms. Of course we saw flying spaghetti monsters!" Jane crossed her arms and peered at the dead lightbulb in its Plexiglas casing high atop the light pole. Maybe it had burnt out. She put the car in drive. "And why haven't I had *my* dream then?"

TJ turned to her and it was all that Jane could hear—no

engine, no road noise, no wind—just TJ's voice from all around her.

"You have."

---

The next week, the two of them scooted across the outdoor bleachers to watch Paul's first home baseball game. It was cold and clammy out, March going out like a cumulous lion. As the opposing team and fans poured from school buses, clouds sailed past the sun, stuttering warmth here and there.

TJ sat huddled in Paul's letterman's jacket, her nose buried in a tattered H.P. Lovecraft paperback. She turned a page.

"I don't know why you bother with him. He hasn't said two words since Roy's funeral."

"We all grieve in our own way. It's a process."

"M'kay, Oprah."

At least he was talking to Brian again. The two stood next to each other at the dugout, chuckling as Gary harried Lincoln Metzger. The unfortunate boy lurched down the track, piled high with equipment bags, a microphone stand, and a PA loudspeaker.

Gary gripped the fencing with his fingers and stuck his lips through, "Come on, Logs, ya fatty." He snort-oinked for good measure.

Lincoln kept his chin up under the load, dropping the bags by the dugout and trudging on past the bleachers.

When he caught sight of Jane watching, his cheeks filled with pink.

She raised a weak hand and waved.

TJ looked up. "What da fuck are you doing?"

"I'm trying to be more mature about things. He can't help how awkward he is."

TJ blew a gust. "Maturity is overrated. Tool of the patriarchy."

As the teams filed onto the field, Ms. Van Laar stepped up to take the microphone stand from Lincoln and set it in front of the bleachers. She plugged in the loudspeaker and dusted off her hands in a theatrical way.

"Oh, shit," Jane whispered. "She's coming over here."

"How are we doing, Miss Render?"

"Fine." Jane turned her eyes down. Sabrina Van Laar was the youngest of all their teachers, and yet she was the most formal, as if she were from the 1800s. She wore antique clothes and always pinned her hair up in a bun. Parents thought it a ridiculous affect, but the nerds loved her. She seemed not to care either way.

"I'm seeing quite interesting essays cross my desk." The woman peered at Jane as if above a set of reading glasses, though she wore none. "And you wrote two. For extra credit? Staying industrious in such trying times."

Jane nodded and averted her eyes. Sabrina Van Laar always locked her up like this. Jane was never sure if she was supposed to start talking in the same stilted way.

The teacher crossed her arms.

"One would be obtuse not to notice you've lost far too many people close to you. But frankly, your coping mechanisms are impressive—more creative than most." Ms. Van Laar gazed upon the crowd gathering around them in the stands. They all looked so tired. Like her mother. Yet Ms. Van Laar glowed with energy. "Don't listen to what the others say, Jane. You possess a truly amazing mind." The woman lowered her voice. "But do be careful in The Thicket. You may not yet appreciate all that you discover there." She tapped Jane's temple with a fingertip cold as stone. "This will take years to ripen."

In a swift movement she took the paperback from TJ and gently rapped her on the head with it. "And asking the big questions, I see." She dropped it back into TJ's lap. "Utter tripe."

As she turned to walk away, the sun flickered across her S-shaped necklace and it glared right into Jane's eyes. The woman moved with a floating gait, down the cinder track toward the school, her long skirt and high turtleneck so out of place with the rest of the crowd dressed in jeans, windbreakers, or tracksuits.

TJ watched her go, mumbling, "What I wouldn't give to be ten years older."

"I thought maturity was overrated. Besides, you wouldn't stand a chance."

"Just you wait."

In the front row, their classmate Jaylene stood up with an old boombox from the 80s. She presented it with a shove to Lincoln, who crouched, fiddling with the loudspeaker, and ordered him to hold it for her. He stood and held it up to the microphone.

"No, dipshit. Then no one will hear me." She grabbed his wrists and positioned the boombox just so.

Jane nodded politely at him. He nodded back.

Jaylene turned to the microphone.

"Testing!"

A piercing whistle crackled out of the PA speaker and TJ burst out with a laugh.

Jaylene cocked her head at the crowd. Their muttering stopped as they stood for the anthem. She kicked sideways at Lincoln who struggled to press the play button while maintaining the boombox at the proper height.

A scratchy orchestra began the opener to the national anthem, but it slowed and then warbled. Jaylene glared at Lincoln and he shook the boombox. It sped up faster than normal and then slowed again. The music sounded like a bad dream, as if it were struggling to breathe underwater. TJ's body shook with convulsions of laughter.

Jaylene clutched the microphone. "Does anyone have any C batteries?"

"I do!" TJ raised a hand. "At home in my vibrator!"

The crowd erupted with gasps and giggles. An older couple scooted away.

Jaylene set her jaw. "Well, this game isn't starting without the anthem!"

"Dear Lord," Jane muttered.

Lincoln gingerly set down the boombox and ran for his car, while Jaylene, hands on hips, stared spikes up at TJ.

High above the field, the lights powered on to diamond brightness, casting down sharp, cold beams. The teams whipped off their caps and slapped them to their chests.

This seemed to buoy Jaylene. And once Lincoln fixed the boombox, she puffed up, ready for the high notes. Moments later she was off to the races:

"Oh, say can you see…"

"That's it!" TJ yelped. "Oh my God, that's it." She ripped her ring-bound notebook from her backpack, took a pen and scrawled:

## THE DONZERLY LIGHT

Jane blinked at the words for a moment.

She had to admit, that's what she'd thought the line actually was when she was a little kid. As if there were some light somewhere which told history, a light that spanned time and space and shed its knowledge upon the world.

TJ did not look up again to harry Jaylene or watch the game or read her book. She scrawled illegibly across the page as fast as her left hand would carry the pen.

---

So, in a matter of days, a common sodium vapor lamp above a water treatment station in an unremarkable stretch of midwestern woods had morphed into a portentous beacon of the Old Ones, cursing everyone who looked upon it.

This proto-tale would land on Ms. Van Laar's desk in the next week. In greater fact, it would evolve into TJ Render's first story published in *Weird Tales* about a boy who gets his revenge on all the kids who bullied him by luring them down to a place called The Donzerly Light, which was actually the tip of an iceberg, so to speak, an eye attached to a massive network of underground tentacles. Like one of those horrifying anglerfish at the bottom of the ocean, it mesmerized them with its light then gobbled them up one by one.

*Burp.*

TJ worked on it with the passion of a writer who obtusely believes it will be her breakout story. The difference was, she was absolutely right. Most kids imagine how their life will turn out, but for TJ, every step directly connected to the next. No triumph was a surprise. If only Jane could have been that sure about anything.

At least TJ had found a simpler drug. After losing Roy, their generation of Thicket Kids stopped gathering fungus. They had ceased playing with fire—foxfire, so to speak. And thus the pilgrimages of fresh acolytes began, with a little help from TJ's pen. As far as she was concerned, the first rule of Light Club was to most definitely talk about Light Club.

———

On a sunny afternoon after class, Jane lay back on TJ's bed, her eyes glazing over as she stared at her homework. TJ sat on the carpet in front of her Nintendo, battling the vampires of *Castlevania*. Green Day hammered from the boombox on TJ's desk.

Jane gnawed on a ballpoint pen already pocked with

plenty of teeth marks, its metal pocket clip bent off. She stroked TJ's Maine Coon, Catthulhu. The feline was the size of a baby bear, with thick gray fur, and a lover-boy demeanor. He made her eyes and skin itch.

Out in the hallway, Ellen Render's feet pounded the floorboards.

"Didn't I tell you to turn that filth down!" she screeched from the other side of the door.

To be fair, it wasn't easy studying calculus this way.

"Please, just turn it off!" Ellen growled just as TJ reached up and flicked the CD player.

"I did! God," TJ said, and under her breath hissed, "*bitch*." And went back to her game.

Jane's Nokia warbled.

Paul.

TJ raised her eyebrows.

Jane punched the talk button. "Hey."

*"Hey,"* Paul said quietly on the other end.

One of TJ's eyebrows stayed up: let *him* do the work. Jane waited.

"So, I know I've been a jerk," he said.

"No, it's okay," Jane said. TJ's eyes fluttered and crossed at this pathetic concession.

"Maybe we could go out this weekend."

TJ made a wanking motion with her fist, put it up to her face and made an o-shape of her mouth.

Jane bit back a grin. "Maybe."

"You still mad?"

She had never been mad. Why did guys escalate like that? She wasn't even sure what she felt. Numb was her best guess. "No, I'm fine." She drew the broken metal clip of her pen lightly across her arm, leaving faint white scrapes.

"Sure wish you hadn't told all those kids about the light."

"Um, that was TJ's idea, not mine."

TJ shrugged. The silence on the other end spoke plenty. She grabbed Jane's notepad and started doodling.

"Paul?"

"I wish you'd stop with her already." He sighed. "I thought the overlook was our spot."

TJ rolled her eyes. On the notepad she'd drawn three spurting water droplets and the words: *thwap, thwap, scloitch.*

*Stop,* Jane mouthed. And then meekly into the phone, "It still is."

"No, it's not! There's a buncha freshmen down there every night waiting for it to go off! They're probably going tonight. You're making Roy's crash into some cheap story."

"Oooh, do you think they're doing 'shrooms?" TJ whispered. "I wonder what that would be like? Tripping next to the light? A singularity maybe. The end of all things." She turned to a new page on the notepad and scrawled.

"What did you say?"

Jane lay back on the pillow. "I said that's not fair, Paul. Everyone is dealing with this differently."

"Um, you bet they are. Did you know Lincoln Metzger is freaking out that it's going to kill someone—again. His words, not mine. It's so ridiculous."

Jane nodded. "They did say the light went off on Friday."

"And nobody died, did they!"

"Well, what about old Jenny Stonefeld?"

"That was yesterday."

"No, Paul, they found her *body* yesterday. Brian said her granddaughter told him that the fire department found a gas leak in the trailer. She'd been dead for days."

"Oh, Brian said that, did he? Seriously? I feel like everyone around me is losing it. I cannot take this, Jane. I really can't."

Paul was right. They were all losing it a little. What had happened to her maturity plan? Blood rose on the back of Jane's wrist now as the pen clip dug deeper.

"Okay, I hear what you're saying. I'm sorry."

"Y'know, I really feel like taking an axe to that fucking light."

TJ's eyes went wide.

"Oh, I don't know," Jane said. "If you *make* the light go out, what if it— I mean, it might…"

Paul's voice grew paternally stern. "*Jane?*"

"Nothing. I mean, that's probably a crime, though. And on government land…"

"Eh. No one will know it was us. Hey, we should take Lincoln! Have him do it. He'll feel vindicated and brave and all that shit, then we can all move on. Plus, we get our spot back."

A crooked grin spread across TJ's face. As if she knew just how this was going to go.

Jane's lip curled. "Yeah, maybe."

"I'll talk to you tomorrow, okay?"

---

Jane sat quietly for a while, watching the twitching cat chase a bird in its dreams, the only noise the pumping 8-bit strains of *Castlevania*.

"Do you think Roy felt it?" Jane asked. "The crash? The impact?"

"I think it was instantaneous." TJ nodded with authority. "Like when you break a chicken's neck." She paused the game. "Dude, what the heck are you doing?"

Jane dropped the pen. Little red jewels gleamed on her skin. "Oh. That." She knew from experience they would form little plasticky mounds that she could smush in a few minutes. If left alone they would become hard, opaque rubies.

TJ rolled her eyes. "Cutting is for the clueless daddy's girls, Jane. You gotta *cat* instead. It's more efficient. That way, you entertain an animal and have an excuse. Unless, of course, you're doing that for attention."

"Screw you. Also, what is this cat method you speak of?"

TJ saved and turned off her Nintendo. She set her chin on the bed, bangs in her eyes, peering at Catthulhu, who now slept upside down on the pillows with his own eyes rolled back. His pale undercarriage lay exposed, a long carpet of furry scallops. She made a ticking sound in her throat and walked her black-painted fingernails across the bedspread.

The glistening white secondary lid of one of Catthulhu's eyes slid open to reveal a pale green iris.

"Gonna get you, kitteh," she whispered. "Gonna get you."

His other glistening eyelid slid open.

"Boop." TJ tapped his pale nose. His secondary eyelids slid shut again.

Jane laughed. He was such a cuddlebear; there seemed no point in teasing him.

TJ ticked in her throat again, this time rapidly, and drew her forearm up above him, shaping her hand like the head of a snake. His eyes popped open and the black oval slits of his pupils widened to circles. He rolled slowly over and flattened down, tracking her hand with a mixture of fear and fury. A low growl rumbled in his chest.

"Uh, oh." Jane backed up.

"Shhh." TJ moved her hand back and forth like a cobra. "Just watch." Catthulhu's eyes followed it and his whiskers fluttered as if he'd spotted a bird—a very large bird that might not go down so easy.

The cat leapt in a flash, taking TJ's arm down onto bedspread in mock battle. He bit gently around her hand and wrist as she playfully shook his head in her palm. His white-socked arms and legs held her tight.

"This lil monster's great." TJ chuckled. "He knows just how hard to bite, just how hard to scratch. Look at those thumpers. He could tear my arm open in two seconds if he wanted to."

Jane didn't doubt her on this point. Catthulhu's fluffy

legs resembled bunny's feet but held large, cougar-like claws.

TJ turned Catthulhu on his back and shook him around, pushing him across the bedspread. His hooks came out, denting and pulling on TJ's flesh.

"This is cutting for feminists." TJ winced. "And it gives him something to do. Reminds him what he is."

"I call bullshit. Teej, stop."

"Oh, we're just getting started." TJ pulled her arm upwards, cat still attached.

As Catthulhu's fangs came out, so too did his claws on both his hands and feet. Pink welts formed on TJ's arms and she cackled at the ceiling, eyes rolling back.

"Teej, stop," Jane demanded, but a shimmering thrill raced through her. Pain spiked across her own arm and ran up her spine.

Ears pinned back, Catthulhu began to thump his legs rapidly. His eyes went wild. Thin, stuttering strips of red gleamed on TJ's arm. She half-giggled, half whimpered as she rode it out.

"Oh my God," Jane said. "Stop!"

TJ lay her arm down in defeat and Catthulhu rolled off her and sat up for a moment in a daze. His body curled around and he strode up to her face, purring, tail whipping back and forth across her nose.

"Good boy." TJ leaned into him, then jumped up. "Of course, it's crucial to wash it immediately." Blood ran in branching streams down her arms.

They hustled to the bathroom, the only room in this house with a lock. Her haven.

"Ahhh," she said as the sink water ran over her arm.

"Don't you think it's animal abuse?"

"What? No! He's having fun."

"But it's confusing to him." Jane stared at her feral cousin in the mirror, this brazen friend of seventeen years. TJ held her gleaming arm up to the light and flexed it with a fist. "Welcome to life, Janey. We have big things to do. Stop wussing out on me."

"What are you doing in there?" came Aunt Ellen's voice.

"Nothing," TJ barked. "Leave us alone!"

"You better vacuum your room, or you can forget about your allowance."

"I should go," Jane said.

"Yeah. Probably."

"Remember when we used to play in the mirror?"

"Yeah."

Jane grabbed the mirror doors. "Let's—"

TJ closed them back. "Don't."

"Why?"

"Evie's in there."

"Very funny." Jane waved at her reflection. "Hi, Evie."

"It's not a joke," TJ said, blocking the view. "She's in there, way far back. I can only just see her a little bit. And she's different now. She looks all out of order and says really creepy stuff." TJ's voice went high-pitched. "'Don't forget us. Don't forget the future.'" She shuddered.

"If you're trying to scare me, it's not working." But it was. Jane opened the bathroom door and headed toward the foyer.

As they passed her mom on the couch, TJ said, "Yeah,

well, behind that mirror a pulsing webwork spreads across the rusted back of the vanity, down the water pipes and into the crawlspace below the house. It's fed by the tendrils rooted along the border of The Thicket."

Jane nodded. "Actually, write that down. That's pretty good."

"I already did."

## Chapter Twenty-One

### OUTSIDE TIME AS WE KNOW IT

The broad alien landscape lay endlessly pronged with pale fingerlike stalks shooting up as high as trees. But they weren't trees. They had no leaves or appendages of any kind. Giant ferns grew all around their bases. The air hung thick and plasmatic.

She floated, minuscule, amongst this odd world, along the banks of a shallow sea that held waving, plant-like creatures. Large green bugs, with a multitude of legs, seemed to swim by more than crawl, like segmented blimps. In the craggy distance, lightning flashed purple fractals across boiling storm clouds. And through the thick atmosphere, came a strange rumble and ping. At this disturbance, a vortex of spores swirled all around, she among them—lost, unformed, and yet she knew no fear.

Lightning flashed again.

The light above the vanity flashed.

My mind woke before my body.

It was still dark outside. I could only move my eyes.

That damn fluorescent light was back on over the vanity, flickering incessantly, sending signals like a beacon. I chanced a look at the corner of the room. Couldn't help myself. My vision was blurry, just like it used to be before I'd gotten Lasik surgery.

An inky presence shadowed the far corner of the room, all the way to the ceiling. A single eye glowed like an amber star.

I yearned to reach for my phone on the bedside table, but still could not move my arms. My heart thumped. At least I could move my neck now.

I turned to TJ's bed. It was empty, entirely made, bedspread and all.

The shadow pulled away from the corner, toward me. Towering high, it had to bend down lest it scrape its antlers on the ceiling.

I opened my mouth to scream; nothing came but a wet squeak from the back of my throat.

The bathroom door opened, and the looming shadow shrank away to nothing.

"Janey? Hey now. It's okay." TJ's face filled my vision. "It's okay. I got you. I got you."

## Chapter Twenty-Two

Present Day

"Welp, here we are," I said as we pulled up to Ellen Render's ranch house, where a plaster garden gnome threw us a cheesy grin from the porch.

"Yup," TJ stared straight ahead from behind a pair of wayfarer sunglasses. The cheap e-cig hung off her lip. She'd really meant it; she was going to wait in the car.

She had grown up on the outskirts of town, in this one-story green-shingled ranch house with a big backyard full of clover that butted up against The Thicket. When we were kids, she and I would play along a spring-fed creek that ran parallel to her house a few yards into the stand of birch trees. In the winter, we would walk its frozen surface as it wound its way out to the Ketchum River. In the summer, we would build dams and whack at the poison ivy that encroached upon our hideouts. Unsurprisingly, oozing blisters often covered our limbs, making us the laughing stock of the neighborhood.

I sat for a moment, swirling my fingertip through the gritty dust on the dashboard, unable to come up with a plan. My mind was still clogged with the dreams I'd had the night before—wild, incomprehensible visions then the abrupt waking to a paralyzing fear.

"Won't be long," I said. "Sure you won't come?"

TJ grunted and e-cig vapor uncoiled before her in wispy bubblegum-scented tentacles.

———

Corroded wind chimes rang on Ellen Render's porch with all the harmony of a pot rack. I climbed the front steps with the Tupperware of sausage tucked under my arm. Up close, I could see that the now familiar dark mold covered the tips of the home's cracked and torn shingles. My stomach turned with the anticipation of standing in line at a sketchy carnival ride, so excited to buy the tickets, but now imagining all the nuts and bolts that could fall off.

The door wheezed open before I could press the doorbell.

Aunt Ellen was smaller than I remembered, in her quilted pink robe, weeping at the sight of me. Her hair was close-cropped and mostly white now, her blue eyes haunted.

"Janey, I prayed and prayed that you'd come down for the reunion. Was afraid you might leave without stopping by." She hugged me tight, humming a faint and far-off laugh that sounded like the olden days. "Let me get you some coffee. I just took some off the stove. Have you eaten anything?"

I followed her through the narrow foyer, which was much tighter than I'd recalled. The stale living room cried out for an open window, or three.

"Watcha got there?" she asked over her shoulder as she padded toward the kitchen in thin house slippers.

"Oh, some venison sausage from one of my classmates. Thought you might like it. We really don't n—"

"Well, thank you sweetie, but you keep it. My freezer's loaded with the stuff." She cackled. "It's coming out my ears!"

I erased that image as quickly as possible.

She waved me off. "Now go sit."

But where? Tables and chairs held books, magazines, boxes, piles of mail, promotional products, laundry baskets full of video and cassette tapes.

"I'm good. Just wanted to see how you were," I said, trying to recall this small home unclogged as it had once been.

She came back and led me through the maze of ephemera to the threadbare couch decorated in flowers and butterflies that I remembered from childhood, an oasis in the clutter. I sat down and a yellow tabby cat slunk across the back of the couch and poured into my lap. My arms itched from the phantom scratches of TJ's first cat.

The shelves around the room still held knick-knacks from the last century: Precious Moments figurines—pink-skinned waifs with oversized heads and black gumdrop eyes—lacquered Asian boxes, a family photo faded to an orangey tinge in the highlights, purple in the shadows, and, inexplicably, a toaster. All of it bought with a sheriff's pension, and by the state of the hardware and woodwork, nothing spent on repairs.

Aunt Ellen shuffled back off to the kitchen. "Oh, I'm getting by, sweetheart."

"We're headed to Florida after this."

She returned with a steaming cup, her hands trembling. "We?"

"Thanks." I took it from her gently. "TJ and I."

She closed her eyes and sighed, sat down next to me.

I cringed a smile. "She's out in the car if you want to see her."

Aunt Ellen gazed far off and put her chin in her hand. Then she looked back and sniffled. "Tell me how your work is. You do books, don't you?"

And we talked about the surface of things, glancing off a thin veneer. I mentioned Nick, pretending we were still together, and how TJ was working on a book and how that might earn the both of us a good payday. Aunt Ellen listed her various illnesses, which were mostly aches and pains save for a gallbladder surgery she'd had last year. I nodded and sipped at coffee that managed to be bitter and weak at the same time.

Above the mantel where the sheriff's prized buck head had once jutted (before its ruination from the spattering of his brain matter) there now a hung one of those folksy Thomas Kinkade paintings. A doe and fawn stood alert in the snow, by a shining river, and across that river stood a quaint home, its lights glowing inside, sheltering the perfect family.

The scene of the crime.

No wonder TJ didn't want to come in.

I wondered how I would extricate myself from this overstuffed situation, then admonished myself for wanting to leave this person who had done so much for me as a child. TJ hadn't been an ideal kid; I knew that. It wasn't easy to have a gay child in this town. But to let TJ just sit out in the car and not run out to see her?

As Aunt Ellen droned on about town gossip, I saw her young again, in jeans, bringing us Kool-Aid and Oreos so that we could keep building an epic fort in The Thicket and defend it from the boys who were firing Nerf guns at us from across the creek.

"I was clearing out a nook a while back and found a few things," she said and patted my knee. "Been meaning to ship it, but never seem to get around to it."

Aunt Ellen set her hand on the couch arm and eased herself up. I set the cat aside and in a dizzy state, followed her through a hallway further narrowed by mismatched shelving and Rubbermaid containers full of crafting supplies, to TJ's old room. Nausea clawed at my stomach like something rotten unfurling. Maybe it was the coffee on a semi-empty stomach. There was a foul smell coming from somewhere in the depths of the clutter. Maybe the cat didn't always use the litter box. Maybe it was impossible to know in this place.

The bedroom appeared so small now and was made smaller by dusty stacks of As Seen On TV products in unopened boxes. The walls had faded a pale pink, and only tape remained from all TJ's posters, which I could draw up from memory: the sexy riot-grrrl bands and gruesome horror movies; the parts of her that Aunt Ellen refused to hoard.

She carefully extracted an old Skechers shoebox from the middle of a towering stack on the twin bed, threatening a Jenga-style collapse. She waited for the tumble, hand quivering, and then handed the box to me.

"You'll get a kick out of some of that."

I took it, and my hands shook. Saliva pooled in my mouth and my skin went clammy.

"Mind if I use the bathroom?"

"Of course not, sweetie. Why would I mind such a thing?"

I backed up and quickly turned to navigate my return down the hall. It slanted, as if the overloaded shelving might collapse and trap me here.

The bathroom vanity flickered on just as I dropped to my knees before the toilet.

I shook with every dry heave until a wave of peace finally came over me. I pushed my hair out of my eyes and instinctively reached up to press the button on the doorknob. This had been the only room with a lock. But the knob was bare now, replaced for lack of necessity, I supposed.

I sat back on my bent legs and looked around the room. It hadn't changed in years. The paisley wallpaper hung in ripples, still a sickly yellow, the bathtub the same pale butter color with rust around the fixtures. It was still a poorly ventilated space, with its dank and dusty smells of toilet tank and scented toilet paper. Yet all of it soothed me and my nausea subsided as quickly as it had come on.

My earliest memory of playing with TJ was around four or five, at the vanity above the sink. It contained three connected mirrors; the middle was stationary but the two on the sides had medicine cabinets behind them—one for husband, one for wife. And I had climbed up, opened the mirrors inward, and tucked myself inside a funhouse reflection. TJ had appeared in there to marvel with me at infinity. It had been our secret little universe. We'd been hard to separate from then on.

I got up, set the shoebox on the toilet tank, and rolled down my capris to pee. The basin rocked beneath me from gaping holes on either side of the floor bolts, where the old linoleum curled up. On the wallpaper before me, roots and horns twisted into faces. The same TJ had pointed out in the paisley pattern thirty odd years ago a pattern we'd thought infinite, until we found the paper's seam around the corner by the tub. Some of the faces laughed, some cried—all were grotesque. Today, thankfully, they were mute.

I flushed, washed my hands, grabbed the shoebox, and turned off the light.

Aunt Ellen met me in the hall. "Everything all right?"

"Yep! Just fine."

"You used to have long chats in there."

"I remember!"

"I need to have that remodeled," she said with a tsk. "You know they do that real quick now, just put a new shower right over the old one. But I really think someone needs to get in there," she grabbed at the air, "and just tear the whole thing out. Get rid of all those mushrooms first." Then she shuddered.

I nodded. "TJ should really see all of this. Are you sure you don't want her to come in?"

Aunt Ellen looked at me with terror and disgust. She shook her head. "I'd be fine never seeing her again."

It hit me like a slap. "How can you say such a thing?" I said breathlessly, staring at her, mouth agape. Could she possibly blame TJ for her husband's molestation? The only thing I could compare it to was a woman scorned, as if TJ were *the other woman* or even the one who had practically pulled the trigger, as TJ had suggested. There was something deeply broken about this family; I could think of no sensible reason why a mother would let her child go when she couldn't even get rid of a broken kitchen appliance. Poor TJ. *Jesus.*

I made my way back to the living room, and snatched the Tupperware from the couch.

*This is why we left Ketchum. This is why! What the hell are we doing here? What have I done?*

"Oh, Janey, don't go. You just got here! Honey!"

At the front door, I looked back and calmly stated, "If you can't accept TJ, you can't accept me."

And I knew it would be the last I saw of my aunt until I read her name on a headstone.

## Chapter Twenty-Three

PAUL: Sorry, running late.
JANE: No worries.

TJ and I grabbed a quick lunch from the Casey's, drove to the edge of town, and parked by the Main Street bridge, where a tributary of the Ketchum River pooled into a pond, which was dammed at the far end. It brimmed with cornfield run-off after last night's rain, chockfull of pesticides no doubt.

We were sick of our motel room but also afraid to drive into The Thicket without Paul, unsure what Lincoln meant about "stopping" TJ. We'd seen what a good shot he'd been with the deer—albeit at close range—and his knife skills...? I shuddered.

We sat in the car and ate our gummy white bread, lunchmeat, and plastic cheese sandwiches while picking through the shoebox of keepsakes. The encounter at TJ's cluttered old house had left me shaken, but I tried not to show it. We hadn't spoken about her mom yet but there was nothing that seemed worthy of relaying and TJ wasn't asking.

Inside the box lay a couple of Barbie dolls with matted hair and mismatched pantsuits. Young TJ had always been making the dolls kiss, even though I distinctly remember telling her they didn't seem all that enthused about it. She'd responded that yes, they were, they were smiling. To which I'd said you can't kiss when you're smiling. On it went.

There were a couple of tank tops, a Rubik's cube, Some of this stuff looked all too familiar; TJ was always taking things and ferreting them away. Clearly her mother's daughter.

"Ooh, Tetris!" TJ plucked a GameBoy out and switched it on. It didn't work. She opened the battery compartment: corroded. "Damn."

Of greater interest to me was her diary, but it was locked with no key in sight.

"Got a hairpin?" I asked.

"Does it look like I have a hairpin? Also, give me that." She snatched it away. "Private property." Then she grinned and tossed it back in the box. "We'll break into it tonight. I'm sure it's full of embarrassing crap in the first five pages then nothing."

I unfolded a signed poster—*my* signed poster—of Green Day, three moody punks with kohl eyeliner.

"Hey! I thought I lost this!" I barked.

"Oh, yeah, that. Well, I liked them better than you."

I gave her my best judgmental shake of the head.

"What? You can have it back."

"Damn right." I pulled out a Sony VHS tape in a striped sleeve labeled *Render Family 79-92*.

"Yeah, you can toss that," TJ muttered.

"Oh, come on. We could have this transferred to digital?"

TJ shrugged, grabbed her laptop, and got out. She scuttled down the hill next to the bridge and perched on a boulder. There she sat tapping away at her laptop with her hoodie up, though it was plenty warm out. I walked the sloppy banks of the stream and watched eddies swirl around corners, little whirlpools reminiscent of the dream from the night before. A great blue heron sailed across the sky like a pterodactyl toward The Thicket. The warm air bathed us with smells of young corn and alfalfa. The breath caught in my throat. Why did this place make me so emotional?

Paul sporadically texted, informing me of his whereabouts. First that he'd had to finish some papers, and then that he'd had to get lunch, refill his car, etc. He was finally on the road, but it would still take a while to reach us. We might not have much time in The Thicket before dark. I let him know where we were waiting.

I gathered bits of trash, candy wrappers, straws, fishing line, and made a pile of it closer to the road.

I called out, "How's it going with *Our Friend Keith and the Girl Who Looks Like Baby from Dirty Dancing*?" This was what we were calling the book now, just the kind of title our demographic would eat up. I could even picture the cover: handwritten white type scrolling across a blue sky, made from the exhaust from a bright-yellow biplane in the bottom right corner.

"Eh," TJ said. "Another chapter."

"That's awesome!"

TJ closed the laptop and seemed ready to cry. She looked so small and un-Valkyrie-like today beneath her hood, though she could still wear the hell out of a pair of tight jeans and checkered Vans.

I gulped. "I'm so sorry I went to your mom's, Teej. Big mistake."

"No. Forget it. I'm just… I'm starting to like this story."

I burst out with a cackle that echoed across the water.

TJ stared at me, injured. "You don't understand, Jane. I get attached. And when it's over, it's like the characters die. It's like ripping away a layer of myself. They become … ghosts. They haunt me." She gazed out over the pond. "Not sure I can do this again."

"You say this every time."

"Do I?" she asked with a delicate voice, so unlike her surly usual.

"Yeah, Teej. But listen, it's that commitment to conjuring a character that makes them so believable."

"I guess so," she said quietly. "I just need to find a way forward after it's over." She seemed hazy to me then, a bit of her rough edges smudged. But I wanted her sharp and on alert.

"When we get back to Chi-town," I said, "you gotta take me to that paintball club you were talking about last week."

TJ grumbled. "You won't last five minutes." And she puffed back up again with a grin. Off came the hood.

A Honda Accord pulled up behind our rental. Paul got out and stretched. Hands on hips, he smiled at the pond and the hollow concrete square in the middle, where floodwaters ran down, underground, and out toward the main Ketchum River.

"Remember when we used to swim to the overflow?" he asked.

"Yeah," I said. "It's a wonder we didn't drown."

When I was very young, riding the bus to school we always drove past the pond and I would look out to the square void in the middle of it, unaware of its purpose back then, wondering where all that water went as it poured over the edge and into the black. For all I knew it was a portal to another dimension that was sucking out the contents of this one. That's when TJ would lean in and whisper that it went to China to provide them water, and that tentacles came up out of it every full moon to bask in the lunar glow, and um, zombies too, every Halloween. When we were old enough, the Ketchum kids did indeed swim out to the spillway, but not for long. Furry green algae covered the sides, which squished and scloiched between our toes and sent us gagging back to shore before we could look down into it.

A gust of wind rolled through town and blew my little ball of trash right back down toward the pond, dispersing it in new annoying locations. There is no way humans have enough patience to clean up after themselves in every damn place in the world. I trudged back to the bank, figuring Paul would judge me if I didn't make at least a cursory attempt to pick it up.

Amidst a tangle of fishing line sat a small white stone, cylindrical, with ridges.

"Indian bead," I called out and bent down to snatch it up.

"Cool," Paul said. "Actually, I learned in grad school that those are fossilized crinoids." He gazed out over the pond. "This all used to be underwater millions of years ago."

I blinked and held the stone up, peering closer. The alien dream! The shallow sea. "Did they look kinda like plants underwater?"

"Yep. But they were actually animals. That's part of its stalk that attached to the coral."

A white truck sped by Paul's car and squealed around the corner.

I yelped. "Did you see that? That was Lincoln!"

"Yeah, so?" Paul said.

"He drives a white truck."

Paul raised an eyebrow. "Do you know how many people drive white trucks around here?"

TJ's voice nudged me out of my calculations. "Show him the email."

"Oh, yeah." I pocketed the stone, dusted myself off, and we scrambled up the hill.

I handed Paul my phone. "He sent this last night. We were afraid to go in without you."

Paul's tongue moved around inside his cheek as he read. He was dressed in tan chinos and a gray three-button henley, with hiking boots. Except for the shiny head and leaner profile, he looked much the same. Life—or the yoga witch—was treating him well post-cancer.

"Oh, by the way," I said with a chuckle. "Want some venison sausage?"

"Made by Lincoln? No thanks. How long has he been writing you?"

"When hasn't he?" I rolled my eyes. "More than a decade. I mean, there were only a couple years after school that I didn't hear from him. But he's written me on average," I searched the air calculating, "probably six times a year since we graduated."

"I'm sorry, Jane. That really sucks. It's hard for some guys to accept no as an answer." Paul squinted down the street. No cars in sight. "Have you filed a restraining order?"

"Guess how many manuscripts I get a year about women shot, stabbed, or mutilated by men under a restraining order."

"Yeah. Okay." He gazed deeply at me. A fond look, not like desire but like family. Good family. "Get in, I'll drive us out there."

Compared to the old sedan we'd rented, Paul's Accord was immaculate, with that pseudo-leather scent of ArmorAll and the tang of Windex. I rode shotgun, and TJ hung out in the back, typing away. It was probably nonsense, just to make it look like she was doing something, letting me have my time with him.

"Watcha writing?" he asked.

"New novel."

"Dedication."

"Yeah, this is making me a little carsick actually."

"Y'know," Paul said as we drove down the county road. "I actually talked to Lincoln some at the reunion. He was really focused on the whiskey fungus, wondering how I was going to get rid of it. As if I can just snap my fingers." He chuckled. "But it was an interesting conversation anyway. For a second, I thought, wow, Metzger's finally gotten his shit together. Then he starts telling me about how the fungus around here is supercharged from too many lightning strikes in the spring, just like it had been when his brother died," Paul rattled off with feigned exhaustion, "just like it was when Evie disappeared, on and on. He's writing a report to submit to the local authorities. Just imagine how that's going to go over."

"Is that a thing? Supercharged fungus?"

"Eh, sorta. Japanese scientists have figured out a way to electro-shock shiitake cultivation beds and jump-start fruiting. But connecting some extra mushroom growth in The Thicket with people dying? Yeah, that's Lincoln Logs for you."

I peered at TJ, who was madly typing away. My guess was that it didn't have anything to do with Keith and the yellow biplane anymore.

We drove past the first pine stands of The Thicket, past the old oak guarding the fence, and toward the access road.

Paul glowered, looking right then left.

"It's the second turn," I said.

"Yeah, I know, it's just … weird." His mouth puckered a

bit. "Lots of deadfalls round here. More than I remembered."

It was four o'clock and the skies had grown overcast. We parked by the Donzerly Light and headed to the hiking trail, where the sour scent of deer scat greeted us.

"Watch your step." Paul wore a backpack over one shoulder as if this were a cross-country adventure and tucked a clipboard under his arm.

We didn't have to traipse twenty feet into the trees before he found a tall conifer with a gaping hole at the base. Black vines, not quite plant roots, climbed the bark, like they had on the brick of the Donzerly Light shed. They looked like shriveled veins of dried blood and gave me the creeps.

"Yep, it's aliens." TJ nodded.

"Rhizomorphs," he said. "They're very hearty. They search for source material, gather information, transfer information, feed the fungus." He bent down and pulled out a knife, then gently turned up the cap of a mushroom which was one of a whole cluster. "Damn, they really do look like eyes, don't they?"

TJ stood, hands on hips. "It's even weirder from far away." She hopped left then right. "It's like they follow you."

Paul shook his head with an amused sigh. I could tell he still indulged TJ's kookiness only for my sake. Just like before we broke up.

"Have you ever seen them before, like that?" I asked.

"No, and I ate plenty of them when we were kids. They didn't have these spots."

"That's what I thought."

He tapped the flat side of the knife to his chin. "Could be a secondary fungus."

"Wait, a fungus on a fungus?" TJ asked, her brow knitted.

"Oh yeah. Lobster mushrooms taste so good because of the orange part, which is actually a parasitic fungus. Wild, aye?" He folded the knife, tucked it away in a pocket, and gently dug his fingers into the soil where whorls of dry rust-colored needles pooled in damp sand from yesterday's downpour.

*Like he used to touch you. Those needles in my back.*

The voice was as clear as if spoken into my ear. A chill washed down my spine and I wheeled around. TJ was busy peering down over Paul's shoulder.

There was a barely perceptible, hollow snap as he pulled the cluster out of the ground.

"Hmm, lots of blue bruising, well-defined annulus."

"That's what she said," TJ joked.

Paul ran the cluster underneath his nose, turned it around, and peered at the stalks and underneath the caps. "Hey, reach in the outer zipper there on the back of my pack and pull out a sheet of paper, would you?"

TJ eagerly went for the task, thrilled at playing scientist. I stood, still locked in a sort of daze, staring at another cluster of mushroom caps nearby. They stared back emptily. Or should I say, without emotion? Like when you check yourself in a shop window and the light hits just right and you realize there's someone standing right there on the other side, gazing back.

"Just set it on the ground there. Oh, and also, there should be a Ziplock in there. Get one of those." He set the cluster on the ground and pulled off two caps. One of the caps he split open slowly so that we saw a sticky film tearing apart between the layers, and he blessed it with more gibberish, "Mmm, separate gelatinous pellicle."

TJ mouthed at me this time: *That's what she said.*

The cap that he had not torn, he set, gills down, on the paper. TJ handed him the Ziplock and he slipped the remaining cluster inside and zipped it closed. "Okay, let's keep going. I have … a theory."

He left the cap sitting there on the paper and strode off the footpath into deeper brush. I thought it odd for him to litter like that and reached down for the paper.

"No," Paul said. "Leave it there. I'm taking a spore print. We'll come back for it."

We scrambled after him, fighting off branches and gnats. His sweeping stare went up into the trees and then down to the ground, up and down as we went. Along the forest floor lay the occasional shotgun shell. Some red and recent, some bleached pink, their brass bases tarnished. Paul halted and we stumbled into him. He stared down at a dead squirrel covered in delicate white webbing. He lifted it a bit with the toe of his shoe and shook his head, amazed. He clicked his tongue and walked on.

TJ kept pace with him, energized and alive.

Occasionally, I glanced back at Paul's quickly disappearing car, and kept an eye out for Lincoln or anything else that might not want us here.

Something rustled down the hill and I stopped,

searching the vast tangle of limbs. In the distance a large tan mass moved. Thorny, brown, leafless branches shifted sideways and then rotated. My mind spun at the impossibility of a tree moving like that. Okay, no, they were antlers. I sighed in relief. It was just a deer feeding off the forest floor. It had a massive rack of spiking horns, much wider than that of the creature we'd felled on the blacktop.

It looked up at me and I choked on a gasp. It had two heads with two interwoven sets of antlers. I placed one hand over an eye, assuming the thatch of branches both near and far was giving me double vision. Nope, still two heads. I closed both eyes and rubbed the lids. When I opened them, the buck was grazing again, and it was impossible to tell whether it did indeed have a second head. I had surely imagined it.

"Jane!" Paul yelled out with a bark that sounded like gunfire.

The buck leapt from its spot and ran deeper into The Thicket.

"Coming!" I called and sprinted up the hill after them. "Deer don't eat people, right?"

"Not last I checked," Paul said.

Ahead, more sickly trees, more mushroom clusters dead-eyeing us from the forest floor, and then we were out in an open clearing dotted with the occasional rotted stump and a single cherry tree already fruiting, no mushrooms at its base. Paul turned around and around, looking back into a Thicket ringed by dying pines with spindly bristling limbs and brown needles.

"What the hell!" TJ whispered, an eyebrow raised.

Paul raised a halting hand and we waited while he walked to the other side, where The Thicket began again. He circled the perimeter, bending down occasionally, collecting more clusters, and writing on his clipboard.

TJ and I sat down in the tall grass and picked red clover, pulling out the tiny petals like we used to and sucking out the nectar. I kept my eyes on The Thicket for any sign of the buck.

After a dozen minutes, Paul walked back, his face pale. "A meadowmaker," he murmured, eyes bulging. "A giant fairy ring essentially."

TJ and I looked at each other, thrilled, and mouthed the word: *meadowmaker*. It seemed so grand for this Podunk location, so fanciful and, well, malevolent. What it had to do with fungi we had no idea.

Paul took off his pack and put another Ziplock of mushrooms inside, along with his clipboard. "These glow, right? They did when we were kids." He slung it back over his shoulder.

"Yeah. I saw them last night," I said.

Paul raised his hands to his lips like he was praying and made little finger claps, considering.

"I'm going to run some tests tomorrow with the electron microscope. But I want to come back on Thursday. With my drone. For the big picture." He nodded, to himself mostly.

TJ sighed. "Dude, I just wanna know if we can eat these motherfuckers."

"Hold off, okay?" Paul stalked off back down the hill and into The Thicket, toward the cap he'd left on the paper.

"Hey are we gonna watch the Donzerly tonight?" I called after him.

"Thursday. I promise."

TJ and I stood up, brushed off, and hustled after him. I stayed close this time, but still glanced over my shoulder for a buck with extra antlers.

---

Paul drove us back to our car on Ketchum's outskirts and we met up at the tavern on the edge of town, where we ordered burgers, fries, and a pitcher of PBR that went down easier than I want to admit.

"I never get to eat red meat anymore. Amanda's got me on bean curd."

"Same. I mean, I've got me on bean curd." I laughed, plowing a floppy fry through the last smear of sugary ketchup. "She okay with you doing all this?"

"Of course. She's as passionate about this geeky stuff as I am. Oh, you mean about me and you? Yeah, she's cool. She'll be more pissed when she smells this grease on me."

TJ snickered at me, knowing how off-putting it was for Amanda not to consider me a threat in any way.

Paul pulled out the Ziploc, snapped off a mushroom stalk, and laid it on the table. Then he retrieved the paper that he'd earlier set the mushroom cap on and pushed it toward us. It was a reverse image of the cap's gills, a round kiss of brownish purple from the spores that had fallen out.

"Psilocybin," he said.

"Yes!" TJ pumped a fist. "So, we can take them."

"I didn't say that." He pointed his pinky near the cap of the little mushroom, at the "eyes," but he didn't touch them. "I want to run tests on these spots. Need the electron microscope. Of every grouping I checked in that meadow, there were seven dots on each cap, no matter the size. Always seven. Some were merely the size of a pinhead, but they were there. I need to know what I'm dealing with here. But even if it comes back negative for toxicity, there's no foolproof way to know for sure. It always requires a fool."

"Well, you're looking at her!" TJ said. "I boiled the one I picked into our chamomile tea last night before bed." She stuck her tongue far out at me and laughed. "So we could probably eat more, don't you think?"

I closed my eyes. *Dammit, Teej.* No wonder I'd dreamt of an alien landscape and a monster in the motel room. Not to mention hallucinated a two-headed deer.

Paul sighed. He looked at the table disappointed. "TJ." He shook his head.

She leaned over and whispered in my ear, "I'll just go and, um, take a leak." I watched as she hunted for the bathroom.

Paul smiled wistfully at me. "I'm sorry I wasn't there for you more. Growing up."

I shrugged at this sudden seriousness. "I had Teej."

"Yeah. I know. But Jane," Paul said. He looked fondly at me again, but this time with a depth of sorrow that raised anger in me, causing little spikes of indignation to flare up my back. "She's not good for you. When are you gonna do your own thing? You really need to find a way to move on without her."

I balked at him and crossed my arms. We'd had a similar conversation just before we broke up. There were people in this town, homophobes, who didn't approve of TJ, but Paul? No, this was about something else. Something too weighty to broach outright, too tiring.

"I'll never abandon her like her mom has. She needs me."

He winced at the mention of TJ's mom and pinched the bridge of his nose. "Okay, well, you've made it this far, I guess. But you've really got to figure your shit out. The last thing you need with Lincoln on your case is tripping on psilocybin. Especially this one." He held up the little mushroom. "This is like nothing I've ever seen before."

TJ returned and scooted back into the booth. We sat there rapt as he talked. Paul loved his work, more than anything or anyone, I suspected. Like so many talented Ketchum kids, his passion was borne of The Thicket.

He counted off on his fingers, "This fungus is ancient, has a massive underground network, is psychoactive, bioluminescent at night to attract spore carriers, feeds on plant *and* animal matter—"

"It's an omnivore!" TJ intoned dramatically. "Like a Venus fly-trap?"

"Oh, it's no plant. Ever wonder why a portobello tastes more like steak than a potato? Fungi are closer to animals than plants. That's why fungal infections are harder to treat. A medication designed to attack fungal cells can also harm our own cells."

"The bridge between flora and fauna," TJ said, marveling.

I cringed at myself. How had I gone so long thinking mushrooms were vegetables?

"Oh," Paul continued, "*and* it will kill its host if it needs to. A genuine meadowmaker. There's a non-psilocybin version out in Oregon—largest organism on the planet. The Armillaria."

"Our malaria?" I repeated.

He chuckled. "Okay, sure. We'll call it that for now. But it needs to be classified on its own. That's why I want to measure its reach. I can do it with the drone by tracking the deadfalls from above, then check for fruiting on foot. Oh yeah, the mushroom stalks are just the fruit. The mycelium beneath the ground is where the real magic happens." He swept an arm across the room. "That network beneath our feet today? It could feel our every step."

"Shut up," TJ said.

"No, seriously. There are mycologists who claim a fungus this age and size is sentient. I don't know if I agree, at least not by human standards. But every time you take a step over their network," he stood his fingers up toward the ceiling and wiggled them upwards, "these roots, these veins, they fork out to scan the ground for nutrients you might have left behind or stirred up. Fungi helped make our environment; they're the architects, in a way. Hell, you wouldn't be here without the fungal microbiome in your body. They were here long before humans and will be here long after we destroy ourselves." He lowered his voice, as if the guys at the bar gave two shits. "There are hypotheses that suggest psilocybin was an evolutionary catalyst in early humans that helped advance our species and even helped us craft our own religions."

It could have been the glass of beer, or it could have been the remnants of last night's dreams, but everything Paul was saying made perfect sense. Any look of disbelief on my face was merely feigned to suggest I could not be easily led into every damn rabbit hole—or two-headed deer sighting.

"… and we came from them! The first living thing on land. Growing tall as trees. Their spores could survive outer space. Hell, they probably even came from outer space. If you were to travel to another goldilocks planet like ours—a young one?—you'd probably see Prototaxites growing everywhere."

"I told you!" TJ yelped. "Aliens!" The men at the bar turned on their stools. She looked at me sheepishly. "What? It even sounds like one."

Paul continued peering at the little stalk as if its "eyes" were hypnotizing him, "but this little guy—"

"Hold on," I said. My heart fluttered as I remembered last night's dream. "Back up a second. Like tall fingers? Really tall and thin?"

"Yeah, they found a fossil of one recently. Massive."

Maybe I'd seen an article and absorbed it subconsciously or something. I pushed my beer away and said nothing more about it; he would really think I'd lost it.

Paul continued, "But this one, even if the underground network isn't as big as the Armillaria in Oregon, it will be someday. Plus, it's presenting that multitude of other features I mentioned. Bonus features. It's like a—"

"Supershroom," TJ marveled.

Paul smiled despite his dislike for that unscientific, hippy-dippy term. "Yeah. I might even get to name this one."

I leaned back. "It goes without saying you'll name it 'Jane,' right?"

He chuckled. "I was thinking something in the realm of Armillaria Oculi Psilocybe, but Jane's probably better. So, stay a couple more days?"

"Of course," TJ said. "I'm not leaving until I collect at least two bags of these mofos."

He glanced at his phone. "I should get going. Amanda Demanda's calling."

───────────

After he left, I pulled out my own phone and opened my email to check the daily flood of book queries in my agency mailbox.

"Oh, no."

"What," TJ said.

**From:** Metzger, Lincoln [hansolo99@frontieronline.net]
**To:** Render, Jane [jRender@stubenliterary.com]
**Subject:** CAUTION

Very clever missy. You know I can't do anything about Paul. But we both know TJ has to go. You'd be better off with her gone forever. If I could put my Luger to her head and not hurt you I would. I'll find a way. Nothing is impossible. Only improbable. Not much time left though. There is the matter of your womb. We only have a couple years to make a family. Do not enter The Thicket again. The fruit of knowledge is toxic to the female mind, my lady.

ATTACHMENT: TJ.jpg

"Fuck me sideways, he's annoying." TJ said. "And oh, yeah, *womb.* Now *that* was a word we hated growing up."

"What do you think he means about the Luger?"

"It means I don't factor into his happy-fappy equation, Jane. But who cares? He's a wet noodle."

"Wait. There's an attachment."

It was a photo of a police practice target, the kind with the black silhouette and concentric circles emanating from the chest. A single bullet hole tore through the very edge of the head, dividing the space between white and black.

"This is a threat, TJ. A clear threat! Chekov's Gun. If you mention a Luger in act one it has to go off in act two."

"Eh."

"Why aren't you scared? You saw what he did to that deer."

"Yeah, an injured animal helped him prove his manhood. He's a fucking pussy. Wait. Pussies are strong. Okay, he's a ballsack, a fucking ballsack."

The men at the bar looked at us again with a mix of alarm and distaste.

I lowered my voice. "I think this is enough to nail him."

In Chicago, Lincoln's emails had been a nuisance, but

now, knowing he lived only a mile or two from our motel, knowing he'd driven past us dozens and dozens of times, meant he was no longer a laughing matter.

"God, wouldn't it be nice to have him off to a funny farm?" TJ went hazy. "We can't afford to be nice to guys like Lincoln anymore. They just glom onto you. We are so set up as women. Compassion is our downfall."

"First thing tomorrow we go to the police."

"Then mushroom foraging, yeah?" She wiggled eyebrows.

I had to admit, The Thicket was calling me back, same as her. Like a holy place.

## Chapter Twenty-Four

"Coffee with cream, two sugars, right?" The pert young woman set the cup on Lincoln's desk.

"Thanks," Lincoln mumbled, and didn't look up from his computer. He sat in his cubicle in the city council offices, running a spellcheck on the most important report he'd ever written. It wouldn't be welcome. It wouldn't earn him any fans. It would cost thousands of taxpayer dollars—millions even.

"Watcha working on?"

Lisa was new in town. Just divorced, cute, with short medium-brown hair, a little overweight. If he weren't already spoken for, Lincoln might have considered it. But give her enough time in Ketchum and people would turn her against him.

Then again, she might be good for making Jane jealous.

"Something big," he said. "Really big." His thighs thwapped together.

"Oh, yeah?"

"Yeah, it's gonna blow the doors off this town."

She knit her hands on the edge of his cubicle and set her chin on it. "Wow."

Cow eyes. She had cow eyes. Like a dumb heifer.

Lincoln went back to spellchecking. He definitely did not want Jane to think he was off the market with this ... dolt. She sauntered away, hips swinging. He tried not to think about them unclothed. Impossible.

Slut.

There were endless temptations from the job at hand. Work of the devil.

Lincoln cracked his knuckles and proofread his report.

**TO: Federal Bureau of Investigation, Drug Enforcement Administration, Army Corps of Engineers, Department of Natural Resources, Rand County Commissioner, Ketchum City Council, Rand County Tribune**

TOXIC FUNGUS OF KETCHUM'S THICKET
THREAT AND REMOVAL

Rand County: A Historic Overview, 1800s

With the removal of Indigenous tribes by General James Ketchum, the territorial government encouraged farmers to settle, log, and cultivate the newly opened land. General Ketchum named one of the last old growth stands The Thicket, for its "deceptive density"[1]

As the century passed, and neighboring villages such as Birkenham expanded into cities, Ketchum's settlement never rose above a few thousand residents. Though situated next to a river, a freight and passenger line, with plentiful farm and hunting land, the only residents who prospered were those who made their way north to Chicago or south to St. Louis.

## Recent History

In 1957, the Illinois Meteorological Society named Rand County the "Lightning Corridor" for the highest number of strikes in the Midwest.[2]

While fishing the Ketchum River in 1962, Edwin Stamets[3], a researcher from Southern Illinois University, discovered a strain of fungus within Ketchum's Thicket that he administered to student volunteers. In 1968, the university shuttered his study due to the criminalization of psychedelics. Stamets left his position and formed the Seven Meadows Society, which held "meetings" in Ketchum's Thicket. After record storms in the spring of 1974, Stamets disappeared the following summer.[4]

In 1995, the suicide of Ketchum sheriff John Render was ruled an accident. Newly discovered files (see addendum) reveal a child pornography ring linking Render with drug and human traffickers in Birkenham. Render's cache of videos and photographs included several packets of dried fungus used as "party favors". The Rand County coroner conducted a toxicology test on Render, but the results are no longer available.

## Today

Arrests for illegal mushroom consumption and distribution in Rand County equal all 58 California counties combined.[5]

In the past two decades, a dozen deaths and disappearances are linked to use of the Ketchum Thicket Fungus.[6,7,8]

Professor Takaki Koichi of Iwate University, Japan discovers a method to electrocute shiitake mushrooms from vegetative to reproductive state.[9]

## An Increasing Threat

With accelerated growth after springtime thunderstorms, and illegal corn distillation increasing, a new strain of black fungus is first reported on barns and silos.

It now covers most of lower Ketchum.

The Ketchum Thicket Fungus propagates the region surrounding Treatment Station #3, endangering the local water supply.

Environmental & Financial Impact

Though the safety of the public is paramount, the destruction of old growth conifer and damage to the deer population cannot be overlooked. Loss of fishing and hunting dollars will result in further devastation to the county long-term.

WHAT CAN BE DONE?

I am proposing a simple, three-step plan:

1. FBI and/or DEA agents must shut down all illegal corn stills to starve the black fungus, which may interact with the Ketchum Thicket Fungus given time.
2. The entirety of the Rand County waste treatment systems must be flushed of contaminants.
3. To destroy the Ketchum Thicket Fungus, we must bite the bullet and remove its source material. **The Army Corps should conduct a controlled burn of the Ketchum Thicket as soon as possible.**

I am available for further inquiry, advice, and assistance in this matter.

Lincoln T. Metzger, Alderman

Well, he'd crossed his t's and dotted his i's. It took all his self-control not to state the obvious. The Thicket was capital-E Evil. But you had to spoon-feed it to these people. They worshipped facts not feelings. If this didn't work, he'd take matters into his own hands or die trying. In fact, he almost hoped it didn't work so he could finally get on with doing it himself. He had parked his father's old F150 in the empty grain elevator, loaded up with a hefty fungicide application for the treatment station and a fertilizer mixture that would blow the Donzerly Light to kingdom come—hit the devil where it hurt—lighting the deadfalls of The Thicket like so much dry kindling.

Then the report would hit the papers and show the government for the tedious knot of red-tape-bound politicians they were. Most importantly, Lady Jane would finally realize that he alone had solved an age-old mystery to save countless lives.

She surely was boiling mad at him right now, the little sassafras. But just because she was visiting a small town didn't mean she shouldn't lock her car.

Last night, she'd gone to the tavern with that baldy, Paul McKenna, who was of absolutely no use to Lincoln now. Too many years at a university had softened the guy's logic skills, made him a bleeding heart who couldn't put two and two together, or make a decision to save his life.

In Jane's rental car, Lincoln had found a shoebox of miscellany in the back seat. He had also spotted his Tupperware of sausage malingering in the stuffy air and had nearly called her the b-word. But the shoebox itself turned out to be a treasure trove and he quickly forgave her carelessness. The unicorn tank top still had her scent from high school on it. He would need to bag it, to retain her essence. But the diary would bring her a world of hurt if she ever read it. He'd make sure she didn't.

Not until the moment was right.

Lincoln printed the report, his lips moving silently at his desk as his fellow city employees passed by and tried to ignore him talking to himself. New girl Lisa sat watching him from across the room, chatting with the front desk receptionist, the b-word already whispering lies no doubt.

He gathered the pages, tapped them straight on his desk, and slid them into a clear binder. This paper copy would go to the office staff, but everyone else would receive a PDF document via email, with links to the footnoted information.

He would give them one week to act. And if the city, county, or state refused, the truck was ready.

The cursor arrow hovered over *SEND* in Microsoft Outlook.

*You're a fool*, his father said. *Never make a damn thing of yourself.*

There would be no turning back from this. Lincoln sat back, laced his fingers behind his head, and shut his eyes, chair creaking, and savored the time before everything changed.

A shadow crossed over his closed lids.

"Lisa, I'm very busy."

He opened his eyes to Deputies Nelson and Yoder, who looked down at him with that same distrustful pity everyone did.

"You need to come with us, Lincoln," Nelson said.

Yoder nodded upward and flicked her fingers in a "come here" motion.

Lincoln smiled and stood up. "What, now?"

*The Birkenham landfill. It must have cameras. It has cameras now!*

"We'll talk about it at the station."

He glanced around at the heads bobbing up like gophers from their cubicles. Lisa had a hand to her mouth. The receptionist's half-lidded stare rolled to the ceiling.

*Or the auction house. The old auction house lot has cameras! Oh Jesus.*

"Am I under arrest?"

"Do you want to be?"

He shrugged and joined them at the edge of his cubicle, trying to appear relaxed, with an elbow on the half-wall. "I've just been minding my own business, working on—" He glanced back at his computer. He hadn't pressed *SEND* yet.

"And breaking into cars, bragging about your guns," Yoder said with disgust.

Nelson sternly eyed his female partner and reiterated, in a measured tone, "We'll talk about it at the station."

Lincoln puckered his lips and started back to his desk.

"Hey," Nelson said with a bark, "what do you think you're doing?"

"I just need to—"

The two deputies sprang forward. "Keep your hands up. No. Stop! Just— Dammit, Metzger!"

He leapt for the mouse and clicked it before the two brought him down in a scuffle, his forehead knocking the edge of the desk. As he tasted the dusty marble floor, and his vision grew dim, he only had one thought.

*This is nothing new.*

## Chapter Twenty-Five

"It really should feel smaller," I said. "Now that we're older." The Thicket still seemed vast, even though I knew it was longer than it was wide. And widthwise we could walk a few miles and be out the other side. "It may be the Tardis of forests."

"I guess we're just not used to the country anymore."

After parking by the Donzerly Light, TJ and I left the footpath and fought our way through the brush, up the hill, and to the meadow Paul had found the day before. The sun warming the wild onion in the clearing filled the day with a savory essence. Without words, we spread out the beach towels we'd packed for Florida in the center, where the view was best, and set out our things like ritual: bottles of water, peanut butter and cheese cracker sandwiches, a deck of cards, pen, notepad, and of course a cluster of the most pristine Armillaria we could find.

We'd found the impressive glut of fungus staring at us from the base of an ashen conifer, where the tree was rotting, and pale wood crumbled in soft splinters. Those creepy black veins that Paul had called rhizomorphs had been wrapped around the bark, like a craggy woman in torn fishnets. When TJ picked the batch, the rhizomorphs shuddered as if they'd felt it, but surely it had only been the force of her tugging.

---

With Lincoln cooling off in the county jail, TJ and I had been free to venture back into The Thicket. Taking care of Lincoln had been easier than expected, though the police station itself left a perceptible residue on our moods. The mint-green walls and dark wood hadn't changed in decades and we became meek little children again. I hadn't thought about how much it might spook TJ until we were standing in its midst. But she kept a stiff upper lip for me.

The sheriff treated us with the same unsettling concern the diner waitress had, and they cringed at the emails I provided. After I signed an affidavit, a male and female officer immediately stalked out to their squad car. They would bring Lincoln back for questioning and if he caused any problems—which they assumed he would or perhaps planned to trump up—they would plant him in a cell right down the hall until I could testify in front of a judge on Friday. When I brought up my fear of his guns, the sheriff thought it likely they would be confiscated, with the evidence and my testimony, and Lincoln would be served a court order to keep away from me, and not to contact me again by any means.

They couldn't promise that they'd find the keepsake shoebox, but if he did have it, it might turn up in the firearms sweep. We hoped they would find it if for no other reason than it would prove his violation of our things. TJ supposed she'd survived long enough without that stuff, but I really wanted to crack open that diary and watch the old videotape.

We then slid, dazed, into the rental car—a man-sized weight lifted—and, elated, drove right to The Thicket. I knew from experience with too many illicit substances that psychedelics were not addictive. I wouldn't wake up craving more upon more, so TJ didn't have to work hard to convince me what great material it would make. While part of me felt a bit ridiculous, like a middle-aged man who buys a sports car to relive his teen years, there was no place I would have rather been than with TJ out on that hill. It was our vacation within a vacation.

I didn't text Paul to say that we were doing this without him. I didn't want his permission or his advice; he'd just told me to get rid of my best friend, as if she were as bad as Lincoln. Besides, all he cared about really was winning some obscure fungus award. We simply left a note in our motel room and a ten-dollar tip in case The Thicket swallowed us, or Greek god Pan turned us into reeds for a new flute. TJ had always encouraged me not to be beholden to the guys in my life: Nick, Paul, my boss David, Lincoln even. No matter their level of importance, I should never assign them a place of authority, never let them get the best of me. There were days I would waver on this. But not today.

---

"All right!" TJ slapped her hands and rubbed them together. "Ready to level up?"

I took a deep breath, let it out slowly, then nodded and opened the bag.

"Are you sure this is the right amount?" I asked, grimacing at my share of mushrooms. With their clods of dirt and little black "eyes" they didn't exactly scream, *EAT ME!* but nor did they frighten me as much as they should have. We'd already tried one in the tea and not gotten sick. I was strangely more wary of harming the mushroom staring back at me. Like meeting the chicken before it's fricasseed. "Seems like an awful lot."

"That's just because they're fresh." TJ brushed soil off the stalks, rinsed them with some bottled water, and held their tan stalks up to the sunlight. "If they were dry, they'd be tiny. Besides, I want to hit the God levels this time."

I scowled.

"What?" TJ laughed. "You want them in a Styrofoam box wrapped in plastic? This is the way people used to eat. Forage, rinse, eat, repeat." She crammed them in her mouth, trying not to make a face.

I thoughtfully flicked the gills of one cap with a dirty fingernail as if they were the pages of a book—a tiny book with a very ancient story. And then I ate it. We chewed the caps and stems of four mushrooms each, their taste wincingly bitter like soil and a bit like anise, just as I remembered. Their flesh was a delicate, spongy texture. We made stank-faces at each other. I tried not to think about the "eyes," which made a slightly gelatinous pop as I chewed. Was that "eye" the one that would kill me? I let out a calming breath. We chased them with plenty of water and the cracker sandwiches, determined to keep it all down.

"Okay," TJ said. "First things first. Let's clear out our shit."

It had always been the rule of the Thicket Kids to air our fears—all the problems that might trip us up before the wave of psilocybin rained down on us. It worked every time—for me at least. Back then it had been about whom we were crushing on, our grades, parents griefing us, our fears about life after graduation. And anyone who skipped the airing of fears invariably had a bad trip as we all watched dumbfounded. *Roy.*

"I have something to admit," I rushed, afraid that if I drew it out, it would still infect my trip. "I have a pill problem."

TJ nodded. "Opioids."

I blinked, incredulous.

"Yeah," she said. "I've known since your shoulder surgery."

Jesus, did I really suck that much at hiding stuff?

"Well, I went to Hazelden. I dealt with it. But, y'know, it's always there—"

"Haunting you?"

"Yeah," I said. "Better though as the years go on. But the icky thing is, Lincoln knows. He's been following me even closer than I suspected. That's the gift he was offering me. More pills."

"That bastard." She looked around. "I wonder if he still has a camera out here somewhere."

I raised both middle fingers.

TJ snorted out a laugh. "You been growing a pair since we got here. Coming into your own." She nodded wistfully at me as if she were going to miss me. I didn't like it. If bringing her down here for closure meant her going soft and shrinking on me, well, that scared me. And then I cringed, immediately guilty for thinking that she needed to carry my water 24/7. She deserved to take her armor off once in a while.

"So," I asked. "Did you really tell me all you remember about your dad? What he did to you?"

TJ hung her head and then looked up at me. "You couldn't handle it, Janey."

"I could—"

"No. You can't." She thumbed her breastbone and nodded. "*I* can handle it. All you need to know is that it happened. Just help me move on, okay?"

I sighed. "Okay." I honestly did not want to know. And besides, I hadn't seen TJ so content in years. When I'd woken this morning, TJ had been propped up in her bed, typing away. I could tell how thrilled she was to be coming full circle today, here in The Thicket. This place had been the source of her creativity, and it was here she hoped to recharge it.

She dealt us both hands of Spit, which we used to play as kids. The cards sat anchored between the pine needles that were poking through our towels. The game was essentially War mixed with Solitaire, except you split the deck between the two players and only used five piles to make your sets. The remainder of your cards were the *spit* cards, for which you called out "spit!" as you drew them. When we were kids, we would actually spit on the ground too, which was half the fun.

The game moved fast, and our hands flew as we laughed and raced to get rid of our cards first.

I couldn't be sure how many hands we played before the black of the spades and clubs slowly deepened, appearing hollow, like tunnels to another place. The space between the white of the card and the black of the ink was sharp and bright, a new color I wanted to name *Mandelbrot*—maybe pink, maybe black, but then again maybe green. I kept this particular absurdity to myself.

We yawned but were not tired. This also made us laugh.

The long blades of grass surrounding us were pulsing now, nutrients surging from base to tip. The rhizomorphs woven around the conifer that bordered the clearing throbbed with the same Mandelbrot highlights in the cards. Knotholes slowly spun. The wind through the leaves gave the trees a voice that said: *hushhhh*.

For me, the beginning of a mushroom trip has always been a fugue state. The type of trance I'd experienced long before I'd ever taken illicit substances and still had on occasion. When I was a child, I would often be in the middle of playing dolls or wandering outside and just … stop. I would stand, catatonic, as life swirled on without me. It was as if I couldn't recall the past or envision the future. Time went still. I had halted on the apex of *Now* and stood in a fog. It was peaceful, actually. Maybe that's why kids often get the reputation for being ditzy. Their mind is growing, neurons ever-firing, hitting the end of the line and forking out at the apex, while the rest struggles to catch up.

I'd forgotten that blissful apex. Until now.

This was our cue; we looked at each other and gulped a silent "Good luck," then raised our eyes to the sky and watched the cumulus clouds rolling overhead.

Their depth increased; their edges sharpened. I could clearly make out the convection, plumes forming, curling outward then inward, whereas most days, I rarely noticed the beauty of such a wonder.

I thumbed at the weather app on my phone. The last thing we needed was to be tripping whilst lying in mud. The reception out here was still terrible, and I could not be sure if the forecast had refreshed, but a hopeful line of sun icons with one white cartoon cloud next to each was good enough for post-sober me.

"I may be a little frightened," I said.

TJ answered from someplace far off, "Don't wrestle the angel, Jane. Let it happen."

We turned our backs to each other and sat spine to spine, propping each other up and achieving a 360° view of The Thicket between us. Like the center of a turntable.

TJ sang softly and I joined her for backup:

> *"Wild on the prairie.*
> *Under the conifer.*
> *That's where we'll hide.*
> *Under the conifer.*
> *Feral and contrary.*

*Under the conifer.*
*That's where we'll lie.*
*With needles in our backs."*

We went quiet; I can't be sure for how long. My shoulders released months of tension and fell to their proper height. Chicago seemed a thousand miles away and a thousand years ago. We could be rapidly aging here as the world flew by and it didn't matter. As we watched the trees in The Thicket, their network clarifying, their purpose simple and beautiful, I felt not so much insignificant but instead *integrated* into their network. A loss of individuality came with it, but I still felt necessary. My mouth hung open at the opulence of nature I'd ignored for so long. Or forgotten.

"Dude," TJ broke the wild silence, her voice cracking. "You and I are like the Armillaria. It's all symbiotic and shit. When something happens to you, I can feel it a mile away. We are probably … a fungus."

A giggle spurted forth. I could not stop. TJ shuddered against me, trying to contain herself. "I'm serious!"

I have no idea how long we laughed. Eventually, I wiped my eyes and my running nose. "Hey, you know what's odd?"

"Um, everything?"

"Yeah, but," I struggled to form a coherent sentence, "I still don't understand why The Thicket feels deeper."

"Technically it *is* shrinking with all the deadfalls."

Something spoke to me from all around, a low gong that

could form words. Male and female voices and something inhuman said:

*He means to destroy us.*

"Did you hear that?"

"Yes."

"Who means to destroy us?" TJ asked the sky.

No answer.

I raised my upturned palms and in the middle joints of both sets of four fingers, in the creases, eight eyes softly gazed back at me. I was afraid if I closed a fist, I would hurt them, but I did it anyway, and when I opened my hands again the eyes were still there. With a forefinger I delicately touched the eye of my other forefinger. It was wet of course, but here's what's even more uncanny: *the eye could feel the dryness of my finger*! Just like when you touch your own eye. Not particularly pleasant, but not horrible if you are gentle. What could it see? I could just about tell—oh, so elusive— like waking from a dream, that world beyond the veil. And the more I concentrated, the less I could perceive. I shook my hands. *Dammit*, why couldn't I see through these new eyes?

Because they were not my own; they were visitors' eyes. I held them up to see the view, but my hand turned back to me. *They* only wanted to see me. I must have stared at my damn hand for twenty minutes like that.

"Janey, you okay?

"Yeah, you?"

"Yeah," TJ said. "I think we are inside its brain." She tapped the back of her head to mine. "Can you see in my head?"

My laugh bounced strangely across the meadow. How alien it sounded. And I didn't stop laughing until snot was running down my nose again.

"Really, Jane. Look!"

I leaned my head back to hers. It was funny because it was true. I *could* see the colors she was seeing, the waves like heat, the richness of texture and the glittering grinning curve of a quarter moon, faint in the sky. Given enough time, enough mushrooms, maybe I could see via my hand. Anything seemed possible right then, even if you didn't want it to be. You could try to get away from it, try to deny the effects, but it rushed back in to fill the space your brain tried to sweep away, like pushing water in a shallow bath.

An old world continually born anew. Everything matters and nothing matters.

I forgot what civilization was, what money was, my own gender, how we would drive the strange vehicle we had arrived in. I could not grasp the old meanings. It frightened me until I heard the voice again.

*All shall pass.*

Peace came over me. I loved this land here and now, had missed it for so long but had denied it. So it had called me home. Through honking cars, sirens blaring, the screeching and clunk-clunk of the 'L' train and the barks of people on Michigan Avenue, The Thicket had called me home.

But why?

---

Somewhere beyond the meadow, there came the rubbery slap of a pigeon flock taking flight and we watched them scatter. The golden sun sat low on the horizon; TJ ordered me not to look at it. I obeyed, unable to move from her back as if we'd grown together while the earth spun, lest we be cast from its gravitational pull. My memories of every day before this one hid somewhere in my mind, muffled and muted, faded and fractured. Who was I anymore?

*Life is beautiful and why am I so cruel to everyone?*

*There is no good. No evil,* came back the answer. *Only survival.*

Was that me or TJ or the Armillaria? Syllables disassembled before I could mutter them. But TJ filled in the blanks by uttering trippy new prose that she couldn't possibly use in her novel. I tried to write it down nonetheless, my eye-fingers unsure what a pencil was for, and I felt an alien joy at the scuffing scratch that the graphite made across the paper pulp.

> Everything's brighter when I close my eyes.
> Oh intangible spirit rise,
> Show us you can materialize,
> The catalyst that sent the dreams,
> The visions and schemes to my throbbing eyes.
> Arise. Arise!

Nothing did rise though—nothing but silence. And then a far-off rustling. An animal of some kind.

"I'm so glad we did this," I said.

"I argee."

"Whoa, did you say argue or agree?

"Yes."

"Aaaa?" Was TJ making fun of me or was I growing paranoid? We were fools. I knew the tricks of a mind on psilocybin and a greater presence assured me that whatever TJ was up to was meant in good faith, as much a joke on herself as on me.

To the south, over the top of The Thicket, a lavender-gray storm was piling up and I remotely grasped that I should be afraid, but still could not move. So instead, we sat watching that single cherry tree dripping with fruit for a while more. An albino rabbit sat under it, chewing clover, keeping a red eye on us.

"If time sped up, we would see all those cherries growing like excretions, little drops of sugar blood," TJ said. And before I could answer, she asked, "Hey, what time is it?"

I picked up my iPhone, an ugly, cold thing, and pressed at it with distaste. The numbers, a blasphemy in our beautiful world, insisted we return to the broken one.

"Five. Three. Zero."

I could picture the neurons firing in TJ's mind-universe as she struggled to do the math. "Four hours."

"Right."

"We should be coming down soon. Don'tcha think?"

"Maybe?"

Across the meadow, the black rhizomorphs lacing the deadfalls slowly pried away and slipped down from their trunks until I could see no more on the trees. Along the edges of the clearing, the grass faintly stirred in an ever-shrinking wave that approached the middle of the meadow where we sat stoned, like a reverse-water droplet and we were the droplet. It could have taken a minute; it could have taken fifteen.

Everything grew suddenly silent, like diving underwater, a rumble and a shimmering ping that grew in my ears, like tinnitus after a rock concert.

I gulped in awe. The pulsing black veins crossed the soil, weaving through the grass roots, searching us out. Even if I could move, I didn't want to and yearned to be touched by something that had just yesterday given me the shivers.

Story of my life.

From far off, yet next to me: "Do you see this, Janey?"

"Yeah."

"He's here."

"Wha'? Who he?"

*Lincoln.*

I was able to turn my body now at least with that onrush of adrenaline.

"Pan. Greek god Pan. He's here."

"Oh, God, Teej, don't make me lau—" My mouth hung open at what faced TJ from the edge of The Thicket.

The buck was enormous, and it did indeed have two heads. The second head was black and grew like rotten fruit from another set of antlers. It took a step into the clearing and bowed its great rack of thorns at us. The eyes of its main head glared a burning amber.

"We've got to get out of here," I whispered. "We're sitting ducks."

"Don't move. Let him pass. This is all part of the hero's journey."

It took long strides toward us.

"Are you sure?" my voice quivered.

I could smell the deer now, rank like piss and roadkill. It was monstrously large, yes, but emaciated, the ripple of its ribcage showing. The antlers of the blackened head looked cracked and the head itself was not connected to the body. The ragged flesh of the neck hung limp and papery. Of all that I had envisioned today, I could not grasp the logic of this creature before us. It was so close now that I could see that the amber in its eyes was merely the reflection of the sun setting on its black pupils.

I crabbed backwards as it came upon TJ first. It cast a hoof at her, and she shielded her face. It lazily struck her arm.

"Um, it's just a deer. And it stinks," she said. It pawed at her again.

"Don't look at it. Don't challenge it," I said.

It turned to me.

TJ scrambled to her feet and stumbled toward me.

"Run."

My feet spun before me, grass blurring by as we bounded down the hill and into The Thicket. The rhizomorphs were back on the trees as if they'd never moved. The buck trotted after us, snorting with annoyance. *My God*, I thought, *we are being chased by a two-headed zombie deer*.

Pan, Pan, Greek god Pan. One half goat. The other half—

With every footfall my breasts ached, reminding me my

period was nearly due. I reached up to cup them as I ran and cackled, out of control, wondering if this was how it would end for me, and even how they might write about it on *Publishers Marketplace*. I stopped laughing, however, when I realized it might not be so swift an end.

Through the woods, scrambling over deadfalls, and jumping white mounds that varied in size. All around, in the periphery of my vision, lay creatures much larger than squirrels wrapped in that strange fungal webbing. They reminded me of those asphalt speed bumps on residential streets. What did Aunt Ellen call them when we were kids? Something whimsical.

"Sleeping policemen," TJ huffed as we ran.

There was no time to marvel or wonder; the zombie deer was upon us. TJ and I took shelter behind the largest conifer we could find. As the buck stomped forward, we turned to keep the tree between him and us, our hands torn and sticky from the sappy bark.

I stumbled and an antler caught me in my upper arm, jabbing me like a broken broom. It could surely gut us. But there was something languorous about it all. As if the three of us were merely doing a drunken dance, responding to each other's moves seconds after we should be.

The buck stopped for a moment, panting, huffing, its neck low and its eyes downcast.

"It's tripping too," TJ said in awe.

As my senses returned, I realized with a glimmer of embarrassment that this buck had torn the head off a dead buck during the rut. I'd heard it happened sometimes. Even the corpse of another male looked and smelled like competition when their hormones raged at full throttle. It didn't help that they might be constantly tripping from the mushrooms that grew so close to the lichen and grasses they normally consumed.

I reached out and touched the living head of the deer. It raised eyes to me, its pelt fluttering with lice and dotted with fat purplish-brown ticks. The blackened head, with its punctured eye sockets, would completely desiccate by winter. The poor beast would be carrying around a white skull if a hunter salivating at all those horn points didn't shoot it first. I tried to see a way of disentangling the puzzle of antlers, which I realized weren't cracked but laced with black rhizomorphs from the Armillaria. In fact, the black veins had crossed from the dead buck and threaded across the antlers of the live deer and had made their way into its—

*It's coming out our ears, Janey.*

I touched the tip of an antler. Gave a little tug.

The buck snorted and jerked away. As we watched, aghast, it strode off lazily, further into The Thicket.

TJ and I then crept back up to the clearing to retrieve our things.

"Hero's journey, you say?" I palpated the bruise growing on my arm, but nothing seemed broken.

"Yeah, sorry about that." TJ cringed and folded our towels.

She grew contemplative as we hiked back to the rental car. "But hey, those sleeping policemen? I jumped one as big as a toddler, Jane. Curled up in a fetal position." She looked around for it, but we'd gotten so turned about, I wasn't sure whether the buck had chased us north or south.

"Must have been a fawn." I flicked a dismissive hand. "Or a raccoon."

"Yeah. Maybe."

My hand fumbled with the car door handle as if it first had to forget its eyes and remember how to grasp.

We slid into the sedan and sat for a while, re-acclimating to the first trappings of civilization. With sap-sticky fingers, I fumbled the key into the ignition and turned. The engine hummed. What a strange contraption. We sat there blinking like dolts with it idling, trying to perceive each combustion.

TJ turned and reached behind our seats, to fish the Tupperware box off the back floor.

"You can't eat that now," I said. "It's been out too long."

"Naw, imma use it for more shroomies." She peered through the plastic then set it on the dash. The sausages seemed blurry. "Mold wouldn't grow that fast would it?" she asked.

"God, I don't know but let's not open it in here."

I set my hand on the gear shift and launched us forward.

We drove at a funeral's pace back to Ketchum, marveling at the ride and my ability to captain this odd rolling boat.

As we approached Ketchum High School, our necks craned at the cars parked in the lot.

"I thought school was out already," TJ said.

"It is."

"Gawd, does nobody buy new cars down here?" She

looked over her shoulder as we passed. "Wow, that looks like Gary's cherry Mustang. He got Lori pregnant in that."

Our tires squealed as I hung the next right turn.

And then the next.

And then the next.

"Dude," TJ said as we sat pointed at the school parking lot.

"Wanna go in?"

TJ's eyes flared, disjointed in space, before me, like the Cheshire cat. Her grin sprouted like a serrated blade.

## Chapter Twenty-Six

B aking bread.
   Sour milk.

Pine Sol.

The principal's Old Spice cologne.

The smells caressed our souls the moment we cracked the double doors. The halls lay quiet, but the lights were on. The floors gleamed, newly polished. We moved slowly, as if walking into a wall of water, down the long row of lockers, past the cafeteria where stout women in hairnets bustled to and fro behind that stainless steel trough we'd spent countless days sliding by with our plastic trays of processed pizza, pudding, celery sticks, and milk cartons.

TJ moved to the edge of an adjacent wall and peered further down the hall as if we were sneaking around without a pass. She covered her mouth, her eyes wide, and signaled for me to join her.

Class was in session. Concert band. Ms. Van Laar was teaching it. *Impossible.*

I stuttered a whisper, "Sh-she's dead though."

I know this day. I know this day.

"We gotta get out of here," I said.

TJ shook her head, searching my eyes. "Let it wash over you, Jane. There's no running from this one."

The bell rang with that awful fire department clatter I hadn't heard in years. We stood back to back as students pushed by us. I knew them all. Jaylene, Roy, Paul. Oh, Paul, with a full head of feathered brown hair. And Lincoln with a bullshit mustache looking like moth antenna on his lip, shuffling by with baggy jeans and chancing a look at me. I smiled politely despite myself.

Maybe we were indeed dead. Maybe the buck had killed us, or we'd already crashed on our way here, or the Armillaria's rhizomorphs had somehow absorbed us via a fine white webbing like it had that squirrel, sorting our memories and preparing to binge-watch them like a low-budget Netflix series.

Paul stopped next to me. "What's up with you? You look like you just saw Hannibal Lecter. Hey, are we still on for tonight at the Donzerly Light? Gary's gonna help us wrangle Lincoln."

"So, you *can* see me then?" I reached out and brushed my hand across his sweet face, which was bristling with a young beard and dried zits.

He laughed and nodded slowly.

"I know this day, Paul," I said. "And trust me, you should study mushrooms."

TJ slapped her forehead, dragging her hand down her face.

"You're really losing it," Paul said, embarrassed of and for me. "I'm serious, Jane." He met up with Brian Milhouse and they bounded toward the doors where many of the seniors ate lunch in the parking lot while leaning on the hoods of their cars.

I turned to TJ. Her face was smooth too, supple (that was another word we'd hated) and unlined, her hair fluffy and directionless, and she was wearing acid-washed … well, everything. On her feet were a pair of chunky white Skechers, untied of course.

"Oh, wow," she said. "Just wow. You look ridiculous in that Cosby sweater."

"How are we *both* seeing this?"

"I think you're in my dream."

"No, because I'm definitely feeling this." I glanced down at the hideous patterned sweater that was stringy between my fingertips. "You're in mine, Teej."

"I'm not going to argue with you about it. Let's get lunch. Oh, I love those rolls. Remember? With the butter on top?"

I could see them. Taste them. Spongy and dense, but not too dense. Slightly moist. Soft air chambers inside when you pulled them apart; that's where the salty butter melted into. Air chambers left by the off-gassing of ravenous yeast. Yeast from decades gone by. An old starter jar of it carried here from overseas by the English lunch lady who married an American because he looked so dashing in uniform. The one who took her innocence and plopped her down in the middle of nowhere—

*Wait. Yeast. Fungus. It's always there. It's always—*

"I'm stealing three this time," TJ said. "What have I got to lose?"

We went with it as best as one can when fully reliving the past. I had never tripped this far off the beaten path. To my knowledge, this level of hallucination wasn't even possible on mushrooms—on anything. It had to be a hyper-realistic dream. I remembered this very day—one of the last before graduation. I knew what was going to happen next and I knew I was powerless to change it, like trying not to nod your head to a really good song. All the things we had just said, what we were about to say, we had said two decades before and I remember at the time we had been late to school, coming down from a trip the night before, and thought we were losing our hold on reality then too. One of those déjà vu moments you have when you're young and your brain is—

Growing. Branching out from the apex.

We stood in line behind some freshmen and leaned on cool wall tiles, tiles I used to trace my finger over because none of us had mobile phones to stare at. I could not shake the tinnitus that had invaded my ears in The Thicket. It was a tiny tuning fork constantly hovering and vibrating in my head, a bow lightly pulled across a fiddle.

TJ spoke to a cute baby dyke she'd had an eye on that year, "Hey, you know what synchronicity is?"

I tried to tune out, but that old embarrassment came back to stand there, front and center. Ketchum had been even less of a gay mecca in the 90s. And after Evie's disappearance, young TJ had grown more brazen, as if she didn't care what anyone thought anymore.

The girl glanced up innocently. "A clothing pattern?"

"That's Simplicity, dorkwad. No, it's when two things happen at once that are related. It's like mystical and stuff."

I cringed. The girl turned to her friend and they giggled incredulously at us.

"Whatever." TJ shrugged and turned back to me. "Ooh, do you think our lunch accounts work?"

"Of course," I said. "If my hair looks as terrible as I suspect, then our money's good here."

Gary Brown galloped by, lean and handsome, no paunch in sight, his hair styled short in back with long floppy bangs.

He sidled up to Lincoln at the head of the line and slapped him on the back.

"Yo, Logs!"

One of the kids yelped. "Hey! No cutting!"

Gary shot the kid a look and the boy turned his eyes down.

Lincoln blocked the door into the kitchen, refusing to acknowledge his classmate. He was taller than Gary, though not as muscular. There was a time when he used to stand up to the bullies. That would end soon. He shuffled from foot to foot, humming a quiet song, hands cracking knuckles at his side.

Gary hit Lincoln's back harder this time—with a fist, so that we could all hear the hollow thump of it in his lungs. "I said, *hey buddy*!" It was sure to leave an ugly bruise.

Lincoln winced. "Hey," he said, back hunched, but he held his ground, refusing entry.

Gary leapt forward, sweeping one of Lincoln's arms behind him and bent it upward.

Lincoln yelped and stood on his tiptoes. The kids in line all took a step back like teetering dominoes. The lunch ladies looked up from their steaming trays, mouths agape.

"Stop!" I yelled out. I couldn't control myself. TJ raised an eyebrow.

Gary looked at me—everyone did—and he let Lincoln's arm drop.

Lincoln turned to me then and I saw it. *The beginning.* His flat smile slightly turned up at the edges. His eyes pouring into me. He let Gary shove him aside and get in front.

Gary pointed at the back of the line. "That's for fucking with me."

"What?" Lincoln said and tried to laugh. It came out an awkward honk.

Gary cocked his head and blocked the door. He nodded to the back of the room. When Lincoln didn't move, Gary jumped at him, feinting.

Lincoln flinched half-heartedly. He sighed and slouched toward the end of the line that snaked out of the cafeteria.

"God, you're such a pussy." Gary laughed.

Lincoln shuffled by us, his frayed jeans dragging on the floor.

"There's room here," I called after him.

TJ shook her head at me. I shrugged; she knew I couldn't help it.

"Thanks," he said, and under his breath, "Lady Jane."

"You're right," TJ whispered to me, her voice an echo of

another time. "We've got to get out of here. I bet if we eat something in the synchronicity, we'll get stuck here." She peeled off the wall and walked slowly, inexorably for the stairs up to the first floor. I had no choice but to follow.

"But wouldn't you like to relive a few things?" I winced at the migraine forming behind my eyes, vision rippling like waves of heat. "Fix a few things? I could tell Lincoln I'm never going to love him."

"You won't get to." TJ trudged up the steps. "We'll only make the same mistakes. Besides, we leave, remember?"

"True. And we get deten—" I halted.

"I missed you in second hour, Miss Render."

At the top of the stairs stood Ms. Van Laar, dressed in her favorite nature colors—tight green skirt, clay heels, rust turtleneck. And down her chest draped the necklace—an amulet more like—with its S-shape and orbiting discs.

"Where have you been?" Her voice seemed to come from all sides of us. "Do you know where you're going?"

My stare followed the silver chain up her bosom and into her face where the corner of her mouth turned up. Her once hazel eyes now gleamed as black and shiny as the dots on the mushroom caps we'd just eaten. And then another eye blinked open on her forehead. Another on her cheekbone.

I began to moan, one of my classic groans warbling up my throat, and bolted around the corner and down the hall, weaving upstream through cliques of students, past the row of lockers, and toward the double doors glowing with warm sunlight. TJ's sneakers smacked the marble floors alongside me.

TJ grunted as we ran. "Epic. Fucking epic."

I banged open the doors as Ms. Van Laar's voice boomed out, splashing along the walls behind us. "Did you find Evie yet?" she called. "Did you find her? Or did she find you?"

TJ hesitated, "Wha—"

"No! Come on, Teej. Don't listen to it. We need to get out of here."

Outside, a crowd of townspeople had gathered, blocking our route to the car.

My headache screeched like antlers across sheet metal as we threaded our way past everyone.

We were no longer in the gravel parking lot of the school, but the asphalt lot behind the police station. A black felt-covered podium stood next to our car—a car which was now shiny and showroom-new, the waxed silver no longer dull and oxidized, the metal flake in the paint alive with speckled brilliance.

"There you are!" TJ's mom called out to us. Ellen Render wore a butter-yellow dress that lit her young face and sent a pang of nostalgia through me. She grabbed TJ's hand and dragged her next to the podium where the new sheriff was speaking. His face seemed familiar. I'd seen it older. Recently. His uniform stretched tight across his broad chest, straining the snaps. God, fucking snaps.

"It's not much," he said, "but we all thought it was the least we could do."

I looked around at the smiling crowd, then at TJ, who shook her head at me.

The sheriff presented Ellen with a wood and brass

plaque, as well as a familiar set of keys, which glittered in the sun.

Mouth gaping, I patted my pockets. The rental keys were gone.

TJ's face matched my alarm.

Ellen stepped up to the podium and bent the gooseneck microphone down.

"I just want to say how grateful we are to each and every one of you. Well, y'all, this is really going to help the two of us." She squeezed TJ to her side. "Thank you so very much for the love you've shown."

She turned to TJ, whispering something at her. TJ didn't move. Ellen nudged her with an elbow this time.

TJ reached out and brusquely shook the new sheriff's hand. This revealed the revolver at his side. I looked to his face again. Marvin. The man who'd been sitting in the middle of the road that first morning in front of the diner.

Ellen's voice grew quivery and choked on tearful happiness. "You've all just shown us so much love. So, so much."

The crowd clapped and kept clapping as they all turned toward me. Each face held seven black gumdrop eyes. My spine straightened and my neck craned backward.

Ellen stepped away from TJ, the new sheriff, and the podium. She tilted her head at me, and her eyes went gray and filmy, her shoulders slumping. Rhizomorphs snaked in forks down her shriveling neck.

"So much love, Janey. It's coming out our ears." Her sobbing laughter went flat and papery. "It's comin' out your ears too. Can't you hear it?"

"Oh, she can hear it," said Marvin the sheriff. "She's the one. It comes from her."

The air erupted in the Mandelbrot color I'd seen earlier —roiling over itself, and expanding in a strobing cauliflower effect. With the now familiar rumble and ping, time slowed as it had when we first entered the school, as if encased in syrup, amber syrup, the color of blood plasma.

The smiling crowd kept clapping, hands slack and slow.

TJ nodded once at me, then leapt. Her arm arced across the air in a gradual, protracted effort to grab the keys from her mother. She gritted her teeth as if it were the hardest thing she'd ever pushed through.

I leapt too, plodding as if walking the floor of a swimming pool. All of it—the yank of the car door, the strain of our muscles, the tumble inside, the click and turn of the key—an unbearably long escape under the multitude of eyes.

*We're coming out your ears, Jane.*

The door latched shut.

Dusk fell outside our honking car.

I let go of my death grip on the steering wheel and the horn fell silent.

Our eyes adjusted.

We were sitting by the Donzerly Light.

"Oh my God. We never left." TJ burst out laughing. She looked down at her clothes—the modern hoodie, jeans, Vans. She patted her hair and sighed in relief.

I sat wincing, my headache subsiding, pulling at the strands of my curls, untangling them again. Even the strands that didn't need it.

"I think we leveled up," TJ said and cracked the window.

On the dash, something flickered at the corner of my eye.

"Stop!" I yelled.

"Why? It's hot in here."

"Look at the box."

The clear Tupperware sat empty.

"Roll it up," I said, still staring at the box.

She did.

The box filled again with quivering sausage.

She cracked it once more and the tubes of meat disappeared.

In the gulley, the Donzerly Light began powering up, the foxfire at the base of the forest glowing too.

"Roll it up! And keep it up!"

The sausages knit back into place.

"Outside is the past," TJ said, matter-of-factly.

"*Okaaay.* What do we do?"

"Lock the doors."

I pressed the button and the latches engaged with a clunk.

"Should we try to leave again?" I asked, hands still searching for new hair strands to untangle.

"Are we sober?"

"Not sure what that means anymore." Down the access road, the lights of a car approached. Multiple cars. "Cops would be a welcome addition," I said.

"Not really," TJ murmured.

The lead car was Gary Brown's Mustang. Following it: Paul's Duster and Brian's Fiero.

"Don't get out," I ordered.

"No way. Not this time."

"And don't roll down the windows."

We wouldn't need to; it would play out before us like a drive-in movie…

## Chapter Twenty-Seven

G ary Brown stumbles out of the Mustang, crunches the beer can in his fist, and hurls it into the brush. His girlfriend, Lori, rolls out the passenger side. He holds his keys high in the air and jangles them in front of the back window.

"You best get out here, or we'll drag you out in pieces!"

Paul McKenna pulls his Duster alongside the Mustang at the side road, which leads down to the light. Brian's Fiero pulls up next to the Duster.

Jane and TJ Render clamber out of the Duster and run laughing toward the light. It has powered up to full and casts its rays through the foggy Thicket like amber swords.

The girls start singing, "Oh say can you bleed, by The Donzerly Light?"

The guys sing too, between huffing and yanking at the boy in the back of the Mustang.

—*How so loudly we wailed, as our jugular lay gleaming*—

"Ah, don't hurt him," Jane says.

"Come on, Linc," Paul says. "Now's your chance to get revenge, buddy!"

—*Whose broad beams and bright core broke the blackening night*—

As Paul and Brian work on extracting Lincoln, Gary stalks to his trunk, opens it, and pulls out a two-handed axe.

—*O'er the whimpers of girls and the boys who lay screaming*—

"Come on, Logs. Now you can chop it down. For Jacob."

—*And the quake broke our hearts, vessels bursting apart*—

"I don't want to!" Lincoln's voice breaks boyishly and then booms low again. "It b-burns," he screeches. "It's on fire, Gary! Knock it off. Stop!"

—*Gave proof to the rites that Cthulhu was still there*—

"Come on, you chicken shit," Gary mutters. He sets the axe down and grabs Lincoln's leg.

—*Oy vey, does that many-suckered tentacle yet wave*—

Lincoln's baggy jeans come off in a tug and the three boys fall to the pavement. The girls giggle hysterically through the last of the song.

—*O'er the land of old gods and the home of the naaave*—

Gary climbs into the car and pummels at Lincoln until he screams and pleads.

Jane's smile drops. "Stop, Gary. Please! Stop!"

"Dude!" Paul yelps. "Just grab him."

Gary draws him out with a headlock, while Paul and Brian grab Lincoln's arms. They drag him, bruised and scuttling in his briefs, down the hill to face the light.

"Face it for your brother," Paul says. "For Evie. For Roy."

"Face it," Gary says. He yanks Lincoln's head up by the hair. "Face. Your. Fear."

Lincoln's eyes remain tightly shut. His hands cup the front of his underwear; his voice is a percussive grunt: "My future is fire, the fire of The Donzerly Light! My future is fire, the fire of The Donzerly—"

"Look at him," Jane mutters. "You're his fear."

Paul shakes his head at his girlfriend. "You don't understand men. This is how it works."

"I call bullshit," TJ states matter-of-factly.

Paul ignores them, turns back to their classmate. "Listen, Lincoln. Just take a whack at it. I promise it will make you feel better."

"Yeah," Brian says. He gallops back to the cars to retrieve the axe. "Come on, Linc. Go for it." He proudly presents it to Lincoln with upturned palms, as if it is Excalibur.

Lincoln takes the axe and it droops to the ground. "I don't want to. It's evil. I won't even leave a mark, don't you see?" he sobs, shivering. "It will kill me, like it did Jacob. *It will take all of us!*"

"You big baby. What?" Gary says, "You gonna make some logs now? It's just a fucking light pole."

Lincoln raises the axe and jumps at Gary. He growls, eyes wild and rolling, teeth bared.

Gary hops backward. "Jesus fucking Christ! Watch it with that thing. You're as crazy as your brother, you know that?" He dances around, faster than Lincoln.

Lincoln stalks after him, crying. "You shut up. I will kill you if you don't shut up."

Gary laughs and circles around him. "You'll always be a pussy whether I shut up or not." He grabs the back of Lincoln's briefs, yanks them to the ground, and leaps away.

The light goes out—

—Screams pierce the thick night air. All is dark save for the faint splash of Milky Way above and the muted foxfire below. The kids scatter, eyes still adjusting, and stumble up the hill toward the cars. Branches snap all around. From far off, the howl and rumble of a freight train grow as it crosses the river trestle.

And then comes the laughter, the jubilant giggles of a young girl. Faint at first and then taunting them from all directions.

"Evie," TJ whispers.

Up the road, inside the car parked by the turnaround, something glows. Two pale orange orbs made of filaments, one brighter than the other, both tethered to each other via delicate threads, hover just above the seats.

Lori screams. "What the fuck is that thing?"

"It's just a trick of the light," Gary says, convincing himself. "A trick of the light. The dashboard maybe."

The Donzerly blazes back on and they all yelp, clutching for each other.

"Did you hear her?" TJ says desperately. "Did you?"

Jane nods and looks around. "Where's Lincoln?"

The boy and the axe are gone.

"Evie!" TJ yells. "Evie?"

"It was just your imagination!" Paul yells. "Where the fuck is Lincoln?"

They search the edge of The Thicket, unwilling to enter it. They check their cars. Gary and Lori peer into the abandoned sedan parked in the circle drive.

"See, there's nothing in there," Gary says. "Just a trick of the light."

"I could swear though," she says.

"Fuck," Brian mutters at Paul. Paul shakes his head.

Gary smacks lips, stumbling a bit. "Eh, he'll turn up. Come on, babe." He and Lori walk hand in hand back to his Mustang.

"What were you guys thinking?" Jane says.

"It was worth a try," Paul says with a grumble. "You sure didn't mind tagging along."

"Did you hear him? Lincoln saw his future. Just like Roy. Just like Roy!"

Lori gets in the Mustang, slams the door, and holds herself.

"Oh, come on, Jane," Gary says. "We can't help it if he's a momma's boy. He needs to buck up and grow some balls. Eh, he's probably just out there staring at you and choking the chicken."

Jane leers back at him. "You suck, Gary."

"Listen, Janey," Brian says, "I saw my future too. It's fine. It's all good."

"But Roy—"

"Fuck Roy." Brian turns away, hooks thumbs in his jeans, and kicks at the rocks. "I mean, I loved him. But Roy was a putz. A coward. I saw how I'm going out and I'm okay with it. We all gotta die sometime." He glowers up at the stars as if to spite the wishes they made. "And I'm here to make sure I get everything I want in the meantime."

"Hell, yeah," Gary shouts.

With TJ still wandering the perimeter, Jane stands there, pleading, quivering. "Paul?"

"Let it go," Paul says. "Lincoln would have gone along with it if you weren't undermining the whole thing." He raises an eyebrow. "You're leading him on."

Jane's glare narrows. Gary makes a girlish squeal and laughs.

"I told you not to involve Gary," she says with a hiss. "He doesn't understand this place."

Gary balks and opens his car door. "You're insane."

"It was all in Lincoln's head," Paul says. He pokes a finger at her brow. "It's all in your head too, Jane. All of it."

TJ calls from the brush. "We *are* our heads."

"You know what?" Jane pushes at him. "We are done!"

Paul looks around at his friends and back to her. "Fine by me. Hang with *TJ* for the rest of your life. See where that gets you." He gets in his Duster, slams the door, and takes off.

TJ returns from the brush, "I am getting the fuck out of this shitty town and never looking back." Her eyes still search the woods. But not for Lincoln.

"Me too," Brian says.

"Eh, you're *all* a bunch of Lincoln Logs," Gary laughs from his car window. He fires up the Mustang and peels out, spraying pebbles at their feet.

Jane crosses her arms. "We can't just leave him out there in his underwear. Lincoln!"

"Welp, he's got an axe." Brian shrugs. "And he only lives a few miles away. He'll be fine. Come on, Jane."

The Render girls get in Brian's Fiero and it pulls away too.

In The Thicket, Evie's laughter bounces from tree to tree, following them out.

## Chapter Twenty-Eight

### Present Day

I came to in the gray dawn—still in the car, still at the Donzerly Light—to the sound of TJ attempting to cry in a dry heaving gasp. I had never seen her shed tears before and she was just on the verge, which was frustrating her even more. She sat dressed in her hoodie, her face thirty-seven years old. And I was in my athleisurewear again. I rolled down the windows to get us some fresh air. The moldering sausage in the Tupperware remained intact.

Outside, no laughter, no wind, no sound at all.

TJ drew on her vape cigarette and wiped her eyes with the meat of her palms, which came up dry.

My throat closed off. How had I forgotten about the filament beings? And Evie's laugh? Clever Evie, whom the boys and I had let ride off into The Thicket alone to cross the train trestle into Ketchum. Evie, who screamed at the drop of a hat—so much that we had grown to ignore it.

Evie, who never made it to the other side of the trestle. Evie, who never turned up in the river either. Evie whom we all adored.

We'd driven out there to the light, Lincoln in tow, to exorcise his ghosts and maybe even wish Evie back into the world. Ignorant, impulsive children.

I swept crumbs from my eyes. At least we were finally sober.

"Maybe she ran away," TJ said, her voice a quiet rasp.

"She had to have been kidnapped. Evie wasn't in the mood to run away. She had no reason to."

"She was gay, Jane. Trust me. And my dad had messed with her too. Remember?"

"But she wasn't depressed, Teej. Tens of thousands of kids go missing every year with no explanation. Most of them are never found."

The Thicket stood still and silent. More than usual. Where was the distant road noise? Insects? Birds? Wind through the leaves? Nothing made a sound. It was as if we were in a vacuum. Maybe we still weren't out of the place we'd come from.

"Lincoln?" she ventured. "He could have got her. What if she was trying to tell us something that night?"

I half shrugged. The answer lay around a foggy corner.

"Lincoln was the only person we know unstable enough to have done it."

I knew what she was thinking: *Since Dad was already dead*.

"No... We all saw him walk home the night she

disappeared. He would have to have doubled back and circled around us."

TJ gave a half-hearted nod and stared out the window.

"It was us in that car," I whispered. "That strange tangle of light. It was—*is*—us."

Another obligatory nod, a glint from the corner of her eye.

The Thicket suddenly came to life with the warble of birds, the hiss of wind through the needles, the light scent of pine on the breeze. Below the front seat, my iPhone purred and we both jumped. It kept purring as my hand scrabbled around for it and fished it up.

PAUL: The dots hold rod and cone cells!

PAUL: Photoreceptors!

PAUL: Amazing

PAUL: Heading back there tomorrow

PAUL: Why aren't u answering?

PAUL: Calling cops if u don't answer

PAUL: Police picked up Lincoln

PAUL: Where r u? We r worried

PAUL: JANE!!

I didn't want to answer, still mad at him for what we had just witnessed from so long ago. The back of my throat, down to my chest, ached with a raw sadness.

But we'd been kids. Just kids.

JANE: Fine. Back now.

PAUL: U SCARED ME SHITLESS!

PAUL: THOT LINCOLN NABBED YOU!

JANE: What are rod and cone cells?

JANE: On the mushroom?

JANE: Please tell me they're not poisonous

PAUL: No Jane, they're photoreceptors

PAUL: For SIGHT

JANE: The dots. Seriously?

PAUL: Unless I've crossed slides with zoology somehow

PAUL: They may be able to see light and dark

PAUL: And with multiple dots

PAUL: Could be compound, like flies see

JANE: Or spiders?

PAUL: That's different, but maybe

PAUL: Keeping under wraps for now

PAUL: Till I can get control of this

PAUL: Otherwise Ketchum will be inundated

JANE: You're coming today?

PAUL: 4pm sharp

TJ yawned wide and stretched. "Should we check back into the motel? Get a nap?"

"Let's check with the police on Lincoln first. I want to see if they found—"

"We're never gonna get that box back, Jane," TJ said, rolling her eyes. "Just let him have it."

Of all the things in that box, I wanted to get that diary back. It wasn't even mine. But a voice deep inside, a voice all around me, told me we desperately needed it. I couldn't explain why, and I knew somehow I shouldn't explain why.

Not yet. My mind was too thick to understand it at the time, but I sensed Lincoln had stolen the keys to this bizarre week.

"It's the principle of the thing." I started the car. The low hum of it seemed normal again, no longer an alien contraption. Yep, we were sober. "I get that Lincoln's had it hard. Lots of bad things happen to kids." I yanked the gear into drive. "It doesn't mean he gets to act this way forever."

TJ stared over at me again, with that proud, wistful look.

"I'm down for whatever you need to do."

## Chapter Twenty-Nine

Hopping mad, his mother used to say. *Your father is hopping mad today, so don't cross him.* Back in the 90s, when Evie Weiss disappeared, his father had been that special breed of furious just after picking Lincoln up from the police station. It was the last time Byron struck his growing son, resulting in a purple stormcloud around the boy's right eye.

Today there was no one left to pick Lincoln up, or punch him out. He looked around at his cell and scoffed. They still hadn't painted the walls.

"What do you think happened to her, Paul?" the quieter of the officers asked.

The boy's voice quavered, "Maybe she got hit by a train?"

"Yeah," Brian chimed in. "Like maybe she got stuck on the front and then fell off some other place."

The officer nodded, slowly at first, then squinted. "Shouldn't someone have found her by the tracks down the line? Why'd she leave her bike a half mile back on the path?"

"The Thicket killed her," Lincoln had offered, in a monotone.

The officers and other boys ignored him.

"What the hell were you doing out there that late on a weeknight!" The older officer slammed his hand on the bare metal table. His bald head gleamed pink under the harsh fluorescent lighting.

Paul gulped. "Just playing hide and go seek."

The angry officer rolled his eyes at the quieter one and lit a Marlboro.

"Really!" Brian said. "Just Ghost in the Graveyard."

"No hanky-panky? Come on, I remember how it was at your age."

The boys looked at one another. Tears ran down Roy's face. Paul and Brian said nothing.

"We played Spin the Bottle," Lincoln offered.

Brian glowered at him.

Instead of a reward for his honesty, the police let the other boys go and kept Lincoln the entire day. Of course, he gave them no help with Evie. He had no idea what specifically had happened to the girl. Well, he did. But they weren't buying literal ghosts in the graveyard.

Since then, every time someone turned up dead or disappeared in Rand County, a cop arrived at the farm. Each time, Lincoln expected them to thrust a photo of the hitchhiker into his face. But no one ever looked for her. She belonged to no one. And the new deputy swore if Lincoln told them his tinfoil hat theories about The Thicket one more time, they'd find a judge who would force him into a psych hospital.

Lincoln knew very well they couldn't. But this time he also couldn't deny he'd been emailing Jane Render and for how many years he'd been doing it. He could imagine how it looked in their dimwitted minds. They'd never understand his destiny.

He reckoned this little stay was God's payback for the hitchhiker. It hadn't been his fault, but he hadn't been a gentleman either.

But this time when he thought about that night, something was lacking. He simply didn't care anymore. He was too angry. If Jane had only come around to things, none of this would have happened. That hitchhiker had been likely to have a heart attack with or without him. She hadn't felt what happened next. So, yes, he hadn't been above board about things, hadn't taken her to the hospital, had undone those shorts instead, and run a hand up her shirt. Had left his DNA on her.

*There's still time. Give her to us.*

This night in a cinderblock jail cell (decorated with a single bunk and stainless-steel toilet) had been a time of much-needed reflection. It brought everything into gleaming focus.

Lincoln's inner thighs banged together, slacks flapping, while he sat on the bunk. As his lawyer finalized the paperwork at the front desk, he rummaged around in his brain for why Jane would do this to the man she was meant to be with. He would go to her now, demand an answer, and if it was the wrong one—well, there could not be a wrong one. Their time had come.

This must be what it was like when couples had their first fight. He'd built up a little resentment for her. Their making-up would be passionate. He knew his way around a woman now.

Though bearing false witness was yet another sin, he'd had to do it to get out of here. He had to tell them it was only a prank. Only symbolic, the mention of the gun, seeing what TJ meant to Jane Render. Didn't they see that too? Jane was disturbed. Much more than he could ever be. They'd both met desolation head on. He was only trying to help her through it, if perhaps worded a bit poorly.

He palpated the impressive knot on his forehead left by the deputies' rough handling of him at his desk. He considered pressing charges for police brutality and then considered just how far that would get him. He would squeeze the knot whenever he needed a reminder.

Truthfully, he was sick of having to navigate this town and its citizens. They wouldn't deserve his sacrifice. None of them were kind to him. Never had been. His farm helped feed the world and this was the thanks he got. No one had shown him the slightest bit of respect in thirty odd years. Save for one person. The woman who was fighting her love for him tooth and nail, fighting their love so hard she had chosen to lock him away. It had to be tearing her up inside to have done it to him. She feared losing herself in him. She feared losing TJ and all the earthly gains she'd made on this sick, sick planet.

He had to be brave now.

No more mumbling.

No more hiding.

Same plan. New schedule.

Jane would go back to Chicago soon and it would be too late. For everyone.

## Chapter Thirty

"What do you wanna bet he's got Mother mummified in the attic?" TJ squinted up at the white paint peeling off the boarded-up farmhouse.

"Um, that is not what you say before breaking in." The migraine had subsided, but my brain was as cloudy as a chalkboard that had been erased too many times. We had no way of knowing how many hours of actual sleep we'd gotten the night before.

We'd never get a second chance to do this. The police had said they could not find the shoebox, nor did Lincoln admit to having it. We were careful not to make a big deal of it. They told us he was talking with his lawyer and they would have an update soon if we wanted to stick around. I gave them my phone number and asked them to text me.

TJ and I had casually sauntered out, then high-tailed it to our car.

We parked a half-mile down the blacktop from the Metzger farm, behind a storage shed that must also be

Lincoln's but hadn't seen use in many years. For cover, we hiked a path misted with fern fronds that abutted The Thicket. Ever since our Armillaria trip, I now feared the forest less than I did the high school or police station, but I kept my distance from the occasional bit of deadfall, where I suspected we were being watched by an uneven number of eyes.

We didn't bother with Lincoln's ranch house, the one the cops had done a cursory sweep of. I knew from his emails this old house was the one he was prepping for our life together.

Our life together.

We traipsed around the property, looking for a way in, moving quickly when we were in view of the blacktop. All along the stone foundation, rhizomorphs had made inroads in the cracks. The Armillaria was watching Lincoln as well.

The front door was boarded up, same as the windows. The back door was not. The screen door opened freely but the old copper knob of the back door refused us. Of course it did. There was a time when people in small towns used to leave their back doors unlocked but that was another century.

"Break the glass," TJ said.

I mulled it over, forehead against the doorframe, my eyes yearning to stay shut for a while. It was hard to think; our brains had been ridden hard and put away wet. My mind no longer seemed solitary, as if wheels turned without me and I couldn't keep up. "If we do that, and he can prove it was us, I have a lot less grounds to fight him."

"Oh, come on."

"No, Teej. We have to get in and get out. He may figure out we were here, but the police can't. I can deal with him thinking I wanna be here, but if the police think it too, I'm screwed."

TJ stomped off.

I followed. "Just … just think."

We stopped at the bulkhead where the double cellar doors lay padlocked with a thick chain.

"Hold up, Lady Jane."

"Do *not* call me that."

"It does have a certain ring to it." TJ knelt beside the bulkhead. She grabbed the combination lock and shook it at me. "What do you wanna guess is the most important number in his life?"

"Do it!"

She tried my birthday month and day: 0708.

Nope.

Then with the year: 7880.

The U-bar slid from the chamber. TJ glinted at me.

I took a deep breath. We were really doing this. Before, I'd counted on the impossibility of it. That we'd given it a try and could go home saying we'd done our best. But now, with the creak of the cellar doors opening wide, I realized we were only at the beginning.

"Turn on your phone light," TJ said as she pulled the doors wide, "we gotta close them or someone might see."

We brought the lock and chain in with us and set them on the steep stairs in case someone noticed them lying on the ground and decided to secure the doors behind us.

The moldering stink of a century-old basement clung to

our noses, and under it lurked the faint anise scent of the Armillaria. I'd read enough crime manuscripts to know we shouldn't be entering a cellar bulkhead and yet here we were and there we went. We shut out the morning skies and carefully climbed down the stairs, scanning with my phone light for whatever goat-man or booby trap lay in wait.

The only thing moving was a two-inch long centipede on a crossbeam, normally enough to pull a yelp out of me, but today it fascinated my fungi-addled mind. I peered at it. It reminded me of the multi-legged creatures in my dream the night TJ gave me mushroom-laced tea. *Trilobites!* It flicked its feelers and shot out of sight.

"What the hell are you doing?" TJ said. "Come on."

We crept down the passageway. The ceiling was low with old pipes running above us. To the left, a wall of crumbling stone lined with crates of Walmart-branded water bottles and towers of televangelist Jim Bakker's survival food buckets. To the right, a wall constructed of old wooden slats held two doors. Rhizomorphs from The Thicket had delved their way into the cracks of the stone wall and between the wooden slats.

The first door on our right was labeled: 319.

My jaw jutted. We eyed each other. My apartment number.

The knob turned, but the door wouldn't budge. It felt like it was bolted from the inside.

We ventured on. At the end of the passageway stood a white chest-style freezer and an old claw-foot bathtub. Above the freezer, a small window allowed daylight in—enough to conserve the battery on my phone. I turned the phone off and tucked it in my jeans pocket. To the left were stairs up to the house. And to the right, the second door.

Dust covered the freezer lid, except near the handle.

"Open it," TJ said with a nod.

I took a deep breath, slowly let it out, and raised the lid.

Cuts of meat lay inside, along with a deer leg wrapped in plastic. We looked to the tub, which had a pink ring around it, and understood its purpose.

As per usual, TJ murmured exactly what I was trying not to think. "Sure don't wanna end up field-dressed in the bathtub like that deer we hit. So let's get in and out."

I shook my head and gave the door next to the freezer a push. It creaked open to reveal a furnished room. Along one wall sat a teal-green mid-century couch, one of those knitted comforters with the colorful squares draped along the back of it. On it rested my Skechers shoebox. Next to the couch, a retro-modern floor lamp that looked straight out of *Mad Men* except for the brown burn in its white shade. On the other side of the couch stood a small drum kit.

Mushrooms fruited all along the concrete floor, where it met the crumbling foundation.

There was an antique round light switch on the wall, with cloth-covered wiring running up the framework and into the exposed beams. I switched it on, and a single bulb overhead lit the room. To our right sat a computer desk with a wide monitor and large hard drive. The lights of a high-speed router flickered. Beyond the desk, on the far wall, stood a bi-fold door for what I assumed was a closet.

TJ gasped at the desk area. "Shee-ut."

Along the wall above the desk, our faces stared back at

us, from multiple locations. Poster-sized printouts, framed photos, Polaroids, 3 x 5s, press clippings.

"What the actual fuck," she said.

"We shouldn't be surprised." I moved trancelike toward it.

"Is that—? Is that your crotch?"

"Oh my God, he upskirted me! He got close enough to upskirt me." I reached out for the photos.

"Wait!" TJ said. "Don't touch the evidence. Take a picture."

"Good point." I opened my phone and tapped the video record button.

"We are in Lincoln Metzger's basement. These are photos he's taken of me without my permission. What the hell is *that*?" I grimaced at a silver tube with a pink vulva on one end.

"Exhibit two." TJ sputtered a laugh. "I believe that there is a fleshlight."

I shuddered at the sex toy and turned the phone toward the couch. "And over there is the box he stole from me."

Above the couch, on a nail, a pair of yellow and blue sneakers with rusty metal spikes hung from their laces.

"Hey, those are my old track sneakers! I thought you stole those. I had to run in a size up and lost that meet."

"Sick fuck." TJ tapped the keyboard of the computer and the monitor came to life. The desktop image was a white tornado against a dark gray sky. In the middle of the screen sat a file titled *LadyJane.avi*.

"Do it." I said, only half paying attention now that a full bottle of oxycodone on the desk had caught my eye.

Instantly the room filled with Whitney Houston blaring, "AND IIII-I-I WILL ALWAYS LOVE YOUUUUU!"

We jumped into the air.

"Shut it off! Shut it off!"

TJ rapidly clicked the volume key to 0. We watched as my history unspooled before us from a baby photo to every class photo I had exchanged with Lincoln as all the children did, and then past high school to photos I didn't know had been taken. Save for vacations out of the country, he had followed me everywhere, caught me on the train, caught me hoarding peanut butter pretzels at Trader Joes, caught me in my bikini on Lake Michigan, caught me peeing in a public bathroom from above.

After it was over, I picked up the pills. The real deal. A fair trade.

"You gotta be careful, Janey. That stuff'll kill you."

I blew a gust. Lectured by TJ of all people. *Swell.* I set them down. And it was strangely easy to let go of them. There was a clarity to my thoughts that I chalked up to adrenaline.

Upstairs, a door slammed. Boots stomped across the old, creaking floors. Dust peppered down from above.

TJ scuttled to the door, turned off the light, and peered out.

"We gotta sleep the computer," I whispered.

"I don't know how to do that on Windows," she spat back.

"Me neither."

And thus we were set to die because we were Mac users.

I clicked to the *Start* menu, which made no sense, but

there it was, a menu within a damn menu. The monitor went black.

I joined her at the door. "He's coming," she mouthed.

We could take him by surprise if we had to. We looked around for anything to use. All we could find were drumsticks. We tried different hand positions, drumming the air. *No!* Stabbing motions. *Maybe?* TJ shrugged. I grimaced. The end of us.

The stairs creaked and then stopped. The door didn't open.

My phone buzzed in my back pocket.

*Shut up! Shut up! Shut up!*

My throat was so dry, I needed to cough. I swallowed it back. TJ hunched, ready to stab eyeballs.

The steps creaked upwards and the clopping around began again above our heads.

"Go," I whispered, and swung the door wide.

"Wait, the box," she hissed.

I ran back and swiped it off the couch.

The stomping came back and the stairs creaked again. Lincoln was shuffling down.

I eased the door shut. *Damn.*

We scuttled quickly backward, drumsticks at the ready. I pulled open the bi-fold doors; we tumbled in and closed them just in time.

The light came on in the first room and sent horizontal beams through the slats. We peered through them at Lincoln as he shuffled past the couch and sat at the desk. I held my chest, willing my heart to slow down; he hadn't noticed the box was missing. He ran fingers through his hair and woke his computer.

An old ballad started playing, tinkling piano notes. One of my mother's favorite songs. Carly Simon. "Nobody Does It Better". Forever ruined, Lincoln joined in with a honking tenor,

> *"Nobody does it better.*
> *Makes me feel sad for the rest."*

He opened his email and typed.

I remotely noticed this closet smelled fresher than the rest of the basement, like eucalyptus, my favorite scent. TJ and I glowered at each other and that's when I saw past her to where we actually were. Though he'd blacked out a basement window, the paint had shrunk in a web-work of cracks, allowing in more light.

This was no closet; it was a bedroom.

*My* bedroom. In Chicago.

It spun before me: the taupe feature wall, fully sheetrocked and painted. Adorned with pictures of my childhood cat, Morrissey, the black and white Diane Arbus photo of twin girls in black dresses, a copy of TJ Render's Lambda Literary Award. And oh, my reading chair, there it sat in the corner, complete with the velour blanket I often curled up in. Looming over it, the mod silver floor lamp that I switched on to read manuscripts and the table beside it for the loose pages. The white coffee mug that read *Drink Me*, full of red fine-point Sharpies.

Beyond that, along the far wall, my queen bed, its chenille bedspread, and decorative pillows. One of them would read *Namastay in Bed* in cross-stitch; I didn't need to check. Next to it, on the bedside table, sat a tall vase of eucalyptus branches.

TJ's mouth went crooked, her lip curling back to bare her gritted teeth. Her eyes rolled wild and twitched with fury. Her fingers curled into claws.

*Oh my God.* She was going to go out there.

As her rage grew, shards of Mandelbrot flickered in my mind and lightning forked across my vision.

My mouth made an equally rabid *NO* shape and I shook my head rapidly. We argued back and forth in silent movie lunacy until we agreed to scrabble on all fours across my faux polar bear rug to the door.

As we passed the bed, TJ stopped.

Someone was sleeping in the bed. A woman.

We backed up along the wall, hoping not to wake her, trying not to shake the contents of the shoebox in my hand. But then I halted. We would need to call the cops, to save her. Should we wake her up?

TJ shook her head rapidly. *What if she screams?* She pointed angrily at the door. We would call for help after we got out.

I crept closer to the bed.

The woman wasn't sleeping. Her eyes stared at the ceiling, her mouth open in a half-smile as if preparing to pay a compliment.

Her teeth were bright white.

Her pale skin was wrinkle-free and without shine but with a few freckles—like I had. Her hair was curly red, like mine, but more primary. Everything about her was like me, but … more vibrant. Perfect. Lifeless.

TJ poked at her face. The woman did not move. I ran fingertips across her soft cheek. And still the same bright-eyed smile: *Hi! You're cute!*

Even in the faint light, we could see that at least it was not a dead woman. It was no woman at all.

I eased back the blanket—*my* blanket.

The doll wore my typical sleep uniform: white T-shirt and blue pajama bottoms, the ones with cats on them. Not exactly like mine, but close enough. Her breasts beneath the shirt did not part and flatten with gravity as mine did. Above the waistband of the pajamas, a black leather belt encircled her torso. I looked to TJ.

TJ bit her lip, held her breath, and pulled open the pajamas.

A leather device encircled her waist with a strap around each thigh, connected to a main strap that ran vertically from her belly button and between her legs, all the way around to the base of her back, I assumed. Four small padlocks held each strap closed.

TJ's and my rage converged. I wanted to leap on him now too. In another time and place, I would be reasonably fine with Lincoln living out his fantasies about me with five and a half feet of silicon, but it's difficult to be reasonable in one's own dollhouse.

The song faded out. A small mercy.

"I hear you, taterbug," Lincoln called from the other room. "Just hold on."

TJ cringed. I covered my gagging mouth.

"Yes, I know," he said. "I want you too, but we need to talk first. I know what you've done."

TJ and I backed slowly to the apartment door and found the bolt.

My eyes crossed as I eased it back and TJ held her cheeks.

We pried the door open.

Lincoln's desk chair creaked and we stopped. His typing resumed and we snuck out, toward the bulkhead stairs and into the dark.

A timer sounded upstairs, ringing and ringing like a fucking bastard klaxon.

We scrambled behind the cellar stairs, opting for a head-in-sand approach—hunched and staring at each other, hearts battering, amongst the spider webs and beneath rusty nails pointing downward. I held the box to my chest like a stolen treasure.

The far door by the window opened. Lincoln came out and opened the freezer.

My phone buzzed again. TJ squinched her face at me. I buried the phone in my bosom.

He dropped the lid and cocked his head.

*Please, please, please—*

Lincoln opened the freezer again, grabbed a cut of meat, and took it upstairs. The timer stopped buzzing.

"If he's in the kitchen, he can see the bulkhead," TJ whispered.

"That window's boarded up," I whispered back. "I think."

So we waited, just in case, adjusting our legs, trying to

slow our ragged breaths.

TJ reached out to a wooden step to steady herself and her hand flew back as if burnt. She shook it out, mouth wide in a silent scream, eyes crossed at me. She showed it to me, revealing a dark hole ringed with blood in the center of her palm. My hand ached in response and I winced for her.

Lincoln galloped back down the stairs, into the room, and slammed the door.

We padded quickly up the bulkhead stairs, grabbed the lock and chain, then opened the double doors. One of them attempted to screech and we glared venom at it. I was tempted to just throw them open and sprint, but we slowly, painfully, eased them shut. We lifted the chain, making sure not to drag it across metal, quietly threaded it back through the handles, laid it down gently and closed the combination lock. We did all of this, not so much to hide our effort, but to stop him from busting out with a *Here's Johnny!*

TJ and I sprinted toward the relative safety of The Thicket, gasping and trading glances over our shoulders.

Pan! Pan! Greek god Pan!

One half goat! The other half man!

At the car we caught our breath, lactic acid climbing our throats like stale milk.

I leaned against the car and gazed up at the blessed sky, thankful to be in the open air.

TJ giggled. "That Jane, she's a real doll, that one!"

"Not funny." But I was chuckling too, happy to be in one piece.

"Gawd, who puts a fucking chastity belt on a sex doll?"

I looked at her incredulously. "I mean, you've bypassed a few other crucial questions."

"What if it's to protect her? You know, historically, they were also used to prevent rape, not just act as a symbol of ownership."

"That's some mental gymnastics he's doing," I said.

"Oh, I'm sure he gets up to all sorts of gymnastics." TJ grimaced. "Jesus. I'm just glad she wasn't a dead woman."

I walked around to the back of the car. "I think we better stay in another town tonight, Teej. Watch our backs."

"Affirmative." TJ removed the diary from the shoebox, and tossed the rest in the trunk. "Ouch. Ooh, look, I'm half Jesus." She raised her wounded hand in supplication and fluttered her eyes at the sky. In the center of her palm the nail puncture had grown pink and oozed blood.

"Ever classy." My phone buzzed. "Damn, I forgot about Paul."

We slid into the car and locked the doors.

TJ gave the Tupperware a little pat. "Good old sausage-clock."

I hummed a pathetic laugh at the inanity of it.

As I pulled the sedan onto the road, I released a long, weary sigh. "I really don't want to go back in."

"The Thicket?"

"Yeah, I just want a shower, a big meal, and I want to sleep. I need to sleep."

TJ leaned her head against the window and cracked open the diary. "Lincoln's going to be so pissed when he sees this is gone."

I glanced into the rear-view window. No white trucks in

sight. "Maybe we should just head for Florida. Christ, we have more than enough material."

TJ went silent for a while, and then, "Are you that scared of it?"

"The Thicket?" I thought about it. "Shouldn't we be?"

"I'm not." As TJ scanned the diary, she flicked glances at me. "I think there's something amazing in there, in that fungus. And Paul is about to figure it out. Don't you want to be there when he does? We may never get another chance."

I growled as I pulled the car once more into the Casey's General Store. "Why are you never afraid of anything?"

"Not the way I was made, I guess." TJ closed the diary. Her gray eyes searched mine and she licked her lips. "This is yours."

## Chapter Thirty-One

"**K**eep an eye out for Lincoln, okay?"

I skimmed the diary and crammed dry wads of poppyseed muffin into my face, chasing it with black coffee. TJ stared straight out the windshield. The occasional customer pulled into the Casey's to gas up at the pumps, then sped off down the county road. Only one white truck drove past, but it had a construction logo on the side.

Multi-colored ink scrawls filled the diary, in two forms of distinctly different handwriting.

Paul finally asked me out today. Things are looking up!
TJ got me sent to the principal's office again, but I only had to serve detention in study hall. Yay!

My brow gathered as I bent my thumb on the end of the pages and they fluttered past.

TJ still misses Evie. I do too. She had everything.

Looks. Brains. Cared about neither. Always curious.
Popularity was such an odd construct to Evie, as was
the split between the genders. She was ahead of her
time. I guess we didn't deserve her.

"God, that's kind of good. I don't even remember
writing this." I chuckled and flicked the pages backward.

Mom's turned into a major bitch since losing Dad. Even
after all that happened. How can she possibly still miss
that asshole? Can't wait to get out of this one-potato
town.

I shook the book at her. "Why were you always using
my shit!"
She still stared out the window. "Read the last one."
I paged forward and found it.

Mom has boob cancer. This is SO not fair. I'm
supposed to take care of her now? She never took care
of me!

"Wait. What? *Cancer*? Whoa, whoa, whoa."
I flipped the pages to the end, but there was nothing
after that and plenty of room to expound on just how awful
it had been. I reached across the car for my cousin's hand.
"*Teej.*"
"Don't."
I wadded up the oily muffin paper into my paper coffee

cup, then quickly turned the key in the ignition. "We have to go over there."

She nodded. "Fine."

"Really? You sure?"

She looked at me. "Are *you*?"

"Well yeah, I think we should go. We owe it to her." My dread organ no longer worked. I think it had atrophied at that point.

"Okay, then. I'm ready."

---

The wind chimes on Ellen Render's porch hung still. I hadn't noticed the yellow foreclosure papers on the door before, but she had opened it so fast the other day.

I rang the bell. She wasn't as quick this time. I rang it again.

I drummed fingers on my lips. "Maybe she's out shopping."

"She's not."

I moved to the living room window, smeared the grime aside, tented my palms over the glass, and peered in. No lights on. "We should wait."

"No. We don't need to." I had never seen TJ so emotionless.

"We're not going to be back down here for a while—"

"Use the key."

"The wha—?"

"The key."

I nodded and walked numbly as my feet carried me instinctively to the side of the porch where the garden gnome sat. I removed his cracked pointed cap and found the key. Just where TJ had always left it when we were kids. I don't remember turning it in the lock, or opening the door, I just remember the darkness of the house. The pull of it inward.

TJ went first, into the foyer, stopping in the crowded living room. I followed. Everything was the same as it had been two days ago—the piles of knickknacks, magazines, boxes—except it lay covered in grime and it rang with silence. Devoid a beating heart.

"Here, kitty," I called faintly.

Where I wanted to go, TJ walked first, ushering me through. It should have been the other way around; I should have been holding her hand. Comforting *her*. Such a coward.

In the kitchen, my fingertips hovered over the refrigerator handle. I bit my lip, arm shaking, and whipped open the door.

Nothing but a box of baking soda and cool, stale air.

I turned to the cabinets and opened each one.

Empty. Empty. Empty. Not even … coffee.

TJ strode to the bathroom and pushed the door wide.

The vanity mirrors hung shattered, most of the glass gone, with large X's of blue painter's tape crossing them to prevent further damage. My reflection stared back, a jagged multitude. Behind me, the paisley wallpaper was torn away in strips.

"Oh my God," I whispered. "I don't— This can't— I was just here."

My heart flubbered in my chest. The dripping tub faucet counted off the seconds.

I rushed to the master bedroom. No sheets. No blankets. The ceiling had partially fallen in, vomiting tufts of pink insulation and electrical wires. The room smelled of books ruined by a flood.

"*TJ!* Say something."

She leaned, arms crossed, against the doorframe, holding me in her merciful gaze.

An orange tail lay curled out from under the bed.

"Hey," I said with a smile. "There he is!" I bent down to pet the tabby that had cuddled with me on the sofa. Instead I touched a furry, flattened disk, eyeless sockets staring blankly.

I yanked my hand away, crabbing backwards. I ran down the hall, out the door, and into the yard, gaping silently at a powder-coat gray sky, unable to scream.

TJ walked out, closed the door, strode to the car, and slid into the driver's seat.

For the first time in our lives I rode shotgun, and let her drive me to the east side of town. To the quiet place I hadn't been to since we were kids.

---

The iron gates stood open, and TJ knew where to park. We didn't really need to get out; the grave sat right by the road. But we did get out, and leaned against the car, just taking it in.

Just taking it in.

The granite etching of a six-pointed sheriff's star topped the broad rust-colored stone.

REST IN LOVING PEACE

JOHN JACOB RENDER | ELLEN MAY RENDER

"I'm sorry I wasn't there for you," I whispered. "I'm sorry I didn't do more. I'm sorry you had to handle this alone." And at that moment, I wasn't sure who I was talking to: Ellen or TJ. Maybe it didn't matter.

TJ turned to me and held out her arms. I fell into them and she encircled me, letting me cry for a while.

Little tufts of cottonwood seeds blew past my smudged vision, the breeze flowing warm and velvety across my skin. Pre-Fourth of July fireworks pattered in the distance. Above the cemetery, a murmuration of starlings painted the sky, swirling and shimmering in a funnel over the prairie like a school of fish.

I gently pulled away, dragging the back of my hand across my wet nose and sniffled. "How do they know how to do it, how to fly in harmony with each other?"

TJ watched them, hands in jean pockets. "Every starling has the ability to interact with seven neighboring birds at the same time. They communicate instantly. Remember when that Marvin guy in the street waved the gun and the crowd fell down in a wave?"

"Yeah," I said airily.

"It's sorta like that. Visual cues, empathy, instinct—all at once."

I brought my shirt to my face and wiped my eyes. "How do you know this stuff? How do you always know about everything?"

The breeze blew through the feathers of her hair. Her voice made jewels of sound.

"I've always known. The birds, the fungus, the living, the dead. You do too, Janey. We've just been waiting for you to catch up."

## Chapter Thirty-Two

Paul's car sat parked at The Donzerly Light when we pulled up.

I slid out and slammed the sedan door with an exhausted shove. It didn't latch. I slammed it again. The seatbelt peeked out of the bottom. I slammed it over and over.

"Jane." TJ gently stopped me mid-swing, reached in, fixed the belt, and shut the door.

"Feh." My reflection in the sedan window was a hollow, dirty shambles; my eyes were bleary and encrusted with dried tears.

We stumbled, dog-tired, through The Thicket and up the hill toward the meadow. Even after the coffee and muffins, I was running on fumes.

Nearby, a wood thrush fluted its song: *Ee-oh-lay!*

"Shut up."

TJ laughed. I joined her. It felt *so* good.

I glanced at my phone as we walked. According to those

inopportunely timed texts that had arrived while we were in Lincoln's basement, he had walked free. After his lawyer had arrived at the jail, the police had released him until tomorrow, when I would need to testify before a judge. So no, there was little point checking back into the hotel. We needed to find a safer place.

I pocketed my phone in the side of my capris. It immediately buzzed with an email notification. Lincoln. Sigh. From a new email address. I read aloud:

**From:** Brer Rabbit [briarpatch99@gmail.com]
**To:** Render, Jane [jRender@stubenliterary.com]
**Subject:** Janey, Janey, Jane

Jane, you're playing a game you never can win, girl.

"Does he think we don't know that's 'Jane' by fucking Jefferson Starship," TJ mumbled, her brow furrowed. "Dad used to play it all the time in his squad car. Christ."

"Guess he knows we were at his house."

"How could he not? You made such a racket."

I let go of a particularly spiky branch of needles and it whacked her in the face. But I loved my cousin then more than I've loved anyone. More than I loved myself.

"Aha!" She opened the Tupperware and tossed the moldy sausage, then knelt for a moment by the base of a conifer.

"Don't bother," I said. "That's the same tree we raided yesterday. There's none left."

"There's tons."

I looked down at the tree. "Can't be."

But there were. There were more mushrooms staring at us, even in the places we'd plucked them from. This seemed the least surprising thing all day.

Ahead, Paul crouched in the middle of the clearing, opening a big plastic trunk.

I trudged up the hill toward him, my mind swirling.

I crossed the clearing to Paul. "Got a big favor to ask."

He smiled up at me and offered his clipboard. "That's a fine hello. Thought you stood me up."

I gathered the clipboard to my chest, tears welling again. I looked away; I didn't like feeling helpless—or looking it either. "We need to stay with you in Champaign for a few days," I said. "Until Lincoln is dealt with."

"You and TJ." His lips pursed. "Sure. Of course."

"We can't take Ketchum another day. And I wouldn't ask if it wasn't—"

"No, I get it. Amanda will love trying to figure you both out." He reached inside the trunk and hoisted up a white quadcopter with a camera mounted on it. It was sizable, with carbon fiber blades, scuffed and dented but pro level, not one of those little drones with plastic blades that kids played with.

Meanwhile, the sun was casting a shadow on the west side of the meadow. TJ wandered east to sit cross-legged and worship the rest of the day. A nap in the grass looked pretty good right then.

"We, um," I said quietly, "stopped by Ellen's house. Then the ... cemetery."

He stopped unpacking and took me in his arms,

crushing the clipboard between us. "I'm so sorry, Jane. Of course you can stay."

"Thanks. Appreciate it," I said, and as much as I liked being held by a man again, TJ needed this more. But as usual, no one ever knew how to approach her. Besides, I smelled sour and dank and needed a shower. I patted his shoulder and pulled away. "I like Amanda. She's great for you."

"A little high-maintenance, but worth the investment. Tried to get her to come down today, but she's too busy with the studio."

"So, how's your health really doing?"

"Honestly? Way better than my prognosis. I stopped chemo midway through. Couldn't take it. Amanda's got me doing yoga under the moon. And I'm taking turkey tail."

"Let me guess, a kind of mushroom."

"Yeah. Sorry if I'm nerding out here, but they seriously work."

"I don't doubt it," I said and gazed around at The Thicket. "Nothing surprises me anymore."

As he prepared the drone, I read the clipboard:

**Armillaria Oculi Psilocybe (AOP)**

A genus of parasitic fungi that lives primarily on conifer and occasionally animal matter[1]. Considered a forest pathogen, the AOP is thriving in response to global warming stressors on host trees.

Unlike similar fungi, which must moderate their

growth to ensure source material, the AOP can also feed on dead plant matter and therefore may kill its host.

To attract insects and small animals for spore distribution, the AOP also displays bioluminescence[2] at night.

Like its relative the Honey Fungus, the Armillaria Oculi Psilocybe is edible. However, the AOP must be cooked and drained thoroughly to remove high levels of psilocybin[3], a powerful hallucinogen.

Chief among AOP features is its wholly unique cap: a light brown shell with black, gel-like spotting found to contain rod and cone cells[4], which are photoreceptors in vertebrates. It is possible the AOP senses light and dark in order to know when to turn off bioluminescence and conserve energy. It is yet to be determined whether the AOP can identify images. Of the two dozen samples collected, all caps contained seven spots each, no more, no less.

— Paul McKenna, PhD
University of Illinois, Mycology

"Armillaria Oculi Psilocybe," I said. "What happened to naming it 'Jane'?"

He laughed and then looked at me again, to see I wasn't completely joking. And like any clever male, he deflected me with my own vanity. "You look tired. This trip has really taken it out of you, hasn't it?"

"We didn't get much sleep last night." The tinnitus was back, a delicate ringing in my ear.

"Yeah," TJ yelled. "We know your big old fungi friend better than you do now, dude."

"I told you not to take it yet!"

"Yeah, well, here we are," she said.

"I had a colleague once who cooked up what he thought were simple straw mushrooms. Said they were the best he'd ever had. They were deathcaps. A week later he was on life support. A day after that?" He shook his head.

I scratched an itch behind my neck that didn't need scratching. "Sorry to hear that."

"The point is, I told you not to!"

I rolled my eyes. "What's done is done." But it scared me. Who would it kill first? Me or TJ?

"Psilocybin is a powerful gift, not a toy, Jane. The mental acuity it provides stable individuals is a curse to those with a chemical imbalance."

"So, it chooses whom to bless," TJ intoned, massaging her chin with her uninjured hand.

"Wait," I said, "A gift from whom?"

"I dunno. Nature. God, if you believe in that stuff."

"Aliensss…" TJ said.

Paul's patience with her was nearly snuffed. With the remote in hand, he backed away from the drone that whirred like a giant angry hornet. I backed away too. It rose a bit, dipped to the ground, and then ascended up and up.

"It's kinda old and clunky." His thumbs moved the

joysticks on the remote. "But it gets the job done. Would you get my iPad there? Just slip it into this slot here."

"What she said," TJ whispered and yet I could hear it right in my ear. There was something about this place that had brought us so close that I could read all her thoughts now. I remembered it from childhood. Since we'd left for Chicago—left Ketchum, left The Thicket—we'd grown further apart. But now? Especially since our little indulgence the day before, the effect was uncanny.

I shook my head and grabbed the iPad off the trunk lid, and slid it into the top of the remote.

"Press that green app, wouldya?"

Mesmerized, we watched as the drone captured video of The Thicket running along the river. There was another circular meadow nearby.

"Looks smaller than this one, but it's hard to tell from above. Let's compare."

The buzzing returned and the screen displayed us standing in the center of our meadow. Paul and I stood in the larger ring; TJ was obscured by a lens flare. He sent it off again, following a path of ashen deadfalls that was clear from above—trees without needles— where you could see the forest floor below their skeletons. The video screen ticked off meters, then kilometers.

"We're nearing Oregonian length."

"Also what she said," TJ whispered again. I looked over at her; she was smiling. It was like something was channeling her voice along an invisible thread across the meadow.

One more meadow appeared before the video ran out of deadfalls and turned to prairie.

"Okay, that's the southern border. Trade me for a sec." Paul handed me the remote and I gave him the clipboard. "It's on autopilot. Just don't touch the stick. It's really sensitive."

I glared at TJ before she could say anything. She clamped her lips, shuddering. Gingerly, I held the remote, with no desire to drive it, figuring I would certainly crash it.

He scrawled some numbers. "Okay, the western border is the river. The east is the blacktop and farmland. Let's check north." We traded back. "If I'm correct, this fairy ring is actually the center of the fungi. Right beneath our feet. Its oldest section. Where the first microbes landed. Probably hundreds of years ago. Maybe a thousand. Or more."

"We think it's sentient," TJ blurted as the murmuration of starlings we'd seen earlier by the cemetery spread out across the treetops and swept overhead like a cloud of spores—spores the birds had surely ingested for breakfast when they ate the worms and seeds beneath our feet. "It spoke to us. It showed us things," TJ insisted. The flock parted for the drone, unfazed by its speed, then swirled around to follow it as it buzzed to the next meadow.

"You don't say," he mumbled doubtfully, only half listening. "Damn birds."

"Remember when we wished out here in that clearing?" I asked.

"Sorta. That one is at the far end, I think. By the Metzger farm. The one with the pond."

"Yeah. That one. But you remember what we wished for?"

He scoffed. "It was two decades ago."

"Paul, we each got everything we wanted. You wanted a better job than your dad, remember? Brian, millions of dollars. Roy, the car he died in."

"Yeah, I remember you wanting TJ back." He shook his head. "But all of those were things we could make happen on our own. We just gave them a voice, Jane, and that made them real for us. That made us really go for them. Besides, Evie sure didn't get what she wished for."

"After the trip TJ and I took the other day, I have a feeling she did."

"Yeah, well, I can't work with feelings, Jane. I need evidence." He drew a hand across his chin. "Okay, listen, bees can do basic math. And I suppose I did find photoreceptors in this fungus. So, I'm not saying it doesn't have simple decision-making skills, but there's no way, without a brainstem of any kind, that it has human-style intelligence. Besides, if fungi could think, they would vote us off the planet."

"Our underlords have judged us unworthy," TJ said.

I waved her off, and tried to speak science-y for him. "But what if their my— The myco—"

"Mycorrizal network."

"Yeah, what if they don't *have* a brain … because they *are* a brain?"

Paul jutted his chin with a not-bad-for-an-amateur look. "Good luck with that theory. Others have tried and now they're doing the same circuit as illuminati conspiracy theorists and supplement hacks. I'd be laughed right out of the scientific community and my job. This place would be over-run with fanatics. I gotta be careful just talking about the photoreceptors at this point."

"You wouldn't believe the things we were able to see yesterday, Paul," I said. "Both of us. At the very same time!" Strangely enough, we'd switched roles with him. He might be looking down from on high through his drone camera, but he no longer saw the big picture anymore; he only saw *his* picture.

"Mmm. You're really starting to worry me with this *we* stuff, Jane. Can I tell you something about TJ that you've never wanted to hear?"

"Um, nope?" I stared at him. How could he still be so jealous of my friendship with TJ after all this time? It boggled the mind. The others were homophobes. But *Paul*?

"Go ahead," TJ said with a grin. "I dare you."

"Jesus, you're exhausting," he said.

I threw my hands on my hips. "Is that any way to treat the people who got you the Nobel prize in mycology?"

Paul sighed, seeing he'd hurt our feelings, and looked back at the screen. "Anyway, I have to do this by the book. I'm not going to posit anything that off the charts, even if part of me wants to. I'm just going to get this all on record. The facts. You know, *reality*?"

He pivoted the joysticks and throttled the drone higher and higher until we could see all the meadows at once.

I clasped a hand to my mouth, saw it immediately, and gasped.

Paul turned to me. "What is it?"

"The necklace," I whispered. "That's Ms. Van Laar's necklace. Do you remember it?"

"I remember she had great tits."

"Yup," said TJ.

Of course.

"Her necklace was that pattern! Seven circles radiating out smaller."

"I'll take your word for it."

My hands hit my hips. "But you're not actually!"

"Fractals are a common pattern in nature and art. Coincidence, Jane."

My shoulders slumped. Maybe I was losing touch after all. I was too exhausted.

Paul glowered at the screen; he shook the controller.

"What's wrong?"

His lip curled. "The Thicket isn't big enough to have this many meadows; you'd be able to see one from another; they'd be that close. It could have three, maybe. But seven? This doesn't make sense." He handed me back the controller, and unrolled the Army Corps map. He turned it sideways, and looked back at the screen. "Either their measurements are off, which I highly doubt, or the drone isn't showing this right. Maybe it's because the lens is too wide-angled." He rolled the map back up and squinted into the middle distance, as if sorting through potential answers, none of them sensical.

TJ chuckled. "We've been trying to tell you, my man. The Thicket is special."

Paul spun and stared at TJ then, no longer with anger, but with amazement—almost smiling—like he was finally seeing her as I did: she was always the only one of us who could handle anything, who seemed to know everything. Her eyes flared back at him mockingly.

He turned back unnerved, released a calming breath, and took the controller from me. "No. Magic isn't a thing. Everything is explainable." The drone whirred high above.

I gazed across our beautiful, private meadow. "Do you really think this could turn into some mushroom tourist spot? I'd hate to see it trampled."

"Doubtful it will go that far. Technically, the Armillaria out west is considered a root disease, an infection. This one would be too. The forestry service will want to eliminate it, if possible, like they're trying to do in the more damaged preserves."

TJ sat up straight. "Whoa, whoa, whoa."

"Are you serious?" I yelped. "No!"

"Yep, it's gotta go. Global warming's wreaked havoc on these trees. They literally can't stand the heat. Doesn't seem like much to us but it's weakened them. Fungi have the upper hand. They've survived other extinctions. And think about it, Jane; we live indoors mostly. A few degrees this way or that makes no difference when you can tap a thermostat. But what lives outside knows the difference, I guarantee you. That new fungal disease *Candida Auris*? It's adapted to the temps. All you need is a cut and it spreads like a wildfire across your body; you're dead in days." He shook his head. "They who can adapt fastest thrive."

"They," I said faintly. "Huh. All you need is a cut."

Across the clearing TJ was peering at her wounded palm. She closed her fist and gathered it to her chest.

He was right of course. The weather was different from when we were kids. Boiling summers that killed the poorest Chicagoans in their high-rise apartments. Unpredictable winters slammed southern Illinois with blizzards that a mere handful of snowplows weren't prepared for. Even the sky had changed. Late summers glowed a hazy peach from western wildfires.

If The Thicket became reduced to just a meadow, the county would be the lesser for it, the oxygen supply lesser for it. But irrational as it sounded, the Armillaria was part of me now and I didn't want it gone either.

"*Everything* steers toward reproduction, Jane." Paul said. "It is trying to spread, trying to exert itself. This is a fungal infection on a large scale. This is my realm, so it's always hard for me to call these things a disease. Gotta put my selfish human hat back on for that. But this strain has gotten greedy, killing off its hosts instead of simply taking what it needs and moderating its growth. If we don't try to mitigate it, it'll run wild."

My ears rung in pain.

*HHHE MEANSSS TO DESTROOOY USSS*

TJ's head slowly turned to me; her eyes dilated black.

"But—" I started.

"Hold this for a sec while I get these numbers down. This is going to rival the Oregonian Armillaria! Just press 'HOME' there and it'll return."

Paul turned over a new sheet of paper on his clipboard. "We'll collect tons of samples, of course. Study it in a controlled environment, but the DNR will want to stop it before it consumes more of The Thicket. Can't burn it. It's underground. Gotta starve it out. They'll do a clear-cut of every host tree in The Thicket and replant resistant breeds." He nodded to himself.

I pressed the HOME button as he scrawled rapidly. He looked so proud. This was going to be huge for him; that much was clear. And perhaps I could agent his non-fiction book. Get him the best publisher possible.

But at the expense of the Armillaria?

The drone whirred back to our meadow, followed by the cloud of starlings. On screen, the view flickered with black blurs as if erupting with static. The air filled with the birds' high-pitched whisper-squawks.

Paul stopped writing, his pen tapping the sum. "Damn." His jaw slackened at his calculations. "I just hit the big time, Jane." He beamed at me. "The largest organism on the planet is right beneath us."

The buzz of the drone and the chirping chorus of birds fell silent.

"What the heck?" Paul took the remote and flicked at the joysticks. He poked at the ON button then squinted up at the sky where the birds had splashed out in all directions toward the trees.

I looked to the video screen and saw Paul's face rushing at me with a look of realization. For an eternal moment we both stood watching it fall from different perspectives. The motor whizzed back on just as it struck him.

I flinched, briefly thinking Paul had spat at me, but my hand came away from my cheek with red across it.

He collapsed to the ground and the drone fell beside his

neck. The carbon fiber blades shot a spray of red into the air like a lawn sprinkler. Paul shuddered and jerked.

I fell to my knees, tugging him by the shirt away from the drone. TJ ran to help, but he was heavy and by the time we got him away from the blades, his face and neck burbled a broken fountain of deep red.

The blades drove themselves into the dirt until the drone silenced. Two starlings had also fallen nearby, both with wings at wrong angles. One of them lay still; the other hobbled off toward the tree line.

The Thicket grew hushed.

"Paul." The voice barely came from me.

The impact had mashed his nose and eyes up into his skull. I had only seen someone like this once before, but there was no time to place it.

My hands shook over his body. "Paul, we're here. Talk to us."

Before I could hyperventilate, TJ whispered, *Stay calm.* Or at least I thought she had.

I swallowed back a sob and pressed quivering hands to the gash on his neck. Cascades of red oozed between my fingers. TJ wadded her hoodie and handed it to me. I pressed it hard into his neck with one hand. With the other I prepared to dial 911. My thumb slid bloody and shaking across my iPhone screen. I had no cellphone bars.

"I think he's dead," TJ said quietly, pressing with me. "It was quick, Jane. It was quick."

"Stay with him," I stuttered. "I'll get help."

I sprinted across the meadow and into the trees, past the dying conifers, whose rhizomorphs were sagging and dropping down like they had the other day. I slowed for a moment, watching them, as they diverted around me, a river of black webs that flowed up the hill and toward the clearing.

I shook my head, denying it. Could I still be tripping, still dreaming? None of it might be real. Paul could be alive in Champaign-Urbana for all I knew. But in case he wasn't, I stumbled toward the path that would lead me back to the cars. Chrome glinted in the gulley by the Donzerly Light. I stopped and skirted around the road, through the brambles. An old brown truck with large milky-white containers in its bed sat backed up to the treatment facility. Clear tubing snaked from the containers and into one of the opened pits. A man in tan camo fatigues hunched down to watch the liquid sluice through the tubes.

*Thank God*, an Army Corps worker could help us carry Paul.

I yelled out, "Hey! Help!" and leapt out of the weeds.

My stomach sank, the dread organ replacing it, as I made sense of the peeled-back fencing. The man had cut it to enter the facility instead of unlocking the gate.

Lincoln Metzger stood up to stare at me, a rifle slung over his shoulder. Recognition overtook his face. He ran as fast at me as I'd ever seen him move.

"No." I swung back the way I'd come and sprinted up the hill toward TJ, racing the rhizomorphs that steadily pulsed through the grass.

"Jane! Stop!" Lincoln lumbered behind me, his footsteps crushing last autumn's leaves further into mulch. He let out a frightened yelp. The Armillaria was aware of him now. I sensed the mute eyes of the fruiting mushrooms watching us. Deliberating.

"TJ, run!" I screamed now, as hard as I could, "Run! *Go!*"

She was already standing, backing slowly away from Paul's body as the rhizomorphs explored the corpse, first the blood running from his head and neck, which made them pulse and thicken, and then into his ears and eyes. They started for his lips, gently, insistently pushing open his jaw. TJ watched, fascinated. A few strands were palpating her jeans as she gaped at the desecration.

*It's coming out his ears, Jane.*

"I see you, TJ!" Lincoln called from the edge of the meadow.

I put my body between TJ and Lincoln's rifle. "Go!"

Obeying, she turned and ran to the other side of the meadow and into the trees.

The rifle's loud cracks echoed through the wood—*tat, tat, tat*—again and again.

As I ran, I chanced a look back.

Lincoln stood firing at Paul's body, at the rhizomorphs gathering and covering the corpse in a black netting. Lincoln looked up with wild, terrified eyes that met mine. Then he ran around Paul, around the pulsing veins, and down the hill toward us.

A flash of brown came at me through the trees. The two-headed buck. I halted, stunned, and cast my eyes down, bracing for it to gore me. It veered past and leapt to stand between Lincoln and me. Lincoln reared back and fell on his butt, dropping his rifle. He scrambled backwards and grabbed for it.

TJ had stopped far ahead, waiting for me. I sprinted at her. If we could just make it to the access road and double-back to our car. *No, he will go there first.* Our only hope was finding the county road and flagging down a car for help, or at least locate a cell tower.

—*tat, tat, tat*—

I looked over my shoulder. The deer crumpled to its fore-knees.

We ran faster, cutting through another circular meadow and then back into The Thicket. A blond sea of tall prairie grasses a half-mile off beckoned, grasses we could get lost in.

It was perhaps the oddest time to realize this, but I had never felt so alive as I did running behind TJ across that chunky ground, leaping deadfalls, scraping our arms on branches, panting in ragged gulps of air. TJ dragged me along, my last link to sanity: tall and lanky with her T-shirt rippling, her thighs pumping, her hair like golden feathers —the Valkyrie blazing a trail.

We had almost reached the edge of The Thicket when TJ halted. She crouched down behind a tree and peered all around. I slid to a stop in the mulch and joined her.

"Listen."

Just beyond us a red-winged blackbird perched on a tan thatch of cattails, and a chorus of tall reeds whistled in the wind.

I panted, heart battering inside me. "W-what?"

She shook her head. "Nothing." She peered over my shoulder back into The Thicket. "He's too scared to come any deeper."

We waited silently for a few minutes in case she was wrong.

All I could see when I closed my eyes was Paul's ruined face. My own face crumpled up into an ugly cry. Poor, poor Paul. My sweet boy, Paul. I would never rid that image from my mind. I thought of TJ's father and what she had seen when he killed himself; somehow I had seen it too—right then, as soon as Paul fell, I saw Sheriff Render. Ever since she and I had entered this wood, I had begun seeing and knowing everything TJ knew. She had been right about the amazing force here, but wrong about whether we should be frightened of it. It was beyond our primitive comprehension. We needed to be on our toes, and not just for Lincoln.

"Do you think the Armillaria somehow controlled the drone?" I whispered. "I had my hands on the controls for a few seconds."

TJ shook her head, "It was the birds, Jane, the birds."

"All I did was press 'HOME' like he told me! Oh my God, he's dead. Paul is really dead, TJ." I shook my head, biting back a new rush of tears. "What have we done? I can't believe we both ate it, TJ. He told us not to! It's in us right now."

"We ate it when we were kids too, Janey. It didn't kill us then or make us kill people. We can't have been fungus zombies this long."

"Maybe I've been a zombie all my life."

"Would you stop?" TJ glanced around. "I bet Lincoln went back to his car to meet us at the county road. He's too lazy to run, that fuckwit."

"What if he's right about this place? What if Lincoln's had his finger in the dike this whole time?"

TJ squinted at me. "You've always wanted to say that, haven't you?"

"This is pretty much the only time." Then I whispered into The Thicket, "Please don't kill us!"

"We don't need to talk to it," TJ scoffed. "Just show it our intent. Show it we mean no harm."

"I think it already gets that. But I don't think it matters. If it has the power and the will, it could take us either way."

*Affirmative.*

"So, yeah, in a way, Lincoln's right, isn't he? Like, not The-devil-versus-Jesus right. But—"

My voice quaked, "Then why did *Evie* disappear"—I snapped my fingers—"just like that, but your dad shot himself? And Roy crashed. They're all such different—"

"Well, I have a theory, if you'd just calm your tits a second," TJ said. She drew her finger and thumb around the edge of her mouth. She sat down from a crouch, while I kept a look out. Her hands hovered over the soil. It was everywhere underneath us and we knew it. "I think it knows who we are. Once it makes contact. Who we *really* are, deep down. And it shows us ourselves. And *more*. Much more. Didn't you feel that yesterday? We were on the cusp of something. And when we were younger, we just, we didn't have the perspective. But it shows us our worth. So, if we can't handle that, well…" She fired a finger pistol at her head. "Boom. That's on us."

"Then what happened to Evie? She was young. She wasn't bad."

"You're right. She was innocent. But maybe that's why she wasn't found. Maybe it *needed* her. And maybe it needs us and hasn't hurt us yet."

"Why? There's nothing special—"

"We're storytellers."

I threw my hands up. "This story requires a fucking journalist."

"A journalist could never report on this and expect to keep her job. It's a fact-checker's nightmare."

A yard away, a black snake slithered through the leaves and for a moment I imagined it was a rhizomorph, engorged from its last meal. But it was just a snake. A creature that would have sent me screaming from the woods just a week before left me strangely pleased that the natural world was going about its business, with or without us.

"I think ... I think the Armillaria classifies humans in one of four ways." TJ pulled back her fingers one by one. "Those who don't matter, which is the vast majority. Those who are worthy: Evie. Those who are not: Dad. And those who threaten it: Paul. Maybe Paul wouldn't have mattered, or may have even been worthy at one time, but then he—"

"So Lincoln may not make it out alive either."

TJ nodded. "And he knows it, in his own way. Maybe he did eat it at some point. Maybe unknowingly. Maybe half the town has. It's growing everywhere. It's probably in the groundwater."

"It's coming out their ears."

"Exactly. And it's the devil to Lincoln. He knows it wants you. He thinks he's protecting you."

"What if he is?"

"Fuck him. You don't need that noise. You can protect yourself!" TJ made finger explosions. "But here's an even wilder thought, Jane. What if the Armillaria is just … a conduit? It isn't even the actual entity itself? It's just the natural world part that we only barely understand. The tip of the iceberg."

I palmed my temples. "Don't start with that turtles-all-the-way-down stuff."

"Well, our primitive minds couldn't even handle it anyway, I'm sure."

I tried to think of it, but my primitive mind led elsewhere.

"Teej?"

TJ kept an eye out. "Yeah?"

"Did you know we were coming down here before I asked?"

"What do you mean?"

"The chapter you wrote about Evie. Did you leave that for me to find?"

She bit at the inside of her cheek, then sighed, and gazed softly at me. "You're waking up, Jane. You got this." She stood up and looked around, brushed off her knees, and winced at the wound on her hand. "We need to get moving."

I got up too, my joints aching.

We stood back to back, as we had sat in the meadow the day before, the world spinning around us. We were back on the turntable, waiting for the rhizomorphs to glom on. Paul had said some fatal toxins take time to release; what if the psilocybin in the Armillaria did too? Still wandering our veins, our brains—searching, testing, finding new doors of perception to throw wide open.

The knotholes of the trees slowly spun into eyes.

It looks. It sees. Through its source material.

Nothing moved to take us; it merely watched. And then my dread organ pumped with a sickening thought. The Armillaria was busy elsewhere. *With Paul.* Covering him in that white webbing soon, like the squirrel and the other bodies. The sleeping policemen.

The head has been fed.

I covered my mouth and tried not to moan.

The woodthrush fluted again: *Ee-oh-lay.*

## Chapter Thirty-Three

"Shit, where's the diary?" I asked.

"I left it on the hill."

"Damn it, *Teej*."

As we made our way back to Ketchum, we skirted The Thicket at the edge of the grassland on a double-track dirt road normally used by hunters and the DNR. We were prepared to use either for cover: the grassland an escape from the rhizomorphs if they dropped from the trees, The Thicket for cover if Lincoln found us.

"It doesn't matter. You understand what was inside it now anyway, don't you?"

"Yes," I said as we staggered along. "And I'm sorry." The adrenaline had subsided, reminding me how weary and thirsty I was. "I'm sorry about all of it."

"Don't, Jane. It's okay," TJ said, her voice hoarse. "We're probably just a mile from town. Be there soon. We'll process this when we're safe. Try not to lose it, okay?"

I thought of praying to God then, but I'd tossed out that contract long ago. If there was a God, he was sitting back, eating buttered popcorn, slurping Dr. Pepper through a Twizzlers straw, and having a bit of a chuckle.

We watched the ground and then my phone, waiting for bars to pop on my cell, just trying to concentrate on putting one foot in front of the other. My phone battery had dwindled to single digits from searching and searching for a signal.

"Don't run. Or I will kill her."

We staggered to a stop. Lincoln trained his rifle on me instead of TJ, which I didn't expect of him. *Bold move*, TJ said in my head.

His truck sat tucked in the big bluestem prairie grass, just waiting there for two worn-out city girls to stumble along.

With the two brain cells I had left, I managed to blurt, "We can't get married if I'm dead."

"Okay, little red riding pants," Lincoln said with pursed lips. "Don't be a sasser."

TJ's face screwed up with disgust. To think these were the kind of words that used to make us laugh. How fatal our hubris. We deserved this.

"Get in the truck."

"I don't love you. I never have, Lincoln!"

He winced at this, slowly inching toward me, the barrel pointed at my stomach. It would be a messy end. Again, the wisdom of the slushpile rose at the most inopportune time, reminding me that if I didn't immediately bleed out, repairing all the organs that the bullet had torn through in time would be next to impossible.

"I'm the only one willing to tell you the truth," he said. "That's got to count for something!"

He reached out and took my wrist, the barrel jammed in my side, and pulled me toward the truck. TJ came with us.

"Tell TJ to stay here." He wouldn't even look at her.

The barrel bit into my hip bone and the pain turned quick to fury. "The hell I will!"

"Then we all die. Leave her here. Leave her where she belongs," he demanded, and opened the truck door. "She's no good for you. Never has been. She makes you look like a fool."

TJ and I gulped at each other.

He raised the rifle to my head. "*Lady Jane*, make her stay!"

TJ raised her hands and backed away, eyes glistening. "You'll be strong on your own now."

I shook my head.

She nodded. "You will. You have to. We both knew this day would come." TJ threw her hands up with a shrug. "Listen, I need some space. We've grown apart anyway."

"What! Why are you saying this?" Now, of all times, when I needed her most.

"I can't leave here this time. I'm done. You've got to handle this one," she began to say it with her usual confidence but produced a sob instead. It reminded me of an old movie where a boy throws rocks at a friendly deer, so it won't get shot. TJ touched her cheek, then peered at her finger, which glistened with tears. She smiled at it with bittersweet wonder—a look I'd never seen on her. She had cried for the first time, and it seemed to strengthen her whole lifeforce.

Beside me, Lincoln's eyes widened, the rifle shaking in his hands. His Adam's apple bobbed as he gulped down the truth of her, silhouetted by the sun.

"Go, Jane," TJ said, glaring at him. "I can't help you … like this."

Lincoln nudged me toward the truck, never taking his eyes off her. He growled his words, low and cautious, "I will shoot her right now if you don't get in."

Lincoln opened the truck door and pushed me inside.

---

The truck swerved onto the double-track and away from TJ. I turned, scrambling onto my knees to look out the back window, over the tanks in the back of the truck, as she stood staring at me. She could hike back to the car, but I had the keys. She could get Paul's keys. But I did not trust the Armillaria would leave her alone. The smartest thing would be to wait until we were out of sight, then make her way to the county road.

TJ turned and walked back into The Thicket and I could swear I saw something loosen and drop from the trees. Disrobing their fishnets for her. She seemed to blur and twist as if spiraling toward a drain.

"No." I moaned and pounded at the window. "No!"

I hated Lincoln then. I had no pity left for him. He put his hand on my leg and I punched him in the face. He cried out and begged me to stop. I would not go into his awful killing jar of a basement shrine to be slowly suffocated.

"Do you really think people won't know that you've taken me?"

"Yes, they'll know. We will have ascended to heaven by then."

"You're an asshole. I hate you. I fucking hate you, Lincoln."

He drove faster through the dirt, the bumps tossing me to and fro in the cab. Tears slipped from his eyes. He took out a pistol and put the cold metal to my forehead.

"I will kill us both right now if you don't stop saying that."

My eyes searched his. I would take the gun from him. Somehow, I would take it. The automatic rifle lay between us, pointed at the floor. *Think, you fool.* What do desperate women do? What would TJ do?

I caught my wild-animal face in the rear-view mirror, Paul's arterial spray airbrushed across my forehead.

Paul.

I let out a ragged sigh and dropped my forehead to his shoulder. Axe body spray. He was just a man, like any man. For one brief moment I would find this within me. If nothing made sense anymore, why not go with it? I reached up and softly clasped his bicep. In my head TJ asked, *Why give him the satisfaction?* I told her I was buying time. She said, *Yes, we've tried that trick before. It doesn't work.*

When we hit the blacktop, instead of turning for the county road, Lincoln turned the truck west, back toward the access road.

I squinted. "What are you doing?"

"Destroying The Thicket. For you. For Evie. For Jacob. For everyone."

I shot a glance back at the tanks in the truck bed. "You'll kill TJ!"

"She's already gone."

"What the hell are you talking about?" I screamed at him. "I don't want this. Lincoln, please don't do this. If you really loved me, you would know I don't want this."

"I do love you."

"You don't. You don't even know who I really am deep down. You've only fallen in love with the idea of me. And by doing that you've shown me who you are. And it's someone I could never respect."

The truck slowed and Lincoln's stubborn leer dropped. He reached up to a black box velcroed to his dash and pressed the button on top. A red digital readout came on.

3:00, 2:59, 2:58...

"What's that?"

"Insurance."

To make sure he got the job done, no matter what happened to us.

"Okay, maybe I was wrong," I said, my lips dry, my mouth pasty. "Maybe I didn't realize what a brave man you are, Lincoln. W-why don't you let me make you happy?" I said quietly, my eyes tracing the wire from the box. It was duct-taped down the dash, onto the carpet, and under the seat.

"You already have," he said, and his flat smile returned. "You chose me. Not her."

*At gunpoint?*

*Don't argue.*

"Lincoln, what is in those tanks?"

He looked at me.

"Insurance?" I asked.

He nodded. "We have to destroy it."

"You can't."

On the access road to the Donzerly Light, he hit the gas. I stared blankly at him.

2:17, 2:16, 2:15…

I leapt into his lap and grabbed the handgun at his side. He clutched my scalp and yanked it backward. The pain stunned me into letting go. I could not let that happen again. My face filled with a rage that reflected in his fear. I fought then. Really fought. Against him. Against every man who had hurt me. Back to the beginning.

I grabbed the rifle and tried to yank it up. It fired into the floor and split my eardrums. We wrestled like that, fumbling two guns in close quarters, my brain ringing out, overloaded. He struck me in the eye, and the ear. It stung hot but I realized I could handle it. I'd grown numb before; I could do it again now. The trick is not minding, as they say.

TJ flowed into my arms, my fists, my teeth, carrying me into the fight, the dirty fight. And the noise that came from me began as a low, guttural blast that rose to an eardrum-splitting scream worthy of a banshee. My vision went white as I shrieked. I don't know why they call it blacking-out when there's nothing dark about it. I stabbed at Lincoln's eyes with my knuckles, grabbed his nostrils with forefinger and middle and yanked upward.

1:55, 1:54, 1:53...

The handgun went off, shattering his window. He dropped it in shock, and it fell beneath the seat. He bent, left hand crabbing around for it as I grabbed the rifle. My left arm went numb and useless.

The butt of the rifle had wedged behind the wiper stalk on the steering column, the barrel pressing on the tip of the gas pedal, revving the engine, and sending us wildly careening across the centerline. He brought up the handgun and fired it at me as the truck swerved toward the ditch. The bullet blew a hole in the passenger window. We looked at the hole, then at each other, shocked at what he had done, neither of us realizing he would ever try to kill me. Heat rose in my left arm and I glanced down to see a pucker of blood oozing from it. He'd nailed me when he'd dropped it the first time. Now I could feel it—really feel it—like a hot poker jabbed deep in between my muscles.

The truck ran off the road, into the ditch, and I hit the roof of the cab. Lincoln wrestled the truck back up and onto the road, swerving and trying to dislodge the rifle at the same time.

I continued to smack at him with my right arm and pull at his hair, when suddenly he just stopped fighting. He simply sighed and stared straight ahead at the Donzerly Light in its gulley a quarter mile in front of us. It first glowed an angry orange and then brightened to a yellow so intense that we could not look directly at it.

0:49, 0:48, 0:47…

I let go and backed away. Staring sadly one last time at Lincoln Metzger, I reached behind myself for the door handle. His face was lit orange and his eyes glistened.

"We will meet in perfection," he said.

Now the truck was moving so fast that my graceless tumble into the weeds produced two quick and sickening pops in my wrist and torso, the sound of branches snapping underwater.

I lay in the ditch, pressed prone against the ground and staring at the fading daylight, wondering what my name was.

A blinding light imprinted pulsing fractals onto my eyes: layers upon layers of lightning, the river network, a crosshatch of sunrays rippling on the water, tree branches, antlers, a spider's web, distant nebulae, the mycelium below me… all of it flashing the same forking shapes that formed my own optic blood vessels.

An enormous whump sounded and a shockwave tossed me into the air. Beneath me, the Armillaria convulsed like a patient after a defibrillator pulse. I covered my head just before the next blast hit. A clanging *TONG!* this time—the propane tank, I surmised.

I peered between my fingers, the fractals dissipating. Birds shot past me. To the south, a red fireball curled in the sky, falling up over itself to form a blackening mushroom cloud. Clots of dirt and branches rained down on and all around me. A steel pipe impaled the earth one foot to the side of me. A hand with only one finger landed with a thump on the road and twitched a few times.

I sat up, the area between my neck and shoulder spiking with pain, and whimpered. My right hand hung at an unnatural angle. My left bicep felt as if someone had taken a whack at it with a baseball bat, but it still functioned.

Flames had engulfed the entire area around the Donzerly Light. There were no trees or brush at all in the immediate blast area. Paul's flaming car blew next and then my rental car. Trees in The Thicket had already caught fire; the dead, dried conifer fell first. The Armillaria screamed in my ears.

TJ.

I set my gunshot arm down for purchase in the grass and struggled to stand. I had never felt such agony in my life, this tearing, this heat, this stabbing. I was so soft, spoiled by an easy life, nowhere close to my ancestors'. Now something had ripped and broken inside me and I quivered like a child with each eruption of pain.

TJ.

I loped into The Thicket, trying to keep enough forest between myself and the raging fire that swept eastward in a wave, up the conifers and sizzling through the needles and broad leaves that comprised the forest floor. As I ran, the ground rippled in rubbery waves. I'd felt an earthquake in California once. This was no quake. It shook only the soil, not the bedrock. All around, dirt piled upward, shaking loose, exposing thick white veins, which branched everywhere. It reminded me of the time I'd cut my wrist so deep I'd seen the pearlescent white of my flexor tendon. At the base of flaming juniper, fruiting bodies of the Armillaria boiled, the rhizomorphs shriveled. A wave of heat pressed at my back as I ran, reminding me the fire was ravenous. It was coming for everything.

---

TJ sat against a tree on the far edge of The Thicket, only a few yards from where I'd last seen her. The vape cig hung from her gently smiling lips. From the waist down an exquisite blanket of white webbing and crosscutting black rhizomorphs covered her like well-tucked bedclothes.

I slowed my stumbling approach to gape as the mycelium steadily knitted white fractals up her body like one of those 3D printers.

"Oh my God."

I fell to her side, the pain in my shoulder and arms joining as one merciless vampire, threatening to suck me dry and knock me out.

"There's a fire coming," I gasped. "Lincoln's dead. Gotta get you out of here."

She closed her eyes and sighed. "Okay, here's the logline," she said. "Two women battle a giant mushroom and get more than they bargained for."

With my gunshot arm I started at her feet, ripping at the Armillaria, flinging it away in patches. I didn't care if it got pissed; it wasn't getting TJ back.

But all that lay where her feet should have been was upturned soil.

Bile rose in my throat. Concentric circles flashed at my vision.

My body quivered and went cold, teeth chattering.

TJ kept talking, "So the *morel* of the story? Maybe you can go home again, but you better have a damn good reason, or you'll never get out."

"Okay, okay," I bargained. "This isn't happening. I think if we just sober up, we'll be in the car."

"You are sober now, Janey. Completely. When's the last time you wanted a pill?" She raised her eyebrows. "Thing is, I have to go. You don't need me anymore. You're strong enough now to pivot." TJ sniffed the air. "Smells like sautéed chanterelles, don'tcha think?"

All around, The Thicket thundered in chaos as deer and rabbits and squirrels sprang from their dens and fled past to escape the flames. The ground rippled, springy and spongy beneath me.

"Nope, this is *not* happening."

The rhizomorphs and webbing held TJ stuck to the tree like a cocoon. In the time I'd wasted negotiating with the unfathomable, it had grown up to her chest.

"Time to face it, Janey. Gotta exit through the wound. Besides, I'm a little uncomfortable being a part of your personal mythology all the time. People judge you for it."

"No, Teej. Fight it, *please*, fight it."

"You don't have a choice." She smiled at me. "Can't unbake this cake. If you never let yourself feel the sorrow, you'll never know joy. Let go, Jane. I'm fine. We'll all be fine. We're all together! It doesn't hurt. It's actually pretty cool.

And, listen, I found Evie! Yeah, she's here. She's everywhere and she's amazing. Ms. Van Laar? She is *vast* now."

TJ's once grey eyes burned green with foxfire, then dilated to abyssal black, like wormholes to a distant place.

"It's preparing us for extinction. Cataloguing us before we destroy everything. Like the lost library of Alexandria. Just like it did when the dinosaurs died. It sets aside our egos, our *selves*, shows us what's next. But you've got to tell everyone, Jane. You have been chosen to make them all see. When you're ready you can come back. But not too soon, Janey. Live your life. Live your life."

The greedy tendrils at TJ's neck unfurled toward my wounded arm; I ripped angrily at gossamer threads, strong as cables. An amber light tore across my vision, a flickering of the vanity light and flashbulbs, the sound of gears and a Polaroid spitting out of a camera. Spheres of information shot me deeper in or further out, I couldn't be sure. As memories spun, it stole my breath from me. The past slid rapidly by, decades fell away, and I saw TJ's monster, her origin, and then that slid away too in another flash.

*No! I'm not ready. I'm not ready!*

Her speech became alien, a barely understandable groupspeak, high like my tinnitus and low like a gong. "You can't get moving without something to push away from. You never had anything to push away from because I pushed for us. This loss will be something you can push away from, Jane. It's time to adapt. *Go! Before it's too late.*"

She was right. What did I hope to salvage? Her head? Tuck it under my arm and cart it home so I could have conversations with it on my desk like an elaborate paperweight?

"Go. Go. *Go*." Her voice, now thin, went papery, a whisper on the wind swirling about me until it was finally lost from this ravaged world.

I could no longer get my mind around what was happening, so it started to unmoor, to ferry away from my basic animal-survival mind. All our experiences together, the heart and soul of our friendship fell away then too, an agony of childhood torn asunder. Time wasted never to return. A part of me, a genuine part of me, would be gone the moment I escaped this flaming forest.

The vape cig fell into my palm. Her face was completely covered now, mummified, quickly collapsing beneath the web work.

Smoke rose around me, a crackling, stinging heat at my back. There was nothing left of my best friend to save. The webs and veins only clasped a tree now. I backed away, toward the double-track and watched mushrooms fruit rapidly at the base of the tree. No sooner had their eyes appeared than they began to bubble and shine. My own eyes stung from the sulfur of ignited fungicide and heat burnt my face like the sun.

In the center of The Thicket, a column of flames twisted and swirled angrily upward—a fire tornado fierce enough to make Lincoln proud. I gasped as air vacated my lungs to feed its insatiable hunger. Now the entire forest crackled in orange and black, pressing me backward, limping as fast as I could down the quivering double-track. Smoke clawed at the back of my throat and I wheezed. All around, the earth indented in reverse mole tunnels as if a portion was falling into a shallow sinkhole.

The wail of the Armillaria grew in my head, threatening to explode my skull. I screamed along with it until my vocal cords surrendered and I tumbled into the county road ditch, sobbing silently onto cool pebbles. My tears quenched the baked dirt. All around, sparks danced and drifted downward. A blanket of darkness fell over me until the only sense remaining was the cry of sirens.

## Chapter Thirty-Four

"I want you to stop talking to the other patients about the mushrooms," Doctor Adelstein says quite reasonably as we meander down the hall.

I hold my laptop like a textbook across my chest, as if a teacher is escorting me through the high school to the principal's office.

"They are still considered a class-A substance, you know."

The doctor knows this route by heart and holds me in her placid stare framed by wide red-rimmed glasses. She's tall and platinum blonde with dark eyes that see through any attempt at deflection. She reminds me of that actor from *Transparent*. What's her name? Judith something.

It's not so bad here at Lakeview Behavioral Clinic, not like an asylum you see in the movies. I don't have to dress in scrubs or anything, just my own athleisurewear. There's a gym, yoga studio, basketball court, and a cafeteria that serves organic meals. They bus us to outings at Navy Pier, our motley crew of troubleds. We ride the Ferris wheel and scream louder than we should, just to let it out.

You can even get a roommate if you're well enough.

I haven't got one yet.

As we walk, I turn from the doctor's withering stare to sneer at the inspirational posters lining the periwinkle walls.

ATTITUDE is a water droplet making ripples in a pond.

GRATITUDE is a cherry tree blossoming pink.

PERSISTENCE is a silhouetted runner crossing a wooded trail.

POSSIBLITIES are the stems of something delicate rising from rich black soil.

MAKE IT HAPPEN features a contemplative man standing atop a mountainous outcropping surrounded by purple clouds.

This makes me snicker. "Tsk. That one seems poorly chosen considering the audience!"

Dr. Adelstein nods calmly. "I'll look into it."

"And how is success like an empty canoe?"

The doctor shrugs and shakes her head in a good-natured way.

The final poster before the double doors to the back garden is simply black with white words:

DO MORE WITH LESS

Seriously? Now they're trolling me. It's all shorthand for *GET YOUR SHIT TOGETHER, JANE.*

My smile goes flat and I think of Lincoln and how his

disappointed leer must have formed. To think that the only person who wandered the same labyrinth of loss was Lincoln; the only guy who truly got me and understood. Maybe he did know the real me after all. If only he hadn't obsessed over me so much, we could have been friends. I could have talked him down from his dogmas. He could have listened to me admit the truths of my past.

Nah. Guy was a fucking monster.

"Can we talk about the light?" Dr. Adelstein asks. "What was it called? The dawn's early light?"

"Judith Light!"

"Hmm?"

"You ... look like Judith Light," I trail off.

She pockets her hands in her billowy slacks. "Yes, I get that a lot."

Summer is in full boil, with cicadas sizzling in the trees. Younger patients, here for substance abuse treatment, play Frisbee barefoot on unnaturally green grass that wouldn't last two minutes in The Thicket. An older catatonic man sits with an orderly on a bench. A sparrow splashes in a puddle, sees us, and gets the hell out. The smells of the city cling to us immediately: car exhaust, the burnt caramel of Chinese take-out, sugar steam from someone's vape down the street.

I pat my capris pocket absentmindedly, where the melted plastic tube from TJ's e-cig sits snugly like a talisman. Contraband. They say I refused to let it go when they found me.

This small act sets off the urge to stretch my neck and roll my shoulder. Then that act sends a fresh pinch of pain through my upper body, a gentle reminder of my first broken bone. TJ would be proud; she'd busted her clavicle in grade school jumping out of a swing. Though she'd be more impressed by the star-shaped scar peeking out below my T-shirt, from the bullet that shot through my bicep. The burns on my back have almost healed. But my short hair and missing eyebrows make me look like a David Bowie fanatic circa the Ziggy Stardust years. A red-haired Valkyrie.

Perfect.

"The light was just a game we played to scare ourselves," I say. "We thought it went off whenever someone died." I roll my eyes. "It was the least of our worries."

"Did it?"

"Go off?" I shrug. Then nod.

"And now you think that was just a coincidence."

"Of course."

"Jane," the doctor says gently, "you don't need to pretend so that you will pass with me. If you believe it went off when someone died, I'm not going put you in a soft cell and throw away the key."

"Okay, yes, I believe it was a manifestation of the Armillaria. I believe a lot of things now that I didn't believe a month ago. Or maybe just forgot I believed." I tap the bullet wound. "It cured me, you know. With the pills. Didn't even need oxy for this or the collarbone. I took Tylenol. Refused the morphine."

"The light cured you?"

"No, the Armillaria. I only ate it once while we were there. It was that powerful, that concentrated. We probably took too much, but there it is. No going back."

I can tell the doctor is selecting what part of this to believe. The scientific part. The ability of psilocybin to reset the brain. Something rattles in her pants pocket as we walk. We cross the gardens where bumblebees struggle into small purple flowers, their fuzzy butts hanging out while they gather their pollen. Somewhere in those woodchips at the base of the plants lies a fungus of some sort. This one is harmless enough for now, but wily and vast beyond the gardener's comprehension. And eager to learn.

At the end of the walk stands our meeting space, a gazebo with wicker couches and plump cushions. We sit cross-legged on opposing couches, gazing out over the manicured lawn, like old friends at a spa—minus the chardonnay. Stuben Literary spared no expense for me. I owe David my best effort to straighten this thing out.

I owe TJ.

I chuckle softly, shaking my head.

Here I'd convinced myself I was dragging TJ down to Ketchum to give her closure and me some way to redeem myself in the eyes of the agency. But in reality (or whatever passes for it these days), I was the hunter taking her old dog on its last hunt, the hunt from which only the hunter returns. I guess this time the dog was in on it, leading me down the path while I stumbled, oblivious. The dog was ready.

Maybe the dog always is.

But that's another story.

I fancy myself a writer finally, as you've guessed. One last gift from TJ and the Armillaria. Both David at Stuben Lit and Dr. Adelstein have suggested that I write this all down (and stop telling my fellow patients) in order to help make sense of it. And I find that I have some of TJ's knack for words. But only some.

*You gotta face it, Jane. Gotta exit through the wound.*

I close my eyes. Oh, how I miss her wild words. I need them so much. And I know it's not fair to want her back when she's happier with Evie and the others. I guess what the Armillaria giveth, the Armillaria taketh away. But sometimes my despair grows deeper and darker than The Thicket itself on a night when the Donzerly Light has gone off. Sometimes, when I can no longer take the unbearable tug of knowing my best friend is not beside me, I remember what TJ said, that we are all together and she is in me and always has been. And a little voice—Evie's voice—says, *Come and get us, Janey.*

Ghost in the graveyard, run, run, run!

Dr. Adelstein sits forward on her couch, trying to mask her anticipation with concern. Because where I see breakdown, she sees breakthrough. I am a rarity in her field. Terms like "high functioning," "substance induced and aggravated," "mixed features," are all bandied about. The way Dr. Adelstein writes in her charts reminds me of Paul at the base of that big, rotten conifer, scrawling on his clipboard about the Armillaria Oculi Psilocybe.

It's a bit greedy, I have to say. But I suppose I'm glad to have an ear, whether that ear is paid to care or not.

"When I touched TJ," I murmur, "right before the Armillaria took her, I saw a vision. I saw through her eyes. She handed everything back to me. She knew I could carry it now."

The fugue state of my childhood returns, that blissful apex, the fine act of ignoring reality, the state of gray.

The doctor softens her gaze, heart fluttering, knowing I'm finally ready to cough it up. "And what was that?"

My lips quiver across my teeth, not wanting to betray TJ.

"I'm in the bedroom, serving the sheriff tea in these tiny cups. There's nothing in them. We just pretend to sip. It's way too late at night to be up. He's wearing his uniform. Brown polyester. He wants me to show him what my Barbies do. He leaves my bedroom door open. Mom's asleep. We are quiet. But because of the angle he's sitting at, the deer head over the mantel in the living room makes him look like he has antlers, like ... like, Pan. Like this cartoon I saw in school. His badge—it's an amber star and it catches the light from the flickering desk lamp. It's all I stare at. I can't look at the rest. His shirt has those pearl snaps on it and they make a little pop when they open.

I sneer. "Snaps." And stop there, blinking. I won't give her the rest. She doesn't need the rest. And she doesn't seem to mind; she wants to reach for me, I can tell, but considers it unprofessional.

"TJ was a fucking trouper," I say.

"How does it feel now, to experience that again after all this time?"

"Strangely peaceful. It's just life on this planet as we know it. Cruel sometimes, beautiful at others. She's been trying to tell me that all these years."

The doctor cocks her head; she didn't see that coming.

"I'm serious," I say. "I have come to accept quite a bit lately." I lean forward, elbows on thighs. "I am a different person from who I was a month ago. There are much larger questions at hand."

Dr. Adelstein gazes off into the leaves of the oaks, which stand like guardians at the front gate. She reaches into her pants pocket and takes a breath through her nose.

"I think we should continue seeing each other after this."

I raise a hairless brow, suspecting she needs me more than I need her at this point.

"I have a colleague at Johns Hopkins," she says. "He just wrapped up a clinical trial on psilocybin. They've opened a center for psychedelic research. First of its kind."

"No kidding."

"I wonder if you would mind me mentioning your case to him."

"Of course not. Go for it. I've got lots to say."

Her eyelids flutter. "Well, I believe they are looking for subjects with no previous experience with the drug, but it's possible your situation may be illustrative in conjunction with his research. No promises, of course."

I nod placidly. But inside I'm already imagining myself as *Jane: Patient Zero of the Armillaria Affair* and I can't fucking wait.

The Frisbee players hike to the badminton net and start hitting the shuttlecock wildly in all directions. Dr. Adelstein smiles at them.

I open the laptop and conduct my daily search for any news from Ketchum.

"Apparently the DNR is clear cutting what didn't burn

in the explosion," I say. "They're replacing the trees with a fungus-resistant breed of conifer."

"Ah." The doctor feigns interest.

I don't bother to warn her how badly the Armillaria will take that. She wouldn't believe me. And besides, I'm sort of rooting for it, like one roots for grizzly bears as a species even though one of them dismantled your friend. The network of underground mycelium, could it take the heat of the forest fire? How many millions of spores made it out of The Thicket in the guts and on the feet of those terrified animals? Lincoln's fire might have only served to spread the Armillaria further. Maybe that was the point.

"I think you're doing well enough to speak to the investigators now, don't you?" she asks.

According to the *Birkenham Gazette*, the firefighters had discovered Paul's body intact, save his face and neck, the drone still beside him. Between the fire, Paul's report, and Lincoln's proposal, the county at large was in disarray and Ketchum became ground zero of an investigation by numerous agencies.

"Sure. I guess."

I wonder if Amanda hates me, blames me. We both know if I'd never sent Paul that photo of the mushroom, he'd still be alive. And I'll have to carry that for as long as I walk this earth.

*Welcome to Wits' End, Lady Jane.*

I nod again. I do a lot of that. But it's only now that I realize how disconcerting it is to others. I can't help it though, you know? It's an age-old habit.

We Thicket Kids gazed into the Armillaria and the

Armillaria gazed back. Some of us could handle its attention; used it to do great things. Others got too close to the edge and slipped. I straddled its abyss. Guess I still am. God, our minds are vast wonders that thwart themselves at every chance, aren't they? By turns they fight us, then defend us. They do neither very well, and yet they do it all so beautifully, so creatively.

Dr. Adelstein rises from her cushions and unpockets a pill bottle. "So, for now, we're going to use traditional methods, all right? We've seen a lot of success with this."

I hold out my hand like a good girl. But why must I let other humans, fallible creatures, diagnose and treat my mind? I gave them my collarbone and wrist to repair, but my mind? They will never understand—these institutions and their factory pharmaceuticals that attempt to mimic a fraction of what the real thing can do.

I'm beginning to think the Armillaria didn't offer a gift or treatment so much as ... an exchange. If Paul was right about its desire to exert itself at all costs, the Armillaria may be sharpening our senses for another purpose.

*The better to know you with, my dear.*

I squint up at the clear blue sky. "What if God was never up there," I ask, "and has been just below our feet this whole time?"

The doctor's dark eyes widen and then she goes blank, saying milquetoast, "What an intriguing idea." But I know she won't give it another thought. Or maybe she will at, say, 3:30 a.m.

I resist the urge to tell her more, to tell her the Armillaria is legion. It makes Greek god Pan look like a grubby toddler. Yes, I know; who but my fellow patients will ever believe such ravings? And those researchers of hers? They'll think my brain is broken and in need of fixing, rather than already in a state of repair and unforeseeable expansion. My ex would be shocked at how good I am at Sudoku now. It wouldn't surprise me if an MRI turned up rhizomorphs threading their way down my spinal column. Probably best if I never let them slide me into one of those noisy things.

Dr. Adelstein turns toward the step, then halts, hand on the archway.

"Just promise me you'll tone down the mushroom talk with the younger ones, okay? It's giving them false hope."

I rattle the pill bottle in my fist like Harvey Milk. "Ya gotta give 'em hope."

Her professional smile twitches and she walks back down the path the way we came, her linen blouse breezing behind her.

I call after her, "Okay, I promise!"

She twiddles her fingers over her shoulder.

I gaze at her going away present:


TORI JANE RENDER


TAKE 1 TABLET DAILY


ARIPIPRAZOLE


There will be no velvet fog with these, a fog I no longer need. But I'll take them so I can get the fuck out of here and stay the fuck out. My hope, my comfort, is sensing that when I am free, these pills might find a home in the bottom of my sock drawer.

And someday, when I've had enough of all this truth-telling, if no one will listen to me, I'll rent another car and drive downstate. But not from EconoCar of course; I'm on their blacklist. When I do get there, I'll go lie down in The Thicket and wish TJ back. And reanimate Evie! And Ms. Van Laar maybe. And if I'm really accomplished, a reconstituted sex-worker.

In the meantime, I open TJ's file on the laptop. My fingers run through my shortened hair, flicking little Valkyrie feathers at my temple. I twirl the empty e-cig between my finger and thumb, jam it in the corner my mouth, and start typing.

I want to tell you about Keith, this Black kid from rural Minnesota.

And a yellow biplane on fire.

And the girl who looks like Baby from *Dirty Dancing*.

## Acknowledgments

A thicketful of gratitude goes to my editor, Bethan Morgan, and the fantastic crew at One More Chapter. It is so, *so* crucial to have a team that totally gets your shenanigans.

Much appreciation also goes to Emmy Nordstrom Higdon and Sam Hiyate at The Rights Factory for ushering me swiftly to OMC's door – as well as Tamanna Bhasin for her thoughtful reading of my manuscript.

Before the above ever happened, I first needed a trusty crew of beta-readers who reeled me in from many a precipice. Thanks to Rebecca Dickens, Jarrod Yantis, Mary Logue, Tracy Laibson, Jo Haugen, Marcie Golub, Joyce Gordon, Philip Elliott, Cameron and Madeline Harris-Gordon, and Amy Dawson Robertson.

Thanks also to my bandmates Riley Kragness and Connor Kuennen for nerding out with me about fungi.

And finally, to my better angel and alpha-reader: Cheryl Gordon, for her brilliance in and out. *Love you.*

— Michele